IMMORAL

PARK AVENUE KINGS

BOOK THREE

BROOKE BLAINE

ELLA FRANK

Cover Design: Hang Le
Cover Photo: Wander Aguiar
Edited by Arran McNicol

1

BENOIT

SEDUCTION WAS A dangerous game. Show your hand too early and you risked giving the object of your desire the upper hand. Come off too strong and you might lose them altogether.

No way in hell was I allowing either of those two things to happen tonight. I had to play this just right, which was why I had been chosen for this particular mission.

After all, there wasn't much I did better than seducing a man.

I slipped on the final piece of my ensemble, a heavy gold brocade robe that gleamed under the light of my dressing quarters. The back collar rose up above the top of my head, fanning out like I was a regal queen—which, *accurate*.

The latest burlesque dancer to take the stage walked back into the room wearing a sequined thong and sweat on his brow. He did a double take when he saw me and let out a curse in Arabic.

I smirked. "I know. But if you think the outside's glorious, just wait until you get a glimpse of what's underneath."

He replied, but I could only translate enough to get the gist of what he said. Something along the lines of "sex walking," which I took to mean as sex on legs—quite a compliment from a fellow performer who could just as easily deem me as competition. Any other night he would've turned my head too. It was unfortunate I had to keep it on straight for now. *Both* heads.

I stepped in front of the full-length mirror, checking to make sure I was a feast for the eyes. The gold-flecked gloss that adorned my lips had them plumped up and extra juicy, and the brown kohl liner around my eyes added to the dramatic flair. It wasn't enough to get the attention of my target tonight—I had to make him desperate with need.

"Benoit." The stage manager gestured for me to follow her, and off we went, through the curved hallway that ran the perimeter of the tallest building in Dubai. We were so high up, the only glimpses I caught of the outside were dark sky and moonlight. "Nervous?" she asked, giving me a smile over her shoulder as if that would help ease any butterflies.

It'd been years since I'd performed burlesque on a stage, something I did for fun in my twenties, but there was nothing but confidence radiating through my body. I'd always enjoyed putting on a show, having all eyes on me. What was there to be nervous about?

The way she was watching me, waiting for an answer, had me smiling back at her and lying through my teeth. *"Oui,"* I said.

She stopped in front of the backstage door and pulled it open for me. "It'll pass," she said, and inclined her head for me to go inside. It was pitch black except for a lit pathway along the floor that I followed carefully, not wanting to catch my four-inch heels on anything hiding in the dark.

I took my cue, center stage, back to the audience—*can't give too much away*—then waited for the music to begin.

The slow, sultry rhythm started, and as the beat of the drum hit, a spotlight lit me up like an exquisite jewel. A priceless gem that none of the men in the audience tonight could resist—which was the plan, of course.

I was there to garner attention. To lure in hungry eyes. I was the bait, and right now, I was up here setting the trap—a delicious honey trap that was going to be sticky once my target was secured, but nothing I couldn't handle.

I'd been in tricky situations before. This one would be no different.

I glanced over my shoulder, searching the crowd, then began to seduce the audience. I swayed my hips to the provocative music and slinked across the stage, the cape swirling around my bare legs as I flirted my way through my routine.

A wink here, a smile there, as one glove, then two, was removed. I tossed them out to the crowd, letting them fall where they may, then continued to peruse the greedy onlookers for the man I was really there for.

He wouldn't be up front, not a man like him. So I needed to be looking toward the back. He wanted eyes on his performers —after all, this was his establishment—so he'd be sure to stay away from prying eyes. Stay in the shadows. That was where he did his best work. But that wasn't going to do tonight. I needed to draw him out, and as I moved up to the center of the stage again, my eyes caught on a tall figure in the back.

Dimitri Stavros.

His name alone was enough to make most men run in the opposite direction. But my goal tonight was to capture and keep his attention, and to do that, I needed to get much closer than this.

With my target in sight, I reached for the gold clasp of my robe and unfastened it, and as the heavy garment cascaded to the floor like a rippling waterfall, I was left in the high, fanned collar, a black, gem-covered corset laced at my trim waist, and a matching G-string that showed off my spectacular ass.

My heels showcased my long legs in ways that would make any supermodel jealous, and what I could do in them made *every*body jealous.

It was a lethal combination, which worked well for this particular man, since that's what he was, and when I executed a perfect flip off the stage and landed square on said heels, my eyes collided with his.

Gotcha.

Not about to roll over and make this easy for him, I started flirting my way through the crowd—fingers through hair, coy smiles offering more than I was giving, whispers of sweet nothings as patrons tried to get friendly and I flitted just out of reach.

It was all about the tease, and I was the master of that. The social chameleon who could slide into any scenario and charm anyone, and who could *especially* fit into this moment.

My eyes tracked back to the man in all black—the one moving when I did to make sure he always had a clear line of sight on me.

Time to give him a little personal one-on-one.

I slinked through the tables until I reached his, and then immediately turned my back on Dimitri Stavros, something no one in their right mind would do. Arching forward, I grabbed hold of my ankles and shook my sweet ass, giving him a view he couldn't resist.

That was the hope, anyway, but just in case...

I straightened and spun around, and sure enough, those dark eyes weren't looking anywhere but right at me.

I'd seen photos of Dimitri, but being in his orbit slapped me in the face in a way I hadn't expected. Of course I knew the man was attractive, even with the scar that marred his cheek, so that wasn't a surprise.

What *was* surprising was the intensity of the power and magnetism radiating off him. It scorched my skin and left me breathless as we locked eyes. There was hunger in his gaze, yes, but also a confidence that would've rattled anyone, and had I not been prepared to seduce, I might've lost my footing.

In one swift move, I lifted my foot onto the table, slamming the heel into the wood and shaking the glasses. Dimitri didn't flinch as his eyes traveled down my body. Taking advantage of his attention, I unfastened the corset and tossed it into his lap, and a thrill ran through me at the way he lifted it to his nose. He took a deep inhale, his eyes meeting mine again until I moved my hips in a way that had his gaze dropping to my covered—and getting harder—cock.

If I happened to bust out of it, that wouldn't be the *worst* thing.

Leaving Dimitri *wanting* was the plan, so as much as I found myself enjoying this little one-on-one, I dropped my leg and continued moving about the room, back toward the stage, shaking my ass in a way that incited whistles and catcalls.

For a brief moment, I wondered why I'd stopped performing all those years ago, until I remembered that being a man of leisure suited me more. That didn't mean I couldn't enjoy the hell out of this rare moment in time.

I sashayed back onto the stage, made a big show of bending over to retrieve my cape, then draped it around my shoulders. I glanced back at Dimitri, and as I reached beneath the luxurious material and removed the final garment, I twirled the G-string around my finger, winked at him, then flicked it off to the side of the stage as the lights went dark.

A roar of applause filled the immediate silence, and though I couldn't see the crowd, I could feel Dimitri's gaze on me as I strutted off the stage.

The manager was waiting in the wings, a smile stretched wide across her lips as she nodded. "I have a feeling they'll be fighting for a seat the next time you're on stage."

"Well then, *très chère*, my job here is done."

She hurried ahead of me, rattling off something in Arabic as we made our way back to the dressing rooms, where a flurry of activity was taking place—garments, makeup, wigs, and heels flying everywhere as the next performer brushed by me and headed toward the manager.

I almost wished them luck, because they were going to need it following after me. But then I remembered the reason I was there and decided to keep my well wishes to myself. I needed Dimitri's focus to remain on me, so maybe I'd work on manifesting an electrical issue with the lights instead.

As the dressing room emptied out and the chaos died down, I slipped into my silk robe and settled into a makeup chair, where I pulled out my phone and brought up a new text.

Fish is on the hook

I hit send.

2

DIMITRI

"WE HAVE TO move quickly if we want to—"
I held my hand up, cutting off Caesar's words
as the performer who'd just given me a private
show took to the stage again to wrap things up.

Whoever he was, he was mesmerizing. Even though the
club offered up some of the most beautiful, talented dancers
for patrons to admire, it wasn't often that one caught my
attention.

The man bent down to grab hold of his cape, giving one
last look at his perfect, plump ass before it was covered up.
Then he turned around, locked eyes with me, and began to
spin his G-string around his finger.

I hadn't even seen him take it off, the sly minx.

Like he knew, he shot me a wink and tossed the G-string
off the stage, and the room went pitch black.

All around me erupted cheers from thoroughly entertained
club guests, but I sat there in stillness until the lights came
back up.

"Like I was saying, I think we need to—" Caesar started

again, but I cut him off with a glance and gestured to one of my bodyguards nearby.

"Get it." Without a word, he headed off, and I turned back to Caesar. "Go ahead."

My treasurer leaned across the table. "We need to wrap these deals up before another arms dealer comes sniffing around our territories. I think you need to get on the road sooner than later to meet with—"

"I don't recall paying you to think strategy. You just worry about the money when I bring it back to you," I said, reaching for the bottle of whiskey and pouring another finger into my glass. I took a sip and settled back into the leather lounge chair.

Caesar's face fell and he looked to Omar, my second-in-command. "But there are rumblings that the Redwater Syndicate is trying to push back against his leadership."

The bodyguard returned to my side and handed me the dancer's discarded G-string, and I fingered the gem-covered material before slipping it into my pants pocket.

"He's not your boss," I snapped, and Caesar's face flushed under the lights from the next performer. "I am. And if someone has a problem with my leadership, let them say it to my face."

Caesar's eyes shifted to the jagged slash running up the left side of my cheek, and the message was loud and clear: *Want to end up like the last person who doubted my ability to steer this ship?* He may have landed a blow, but *I* was the one who'd ended up at the fucking helm.

"Of course." Caesar swallowed. "I didn't mean anything by—"

"Stop talking," I said, and turned my attention to Omar. "Is everything set up for next week?"

"It is. The gala is next Friday; you fly out Saturday. All

prospective buyers have agreed to a face-to-face, and I'll send word of time and location upon our arrival."

"Good." I leaned back in my seat and ran a finger around the rim of my glass, running over everything I needed to get squared away between now and next week. There were a lot of variables when one was about to broker a deal, or *several* deals, as large as I was about to, and I needed to make sure everything was in order.

Including my fucking men.

"It's important we secure these deals," I said. "Establish that I'm still the top supplier in the market. I'm not about to be run out because some wannabe crew thinks they're about to encroach on my business."

"Understood." Omar looked to Caesar and gestured for him to get up. "If I get a hint that anyone is talking shit, they'll be dealt with—"

"By me," I added, and Omar nodded.

It was clear that the only way I was going to gain respect from my men was to stand up and fight for the position I claimed I deserved. Plus, what self-respecting leader would send someone else to do their dirty work?

"Right." Omar shoved Caesar through the tables, about to leave. But then he stopped and asked, "Anything else you needed tonight, boss?"

I looked to the stage and had a flash of supple skin, sparkling gems, and a flirty wink, and was close to requesting that a certain dancer be brought to my room. But I had too much to do tonight, and shook my head. "No. I'll be leaving soon enough."

Omar and Caesar exited the club, leaving me to my drinks and dancers, while my bodyguards stood off to the side, watching over the patrons.

I always thought it was an interesting dichotomy, for the

biggest underground arms dealer in the world to require body-guards to keep himself alive. Then again, it was nice having a set of eyes at the back and sides of my head, since many would like to put a bullet through it.

One of the downsides of the new position I now found myself in. Maybe if my predecessor had been less sure of his own invincibility, he might still be alive today.

No. That was a lie. He would've died no matter how many people stood in my way.

I pulled my phone from my inside jacket pocket and looked at the time. It was closing in on one a.m. and while I enjoyed a late night out, I hadn't been sleeping much the past week.

Despite what I'd told my men, I was well aware that there were people talking about the new head of the organization, and how I'd come to power. It'd been bound to happen. After decades of rule under one man, you weren't going to win everyone over just by telling them you were in charge. They were going to need proof that you were capable of not only supplying the goods they were after, but of keeping in line the kind of clientele who dealt in the darker shadows.

I knew I could do it; I was more than capable. Now I just had to prove it.

I took another swallow of whiskey and refocused my attention on the stage for the few minutes of pleasure I'd allow myself tonight. But the dancer currently making eyes at the crowd didn't make my cock stir, not the way the dark-headed one with the sultry mouth had. He'd been a surprise, one I hadn't seen in the club before. The scrap of material he'd been wearing burned a hole through my pocket, and the ties on the corset he'd left behind made my hands itch to touch, but I wouldn't let temptation override my plans. I hadn't gotten this far by letting my dick take charge.

A familiar face entered my periphery, and I nodded,

allowing the club manager to slide by the bodyguards and approach.

The forced but polite smile and the edge of fear in his eyes told me just how uncomfortable he was in my presence, like he expected me to lash out at any moment, the way my predecessor had.

Not my style.

"Everything is to your liking this evening, I trust?"

I threw back the rest of my whiskey, my eyes drifting back to the stage. "And if I say no?"

I could feel his instant panic and couldn't help but smirk.

"Relax. All is well."

He didn't seem to heed the message, remaining tense and on alert. "Can I bring you another bottle?" he said, gesturing to the empty one on the table.

"No."

Drumming my fingers along the arm of the chair, I waited as the next performer took the stage, but when the man's hood came down, it wasn't the one I was hoping to see again.

The manager must've heard my sigh, because he cleared his throat. "Are you...satisfied with the dancers this evening?"

Lights reflected off the performer's dark, oiled-down skin as he lowered into a split and ripped off his skirt. "They're fine," I said.

"Perhaps there's one who caught your eye that could entertain you? Or two? Three? However many you'd like."

I turned to the manager and cocked my head. "There *is* something I would like."

"Of course. Anything."

Reaching into my pocket, I pulled out the G-string and held it up with the tip of my finger. "The one who wore this. I want him at my gala next week."

He hesitantly reached for the thong, but I balled it in my fist and shoved it back in my pocket.

"Uh, I'm not sure which of the dancers that belonged to—"

"The new guy."

"Benoit?"

"Have him at my place."

"Consider it done." He lowered his head in a bow that I didn't acknowledge as I continued mindlessly watching the show.

Tonight wouldn't be the night to indulge in my baser desires, no. But I was used to biding my time, waiting for the right moment, the right person, the right opportunity. This would be no different.

Friday, Benoit would be mine.

3
DIMITRI

"ANOTHER ROUND OF applause, if you please, for the breathtaking Benoit Olivier."

The gala attendees exploded into cheers as Benoit stepped to the edge of the stage and basked in the adulation cast his way.

I'd been making my rounds at the gala, touching base with each and every guest on the exclusive list, but when Benoit performed I made sure to stop and watch. He was just as mesmerizing as he'd been that last time I saw him, even without the private show.

He blew kisses out into the crowd, his toned body on full display with just a scrap of red lace covering his impressive bulge. With the way he captured the attention of everyone at the party, it'd been a wise idea to bring him, and not only for my...personal inclinations. There were conversations that needed to happen between me, my team, and a couple of buyers that wanted to keep their presence unnoticed, so Benoit would be performing an encore within the hour.

The man was an impressive distraction.

Like he could hear my thoughts, Benoit turned in my direction, finding me immediately and winking. Then he slid his thumbs beneath the sides of his G-string again, only this time he didn't pull it off. He lowered the strings down below his pelvis, teasing in a way that felt personal. At least, my dick took it personally. This little show was for me.

An appreciation for the booking? A way to tantalize the boss? Something else?

Sliding my hands in my pockets, I cocked my head, daring him to add another G-string to my collection. Benoit arched a brow, sliding the sides down lower until we could glimpse the base of his cock.

A man who flirted with danger and tested the boundaries of how far he could go? I could use someone like that, especially when they moved their body the way Benoit did.

Unfortunately, as luck would have it, the lights and music went dark, sending the guests into a collective groan.

"That's a fuckin' shame," Omar said, crossing his arms as he narrowed his eyes on the now-empty stage.

"Is it?"

"That's the guy from the club last week, yeah?" When I didn't respond, he added, "Seems to be a...crowd pleaser."

"Is there something you need from me?"

"Just letting you know the guys from Redwater haven't shown up yet."

"I'm not surprised."

"You don't think they will?"

I gave him a sideways glance. "If they want to prove themselves as a threat, they'll wait to make an appearance until last minute."

Omar fidgeted by the waist of his coat pocket, itching to palm his gun.

"Not tonight," I said, giving him a pointed look. "Not here."

"But if they try—"

"They won't. Too much on the line to try to take us out without a guarantee from the buyers."

He snapped his mouth shut and nodded once, but his shoulders remained tense. The man needed a distraction so he'd stop watching the door.

"The dancer," I said. "Bring him to me."

"On it, boss." He slipped into the crowd, and I headed toward the private lounge set up for the meetings tonight, my bodyguards trailing a few feet behind me.

I nodded an acknowledgment to those I passed, and they gave me a wide berth. It wasn't a carefree group of attendees gathered tonight, though everything about the party gave the appearance of a good time. The location itself, the entire exterior of Dubai's exclusive seven-star hotel—the only one in the world that could boast that honor—was designed to look like a private club under the stars. Nothing but pure luxury for my guests, designed to show unlimited resources, money, and power. Just in case anyone, including the Redwater Syndicate, wanted to test my rule.

The curtains of the cabana were drawn open on my approach, and one of my bodyguards did a sweep of the interior before I took a seat on one of the plush couches. My favored whiskey sat on a bar cart along with glasses and an ice bucket, and a box of cigars. A butler stood to the side, waiting for my cue, and as I settled back in my seat, I gestured for a glass.

Not usually the kind of man to be distracted by a sensual smile and a sexy body, I figured the best way to combat the intrusive thoughts was to face the problem head-on. This dancer, Benoit, had been playing havoc on my mind all week, slipping to the forefront of any and all plans I'd been making. So it was time to deal with the issue and make a different kind of plan. One that would allow me to assuage my lust for him and put this fixation I'd developed to rest.

The curtain to the cabana was pulled aside, and a second later the stunning man from the stage stepped inside my domain.

He was dressed in a silky, plum-colored robe that seemed to shimmer under the lights, the garment flowing over the regal set of his shoulders and dipping into a deep V at his trim waist, where a sash held the material together with an emerald clasp.

The luxurious material swirled around those exquisite legs as he came to a stop in front of me, and if I were to hazard a guess, there wasn't much else on under that robe.

My eyes shifted to Omar, who stood off to the side of Benoit, and I inclined my head.

"Leave us."

I wasn't sure how Benoit would react knowing I wanted to see him alone, but when he glanced back at Omar, giving him a flirty little wave goodbye, I had my answer.

It appeared the confidence he exuded on stage was an integral part of him, and I found it more than a little arousing that he didn't seem intimidated by me.

"You wanted to see me, *mon cher*?"

My eyes trailed down the smooth skin of his chest that seemed to sparkle along with his robe, then back up to see his mischievous eyes twinkling at me.

"I've *seen* plenty of you." I gestured to the empty couch beside mine. "Tonight, I want to talk to you."

Benoit gracefully took the spot offered to him. His robe parted as he crossed one leg over the other, sliding up his thigh.

"Only talk?" He leaned toward me, resting an elbow on the arm of the chair and batting his lashes. "Now *that's* disappointing."

There weren't many people in the world who would dare talk to me the way this man was, but as he stroked the stubble covering his jaw, my dick reminded me of the reason I'd summoned him here in the first place.

I slipped my hand into my jacket pocket and fingered the gem-covered material that had been burning a hole there all night. That seemed to have seared a hole in my brain sometime last week.

"You're very confident for a man who's just been summoned to his boss's private cabana. What makes you think you're not here to be fired?"

Benoit slid his tongue over his glossy lips. "If I had to guess, the hard-on in your pants for one"—his eyes shifted to my hidden hand—"and my G-string's being in your pocket for two. I think it's sweet. Do you want me to sign it for you?"

His boldness had me dropping my hand. "I'm not keen on anyone touching what's mine."

"Even if it was mine first?" The teasing glint in his eyes had me imagining the way he'd look on his knees. Benoit inclined his head toward the whiskey. "Aren't you going to offer me a drink?"

"No. You have another performance."

"Maybe it'll only encourage me to take *all* my clothes off this time."

That *was* tempting, but I could just as easily have him naked right then if I wanted to. I didn't need to share his incredible body with others.

His leg shifted, drawing the robe even higher up his muscled thigh.

Plan change.

"You like to play with fire," I said, and took a sip of my drink, letting the whiskey burn its way down my throat.

"I wouldn't do that with someone like you, *mon monstre*. Not when I'd rather play with *you* instead."

I'd been called many things in my life, monster being one of them, but it'd never sounded as sexy as "my monster" did coming off Benoit's tongue. And for that, I'd let it slide.

He leaned over the small table between us, and this close I could make out the green that flecked his brown eyes. They sparkled with mischief and more sex appeal than could be contained in this cabana.

I lifted my glass to his lips, but before I could tip it forward, Benoit's hand covered mine, scorching my skin as he swallowed down the alcohol.

My cock jerked as I watched his throat work, then I set the empty glass aside and leaned back into the couch, crossing my ankle over my knee.

"I've got business over the next month. You'll join me."

Benoit didn't blink. "I can join you tonight, but I can't neglect my job. I'm sure you understand."

"A job I pay for."

He parted his lips like he wanted to refute that, but then closed his mouth.

"Exactly," I said. "You'll spend the month with me."

"That's a very kind offer, but—"

"A million dollars."

Benoit's eyes flared. "I beg your pardon?"

"I'll give you a million dollars at the end of the month."

"For little ole me?" he said, batting his lashes as a smile curled his lips.

He knew as well as I did he was worth it and more, and I waited for his counteroffer. I'd give him a hell of a lot more than that if he asked for it.

Benoit tapped his chin with his gold-tipped nail, his head tilted as he looked at me, pondering my proposal.

"I'm flattered, but I don't think so," he said. "But thanks."

I didn't show my surprise. "Two."

"Two million dollars? Surely you could find someone who'd enjoy a month with you for free."

"I could. I want you."

A slow smile crossed his face, and I knew I had him.

Until he checked the dainty, jeweled watch at his wrist.

"It's been a pleasure, *mon monstre*, but it's nearly time for my next show. I hope you'll be watching." Benoit rose gracefully to his feet, his robe falling closed and cutting off the view of all that tanned skin. "Oh, and if you change your mind about that signature, I'd do *that* for free."

Not about to show all my cards, I let him strut out of the cabana thinking he'd gotten the upper hand tonight.

I wanted Benoit now more than ever. But there was one thing he underestimated—I wasn't the kind of man to give up so easily.

4

BENOIT

"WE ALL KNOW your body's a work of fuckin' art —you don't have to show up to this shit naked," Alessio said the second I logged on to the video meeting with all of the other Kings later that evening.

The Kings of Libertine, our ultra-private and exclusive society of powerful, rich men from across the globe, not actual kings of countries.

Yet.

I glanced down at my bare chest, still damp from my shower, and was tempted to lower the camera below my waist just to piss him off.

"I didn't hear any complaints tonight," I said. "In fact, they were begging me not to leave."

"Did the begging also extend to our target?" Shep asked, always the one ready to get to the point. Being the son of a former U.S. president meant years of learning how to sift through the bullshit and use it to his advantage. And now *our* advantage.

"Of course it did," I said, balking at any speculation that I couldn't follow through on the job. "You think I put on a wicked pair of heels and rhinestone G-string with nothing to show for it?"

"I don't know your sex life," Lachlan muttered as he sharpened a knife on a rod of steel.

Theo, the only one of us who could actually claim to be royalty, as a prince of Monaco, said, "Doesn't look like much of a sex life at all, considering you're alone in that hotel room. Wasn't the point to end up in someone else's bed?"

I ran a hand through my wet hair, tousling the strands a bit, and ignored the insinuation. "You underestimate me. That's adorable."

Tyrone Kingston, better known as King, the founder and leader of Libertine, sighed. "Can we get back to the brief, please?"

"Oh, I don't think he's wearing any of those," Lucien said, a mischievous twinkle in the sex club owner's eyes.

I shot him a wink. "You're right about that. In fact, I'm not wearing anything at a—"

"Benoit." King's voice switched to that deeper, no-nonsense tone he always got when he was ready to lay down the law. "We need to know what you've learned about the target."

I, on the other hand, liked to... How did Dimitri put it? *Push the boundaries?*

"Well, for one thing, he's a lot sexier in person than his photos let on," I said. "It's his vibe—it's super intense and hot, especially when he's eye-fucking you—"

"*Benoit,*" King growled, and it seemed that maybe I'd pushed a little too far. "Get to the point."

"Our intel was right," I said. "Dimitri *is* about to leave the country. For a month."

"You heard him say that?"

"No." I preened a little, a grin curling my lips. "He invited me to go with him."

"Holy shit." Alessio shook his head. "You really did it. You seduced that cold-hearted motherfucker."

I wasn't sure *cold* was how I would personally describe Dimitri, especially after the way he'd looked at me tonight. "Was there ever any doubt?"

"I mean," Lucien said, chuckling, "it's been a while since you've worn the heels. Turned me and the club down several times."

"Yes, well, they only come out for special occasions. This was one of them."

"So you got him to ask you to join him," Shep—King's right-hand man—said.

"I did."

"So when does that happen?"

"Don't know." I shrugged. "I told him no."

"You did what?" Shep's jaw twitched, and I laughed.

"Relax. It's all part of my plan. Haven't you ever heard of playing hard to get?"

Theo snorted. "It's been so long since he played with anything, he probably doesn't even remember how to get hard."

Shep's eyes narrowed, but before he could reply, King shut it down.

"I didn't set up this chat to talk about what everyone is or isn't doing with their dicks. Benoit, report."

"*My apologies.* Tonight at his gala, Dimitri requested my presence in his VIP cabana. There, he invited me to spend the next month with him while he conducted business for a million dollars."

"Only a million, huh?" Lachlan's smartass mouth got him a flipped finger, but I kept on going.

"I, of course, played the shocked, but flattered, little dancer and refused. You know, morals and all. Then he offered me two million."

Alessio whistled. "That's some serious cash for flashing your ass."

"What can I say, it's a spectacular ass."

"Okay, so he offered you two million? And..."

"I told you. I said no. This isn't the kind of man who is turned on by someone who easily capitulates, boys. He wants a challenge. So I gave him one."

King nodded and rubbed at his jaw. "It's a risky move. What if he decides to invite one of the other dancers in your place?"

I put a hand to my chest. "I'm going to pretend you didn't say that. You sent me in here for a reason: to read our mark and get close to him. You have to trust me. This is what Dimitri wants. What he needs to tempt and distract him. From the first time he saw me last week to an hour ago when I left him sitting in his cabana alone, that man hasn't been able to stop thinking about me. Trust me, I have him right where I want him."

"You better, because this is our only shot at this. We need you in place to see who he's meeting with. I'm not about to get into bed with drug lords and terrorists."

"I'll be able to find that out and more. Really, the lack of belief in my abilities is telling. I don't question it when Lachlan's sent out to take care of an enemy. Or when we have to trust that Alessio can break into an offshore account and steal millions—"

"Steal's a strong word," Alessio interjected.

"And I don't see you complaining when I eliminate any threats," Lachlan added.

I lifted a shoulder. "Just saying, you do your jobs and let me do mine."

King's brows pulled tight as he lowered his chin. "All this aside, you do know you don't have to do anything you don't want to."

I heard the warning, but he knew as well as I did that I wouldn't put myself—or my body—out there if I didn't want to. I appreciated the gesture, but it was unnecessary. Dimitri was a man I was interested in getting between the sheets, mark or not.

"Trust me, I know," I said. "This is not going to be a hardship on my part. At all."

"You have a plan B, though?" Theo asked, and when I shot daggers in his direction, he held his hands up. "Not that I don't believe you can persuade anyone, but backtracking and taking the two mil after all this would be embarrassing."

"I—" My words cut off at the knock on the door, and I held up a finger to the guys. "You're all about to eat your words," I said, standing and refastening my towel so I flashed them all. Their groans were audible as I headed to the door and pulled it open, and the two bellhops on the other side took one look at my half-naked body and quickly looked down at their feet.

The top of the first one's head flushed a bright shade of red as he held an envelope out for me. "This came for you, sir. We were told to bring it to you straight away."

"Ah, *merci*." I plucked the envelope from his hand, loving that my instincts were right.

"And also this." The second bellhop stepped forward with a large, intricate box in his arms. The box itself was gorgeous, like an ornate vintage jewelry box, only much too big.

I bit back my smile and slipped them both a few bills from my nightstand before taking the box and heading back to the laptop.

"My oh my, will you look at this," I said, setting my gift on the bed in full view of the camera and then sitting down behind it, fanning myself with the envelope.

"No fucking way," Shep said, shaking his head in either disbelief or admiration. Maybe a mix of both.

Lachlan narrowed his eyes. "Okay, but what's in the fucking box? A bomb?"

I arched a brow. "And the point of that would be?"

"That he knows you're a spy," Alessio said. "Don't open it."

"You're ridiculous. I'm not ignoring a gift, especially one this nice."

"You won't think it's so nice when what's inside blows your face off."

"Well then, I suppose you'd better get a good look at it now." I turned my face to each side before sliding my finger under the envelope's flap and ripping it open.

It wasn't like I even needed to see what was on the card, but humoring them was too entertaining to resist.

There, in handwritten black ink, was the summons I'd expected:

I don't take no for an answer. Tuesday. Noon.
~Your Monster

I read the card aloud for them and then flipped the latch on the box. Another note was placed on top of carefully bound hundred-dollar bills that filled the interior to the brim.

Two million now. Another two at the end of the month.

"Shit, you did it. You really fuckin' did it," I heard someone mutter, but I was too busy grinning like a Cheshire Cat at my victory to notice who it was.

"What did I tell ye of little faith?" I said, taking one of the bundles of crisp bills and fanning myself with it. "Got him, boys."

5
DIMITRI

Location: A Snow-Covered castle in Prague, Czech Republic

THE WARMTH OF my breath cut through the frigid air as I stood alone on an upstairs balcony at the castle I'd commandeered in Prague. Several feet of fresh snow had fallen overnight, blanketing the grounds and giving the illusion of peace. Safety. Beauty.

All things that were unfamiliar to me, but made this the perfect hidden place for business.

"ETA two minutes," Omar said, coming to stand beside me.

I nodded, scanning the distance before I headed back inside, Omar following after me silently. At least until we started down the grand staircase.

"Are you sure this is a good idea, boss? Not saying you don't deserve it, but now's not the time for distractions."

I turned around so fast that Omar had to reach for the railing to catch himself.

Taking a step back up so we were eye to eye, I said, "That'll be the last time you question me."

He nodded. "Understood."

Without another word, I started back down, and another member of my team opened the front doors so I could be there to welcome my guest when he arrived.

Benoit Olivier hadn't been an easy one to pin down, and that was half the reason why I'd wanted him to join me. No one in their right mind would acquiesce so easily to someone with my reputation unless they had ulterior motives. That Benoit had turned me down not once, but twice, only upped the ante, and I'd given him an offer he couldn't refuse.

A demand, really. One I hadn't been sure he'd follow until I got word he'd boarded my private plane. Now here he was, willingly stepping into my world for the next month, and I planned to keep him as close as humanly possible.

The car pulled to a stop on the snow-filled courtyard, where the driver emerged and immediately moved to open the back door.

A second later, a leather-covered hand took his and Benoit emerged, elegant as ever in a pair of tall winter boots lined with fur, tight tailored pants, and, as always, his signature cape. He had on a pair of sunglasses to ward off the glare from the setting sun, and after scanning the sparse white landscape, his attention finally locked on to me.

"Well, if this isn't a fantasy come to life." He lowered his glasses to look me over before sliding them back up. "You're forgiven for not mentioning we'd be vacationing in a winter paradise. If it hadn't been for your driver suggesting I put on something warmer, you would've missed out on this entire look."

I slid my hands into my pockets and walked toward him, eyeing the driver taking bag after bag after bag from the trunk. "It seems you would've found something."

"I wasn't told where I was going, so I was forced to pack for every occasion."

The sheer amount of suitcases spoke to that fact, but I wasn't giving away details regarding our whereabouts this month. The last thing I needed was a spy in our midst.

"I hope you also packed wisely," I said.

"Meaning?"

"Your bags will be searched for weapons. You better hope they don't find any."

Several of my men exited the house to collect the luggage, and as they disappeared back inside, Benoit let out a laugh and took hold of my arm.

"Oh, Dimitri," he said as we entered the foyer. "Are you always this paranoid?"

"Careful, am I always this *careful*, and the answer is yes."

I steered him toward the parlor off to the right, and he removed his glasses to take in the antique, old-world interior.

"Next I suppose you're going to tell me they're going to come in here and search *me*." He dropped his hold on my arm and continued into the room until he realized I wasn't following and spun back around.

I shut the doors behind me and flipped the lock.

"No, they won't be searching you," I said, closing the space between us. "That's my job."

"Oh, I see." Benoit arched a brow, his eyes roving over my face. "Tell me, *mon monstre*, do you search all of your guests this way? Or am I lucky and getting the hands-on treatment from the head of the house?"

If I'd thought Benoit would balk at my announcement, I

was dead wrong, as he reached for the clasp of his cape and unfastened it.

"I don't have guests at my house."

"And yet here I am." The cape parted and Benoit removed it from his shoulders with a quick flick of his wrist.

The black turtleneck he revealed molded to his fit body like a second skin, and paired with the tailored pants and boots, he could've passed for a cat burglar on the prowl. Another good reason to search the man. Though, truth be told, if he *were* hiding a weapon, I was going to have to go hunting for it.

The thought had my lips curling.

"Something amusing?" Benoit asked as he dropped his cape over the arm of the antique couch facing the fireplace.

"Not at all. Arms out."

"Oh no you don't. I saw that smirk." Benoit glanced over his shoulder as I moved around behind him. "You were almost smiling."

"I don't smile."

"Why not? Worried it'll ruin your fierce reputation?"

I stepped in behind him and clasped the back of his neck. "Eyes forward."

Benoit licked along his lower lip and turned back to face the doors. "Would you like me to bend over, too?"

Yes, I would. But I needed to search him, and I wouldn't get through that if he was bent over.

"Don't tempt me," I growled, then slid my hand from his neck across his shoulder, my free hand searching his other side.

Down his arms, then up and under to his ribs, where I trailed my fingers along the soft material, searching for any kind of weapon. A small gun or knife could be hidden just about anywhere, and in Benoit's line of work I wouldn't have been surprised to find either one on him.

I slipped my hand under the hem of his sweater, checking along the waist of his pants, and at the touch of my fingers against his bare skin, Benoit trembled.

"*Merde.* You could've warmed your hands before putting them all over me."

My dick kicked against the zipper of my pants at his suggestion, but I merely grunted in response before running my palms over his ass, then down to feel along the legs of his pants.

It took everything I had not to linger there, remembering how good those legs had looked naked and shiny under the lights. Instead, I moved to the front.

My cock throbbed as I placed my hands on his shoulders, and when Benoit looked up at me from beneath his lashes, I was close to saying *fuck it* and strip-searching him the way my dick wanted me to.

"I have to admit, I was a little worried when you mentioned this search as a welcome. But I'm starting to think if you greeted everyone this way, you'd have a lot more friends than you would enemies."

With my hands at his neck, I moved my thumb up to the top of the turtleneck and drew it down so I could see his Adam's apple.

"Who said I want friends?"

Benoit swallowed, and I watched his tanned throat work under my thumb.

"Right, well, maybe just someone you wouldn't have to *pay* to be here."

"Maybe so. But I don't like leaving things to chance." I moved my hands to his shoulders once more and glided them along his arms, ribs, and then down the front of his sweater to the button of his pants. "I wanted you here, and now I have you."

I shifted my hand down to cover an erection that rivaled my own, and Benoit sucked in a breath and reached for my arms.

"Uh, no weapon hiding in there, *mon monstre*. But if you want to look closer, I won't stop you."

I was tempted as Benoit arched forward into my touch, but I had a few more places to check before I did anything like that.

"If I didn't know better"—I curled my fingers around him—"I'd think you were trying to distract me."

Benoit chuckled, a low, throaty sound that sent fire licking through my veins.

"*Au contraire.* You're the one whose hand is around my cock."

"Just being thorough," I murmured, then released him and continued before I changed my mind.

I crouched down, and if I thought I'd been tempted by merely a touch, seeing his hard-on outlined behind the wool of his pants was fucking torture. But again, Omar's warning of becoming distracted ran on a loop and wouldn't leave me be. So I felt my way up and down each of his legs until I got to his boots.

That was when I saw it—the shiny glint of a handle tucked inside those tall fur boots.

I dipped my fingers inside the leather and fur and removed a slim knife with a jeweled handle.

I glanced up at Benoit, who was looking down at me. When I held the knife up, the sassy minx grinned.

"Whoops."

Narrowing my eyes, I quickly checked the other, and when that was clear I got to my feet. "*Whoops?*"

"*Oui.* With the excitement of packing and being whisked away, I must've forgotten I put that in there."

I flipped the knife in my hand and held the pointy tip just under his chin, angling his face up to mine. "You forgot? I specifically asked you about weapons. *Told* you I was going to search you."

"Well, it sounded like a fun get-to-know-you game." Benoit winked at me. *Winked*, while I was holding a fucking knife under his chin. Ballsy. I liked it. "Plus, you can hardly blame me. You are a strange man paying for my company... One can't be too careful."

Ah. He wanted to play, did he? He'd spent every encounter we'd had teasing my dick, and now it was time he paid for that.

"You're right," I said, lowering the knife down his body to the button of his pants. "You can't be too careful."

With a quick flick of the knife, the button went flying across the room, and Benoit sucked in a breath. But given the way his cock throbbed against my hand as I lowered his zipper, it wasn't a gasp of fear.

I tucked the knife into the back of my pants and then slid my hand inside Benoit's open zipper. He was so hard, the heat of him scorched the thin fabric of his briefs.

I let my fingers wander, up and down his straining dick and underneath to cradle his balls.

"Now this is what I call a welcome," Benoit said, his voice low and full of arousal as he pushed his hips toward me.

Taking full advantage of his enjoyment, I curled my palm around his length and stroked him, once, twice, then got into a steady rhythm that had him breathing more erratically.

It was tempting to continue, to get him naked and writhing beneath me. I could almost hear the way he'd come apart, the sounds he'd make as I fucked him into mind-blowing orgasms all night.

That would happen. But for now, patience.

I removed my hand and backed away, grabbing the knife so I wouldn't do something stupid, like reach for him again.

"You're clear," I said, and held up the knife. "But I'm keeping this."

A groan ripped out of Benoit, followed by unintelligible French curses. He pinned me with narrowed eyes. "You brought me all this way to be a tease?"

"You should know. You've been teasing my dick since I met you."

"Ah, so this was payback." He pulled his zipper up. "Well done. Just remember, two can play that game."

Twenty minutes in and this month was already off to a tantalizing start. I just needed to get him out of this fucking parlor, because otherwise we might not leave it tonight.

"Come," I said, and opened the door. "Let me show you where we'll be staying."

6

BENOIT

DIMITRI FLIPPING THE script and teasing my cock without following through should've frustrated me to no end. Instead, I was intrigued as I followed him up the grand staircase, albeit a bit uncomfortably with my erection strangled by the tight fit of my pants.

Who was this man, really? That was the question I was determined to get the answer to before this month was up. If the thorough way he searched my body was any indication of his prowess in the bedroom, it was going to be an enjoyable few weeks on the job.

Add in that we were in Prague, one of the most beautiful cities in the world, and I was in heaven.

As Dimitri led us down a long, dimly lit hall, I took in the elaborate paintings surrounding us on both sides, almost all of them depicting an architectural masterpiece somewhere in the city. I'd only been here once or twice in my life, so I hoped he was up for a little exploring during this trip.

"This is where we'll be tonight." He made an abrupt turn, and as we headed into the decently sized but not overly large room, he nodded at my bags, all perfectly lined up against the wall like they hadn't been searched.

"Not obsessed with size, I see." I ran my fingers along the edge of the bed, the material softer and more plush than it looked.

"This isn't up to your standards?"

"I didn't say that." As I regarded our accommodations, I lounged back on the mattress, resting on my hands. "It might be a tight fit for all of my clothes, though. You don't mind a tight fit, do you?"

Dimitri's dark eyes narrowed a fraction before he ran them down my body, where the waist of my pants lay open without the button closure. I was tempting, I knew that much. Dimitri knew it too, judging by the impressive erection tenting his pants.

Feel free to give in, I thought, waiting for him to take the bait. After a long trip and his cock-teasing body search, I was horny as hell and could use a good fuck to take the edge off.

And I knew without a doubt that Dimitri would be a *very* good fuck. Something about that stoic nature told me he only let loose on his sexual partners, and I was willing to offer myself for the taking.

Really, this whole mission was entirely selfish at this point.

"Don't bother," Dimitri said, but before I could protest, he continued, "unpacking. We'll be moving rooms tomorrow."

"Moving rooms? Why?"

"I never stay in the same place twice when traveling."

So he *was* paranoid, because who changed rooms every single night? At least it explained why we weren't in the largest suite of the castle. At least, I hoped this wasn't, or it didn't bode well for the other rooms.

"You do know you can simply have someone change your sheets every night instead of having to change rooms," I said.

"And give my enemies an advantage?" His jaw tensed, accentuating the hard lines of his face. "Predictability gets you killed."

"So you move rooms like musical chairs."

"Exactly."

"That's got to be exhausting."

Dimitri shrugged. "Better to be exhausted than dead."

Now *that* I could agree with. I ran my hand over the luxurious covers and patted the spot beside me. "What do you say, then, to a little...nap?"

"If you think the first time I get in a bed with you is going to be to sleep, you're not half as intelligent as that quick wit of yours led me to believe."

I preened at the compliments. "Well, you wouldn't hear me complaining."

"No, your mouth would be too busy."

My dick stiffened at the suggestion as my eyes traveled down to what I assumed he'd shut me up with. Pleased to see the sexual tension sizzling in the air was coming from both sides, I arched my hips.

"If this is another version of teasing my dick, I have to admit, I preferred the one where you used your hand."

"I'm not teasing you this time. Just stating facts. Something I'll be happy to prove, after dinner."

My stomach growled the second food was mentioned, and it wasn't until that moment that I'd realized I was a little hungry.

I licked at my lips. "I could eat."

I couldn't be sure, but I could've sworn Dimitri's lips quirked. I was determined to make that man smile, even if it killed me.

Which it might.

"I'll expect you downstairs in an hour. If you need anything pressed, washed—"

"My back?" I suggested, then batted my lashes. "Or maybe my...front."

"Clothes-wise." Dimitri pointed to a panel on the wall. "Hit this button and someone will be up to assist."

I got to my feet and inclined my head. "Thank you, *mon monstre*. I think I'm going to take a shower, since you're hell-bent on leaving me all alone."

I reached for the hem of my turtleneck sweater and drew it off, tossing it on the bed. Dimitri's eyes flared and he grunted, then he turned on his heel and headed to the door, where he stopped and glanced over his shoulder.

"But don't think for a minute you won't be in there with me." I slipped my hand down my pants and gave myself a firm squeeze. "You'll be there in spirit."

Dimitri shook his head then marched out the door, slamming it behind him. The second I heard him head off down the hall, I zipped up and raced over to the door to put my ear to it.

I waited there for a good minute, maybe two, to make sure he wasn't going to turn around and come back before I did a quick visual sweep of the room. Everything looked standard enough—queen-size bed, nightstands, a chest of drawers, and a couple of paintings hanging on the walls—but you never knew what could be hiding.

First things first: I needed to check for bugs—though that might be even a little too invasive for Dimitri, given what he'd promised would be happening after dinner. Either way, I wasn't leaving anything to chance. I checked the wall hangings first, the frames, behind the canvases, sweeping my fingers along the gilded gold and under any latches or hooks.

Nope. Nothing.

Next on the agenda were the lamps. I checked both, taking

the shades off and looking at the base to see if anything could be planted there—again, nothing.

The bed was next—the frame, underneath, and under the mattress until I was satisfied there was nothing that would be recording any of my secrets, whether they be business or pleasure related.

Not that it would be the first time I'd found my sexual escapades on tape. I mean, who wouldn't want to record something so spectacular?

After searching the drawers and every other nook and cranny I could find, I was fairly confident I was alone. But not about to take any chances, I opened my suitcase and grabbed a change of clothes, underwear, and my makeup bag, then headed into the bathroom and shut the door.

Like the room, the bathroom was nothing showy. It was a decent size and hosted an average shower, bathtub, and vanity. That was interesting. A man like Dimitri could afford the best of the best. Instead he'd chosen to stay in some secluded castle in the middle of nowhere, which I assumed was the appeal. No one could get to him.

Or maybe it was that *I* couldn't get away.

It should've alarmed me, but I didn't hate that idea. In fact, I kind of liked it. People always underestimated me, and the fact that Dimitri regarded me with as much caution as I regarded him made my dick hard.

It wasn't that I thought he was threatened by me. But he was distracted by me and knew that made him vulnerable. Something I planned to take full advantage of.

After hanging my clothes, I went to the shower and got the water running. But instead of fully undressing and stepping inside, I went back to where my makeup bag sat on the vanity and unzipped it.

I rifled through the contents—lipsticks, eye shadow, foundation—until I found the small compact I'd buried at the bottom. With the jeweled case in hand, I tiptoed over to the door and opened it a crack, making sure no one had entered the bedroom. When I was satisfied it was clear, I closed the door and put my back to it. Then I flipped open the compact and removed the powder and brush from inside, revealing a small pocket phone.

I grinned, remembering how pleased Alessio had been with himself when he first presented me with this.

"You can beat your face, isn't that what you say? Or call someone to save you from a beating."

He'd been totally off with his terms, but I appreciated the thought behind it.

My heart pounded as I dialed the number, knowing that if Dimitri came back, if he knocked on the door and caught me, I'd be as good as dead.

It didn't take but one ring, and I didn't bother with any small talk. I merely confirmed my arrival, then gave them the intel they needed for what I had planned next.

"Tomorrow night. Christmas market."

I ended the call.

7
DIMITRI

I T HAD BEEN a monumental feat to walk away from Benoit's undressing upstairs. That was three times now that I'd denied myself, and I wasn't keen on a fourth.

Even now, in the middle of my meeting with several of my team, my dick was hard as I pictured him stroking himself while backing into the en suite, half naked and giving me a daring smirk, as if I wouldn't have him bent over in a heartbeat.

"Boss?" Omar looked pointedly at my clenched fists resting on the table. "You good?"

Good? I was wound up so tight I could spit nails that would kill a man.

Ignoring his question, I took a look at the rolled-out map on the table. It was safer to keep our plans on us and not online somewhere anyone could hack into.

"We'll make the sale early morning. Here." I pointed to the destination just outside of Prague's city center. "A flower shop right off this street. Hugo, you'll lead team two to cover all exit points surrounding the shop. I don't want anyone who shouldn't be there within a block's radius."

"Got it," he said, nodding.

"Omar, you'll be with me, along with the guards. We'll enter from the front, meeting time no more than twenty minutes."

Though we wouldn't be handing over the weapons right then and there, it was still an intensely dangerous situation we were walking into. The possibility of capture was always top of mind, as well as the many others who would kill—literally—to be in my position.

But negotiations could only be done in person with the amount of money and weapons on the line. I wasn't a stranger to these deals, not when I'd been the number two for well over a decade, watching and learning, filing away what I'd do differently in the back of my mind for if there ever came a day I was the man leading the charge.

That day had come sooner than I'd expected.

Omar smoothed his hand over the second map, one of Europe. It had several dates and times, along with a few Xs by main cities, and a couple more with question marks.

"We haven't confirmed the meeting yet for Budapest, which we'd originally planned for Sunday. We may need to change up the schedule for—"

"No one told me this was a party," Benoit said as he swept into the room. All heads immediately swiveled in his direction, and with the way he was dressed, he certainly caught their attention.

And mine.

In a pair of black-and-white pinstripe pants and a satin cowl-neck shirt that dipped low enough to show off his smooth chest and the set of pearls he had clasped around his neck, Benoit had clearly done what I'd suggested and cleaned up before dinner. His hair was slicked back, and his face was devoid of any makeup, save his glossy lips.

He looked fresh, rejuvenated, and one hundred percent fuckable.

The conversation fell silent as he entered. Benoit all but floated into the room, his walk almost as rhythmic as his dancing, making his way toward the head of the table.

"Oh, don't mind me," he said with a dismissive wave at my men. "I just thought I'd come and see if there was any wine in this place. I'm feeling a little parched."

His eyes glittered at Omar, who was frowning at him over his shoulder.

"What?" Benoit said. "You don't like wine?"

That wasn't the problem. Omar didn't like interruptions, and neither did I when we were covering sensitive information. But in this case, I thought he was being a little *too* paranoid.

Benoit and his cases had been searched, and even if he planned to run off into the snow-covered wilderness, he wouldn't skip town with any pertinent information.

"He likes it just fine." I eyed my second-in-command in a way that told him to back off. I had this under control, had Benoit under control. I didn't need Omar acting like my babysitter.

Benoit came to a stop beside me and sidled in close enough that I could feel his heat through my shirt.

"Oh, are you planning out our next stops?" He leaned down closer to the map, pointing to St. Anton. "My vote is Austria. We could book a little chateau in the mountains and hire some skis, and I could live out my dream of being someone's ski bunny for the season."

The idea was so far removed from what Omar and I had been planning that I almost laughed—almost, because we *would* be going through Austria. But not for skiing and definitely not to live out any ski bunny fantasies.

No matter how tempted I might be now.

Omar started to roll up the map, but got stuck when Benoit turned and sat on the table to face me, pouting.

"You don't like that idea?"

I arched a brow. "You have an outfit to *go* with that idea?"

Benoit's laugh chimed around the room as he ran a hand up my arm and squeezed. "I told you, I brought outfits for any and all occasions, *mon monstre*. But in this instance, a couple of cotton balls as a tail is all I'd need."

My cock immediately hardened at the visual of Benoit in nothing but a cotton tail, and while it should've been ridiculous, I wanted to see that now more than I wanted my next breath.

Omar and a couple of the others coughed from their side of the table.

"We'll leave you to it," Omar said. "We can pick this up later."

I was about to nod when Benoit got to his feet and turned back to Omar, reaching over the map and table to put a hand over the top of his.

"Don't go," he implored. "Stay and have a drink with us."

"No." Omar removed his hand, and Benoit straightened. "Boss," he said, then finished rolling the map and shot out the door, the rest of the crew following.

"I can't be sure, but I don't think Omar likes me," Benoit said.

"Omar doesn't like anyone."

His eyes widened. "Not even you?"

I didn't really have an answer for that, because honestly, I didn't know whether Omar liked me. Nor did I care. All I was concerned with was his loyalty, and he'd proven that on many occasions over the last several months.

"You must be hungry," I said.

Benoit perched on the table and reached for the bottle of red wine that had been pushed aside during the meeting. As he ripped off the foil from the top, he said, "Well, if *that* nonanswer doesn't speak volumes... Surely there's someone in your inner circle whose company you enjoy."

"Not in the way I plan to enjoy you."

"Ooh, now you're talking." Benoit stabbed the corkscrew into the top and began to twist, somehow making even that look suggestive. "Do I get all the dirty details now, or do you prefer a sexy surprise?"

I popped the map into its case and hung it off the back of my chair before taking a seat at the head of the table. The way Benoit made himself at home, casually posed to his best advantage on the cherry oak with his hands working the corkscrew like he was handling a cock, had me feeling even more confident about my choice of travel companion. There was a lightness to his temperament that somewhat eased the weight from my shoulders when he was around. A sense of humor wasn't one of the top five qualities I looked for in those who worked for me, but with Benoit it was a welcome trait. Sex had been at the forefront of my mind, still was, but that didn't mean I couldn't enjoy the man himself too.

"Another nonanswer," he said, shaking his head as he popped the top off the wine and poured us each a glass. "And here I thought we were getting to know each other."

"That wasn't one of the terms of our agreement."

"As I recall, the terms were *astonishingly* vague." Rising to his feet, he sauntered toward me, the satin cowl neck dipping to mid-chest and giving a teasing glimpse of skin. He held one of the glasses out for me, brushing his fingers along mine when

I reached for it. "I'd like to know more about the man I'm spending the month with. Don't make me beg..."

But he would do it so well...on his knees.

I gestured toward the chair to my right. "Why don't you have a seat? Dinner will arrive shortly."

"How do you know?"

The doors opened suddenly, and two of the kitchen staff entered with silver-domed serving trays.

"Oh." Benoit took a seat beside me, gracefully placing the linen napkin in his lap and offering up compliments to the chef once the domes were lifted.

That was one thing I'd noticed about my companion—his unfailing politeness, not to mention his enthusiasm. A far cry from my disposition, and one the staff no doubt reveled in.

He waited until the servers left before lifting his wine glass toward mine. "To you, *mon monstre*. And a month of delicious devilry."

Those hazel eyes practically twinkled as I tapped his glass and then took a long sip of cabernet. I wasn't usually a wine drinker, but it paired well with the roast pork, dumplings, and sauerkraut we'd been served.

"Mmm." Benoit closed his eyes and moaned around the fork in his mouth. "That is heaven."

"First time having *Vepřo Knedlo Zelo*?"

"First but definitely not the last," he said, tapping his mouth with his napkin. "And what about you?"

"No, it's not my first."

"What's your favorite? If you could have a final meal of anything in the world, what would it be?"

"*Pastitsio*."

"That didn't take you long. Is there some deeper meaning behind it?"

I kept my eyes on my plate as I scooped up another bite. "Just a reminder of home."

"And home is in Greece, I take it. Athens?"

"Santorini."

"Even better," he said. "Though horribly overrun with tourists lately."

I arched a brow. "You've been?"

"I might've performed there once or twice. Years ago." He ran the lip of his wine glass along his mouth as he tilted his head at me. "My very own gorgeous Greek god. Whatever will I get to do with you?"

That suggestive comment was accompanied by his foot sliding up the inside of my leg.

"I'm sure you'll come up with something. You don't seem lacking in ideas when it comes to the...physical side of your nature."

Benoit's foot stopped. "I believe I'll take that as a compliment."

"That's how it was intended. Although I have to admit, your confidence in that department makes me—"

"Horny?" My lips curled around my fork, and Benoit chuckled. "There, I did it—you definitely smiled that time."

I didn't even bother refuting his claim, because he was right. "I was going to say—"

"Jealous?" I lowered my fork to the plate, and Benoit held up his hand. "Okay, okay, I was just playing. But it would be hot if you *were* jealous."

Then I must've been on fire, because the more I sat there thinking about him acting this way with anyone other than me, that green monster was starting to lurk.

"Go ahead." Benoit relaxed back in his seat with his glass. "You were saying my confidence in that department makes you..."

"Curious," I finally said. "About your past and any significant others you might've had."

Benoit took a sip of wine then aimed a sultry look my way. "Who says I don't still have one?"

That was the last thing I'd expected to hear, and it was obvious by his sly grin that my expression gave that away.

"Again, just playing with you. I'm free as a bird—or snow bunny. I don't do relationships."

Interesting...

"Really?"

"I know it's hard to believe. And trust me, many a man has tried to tie me down. But once the fun and orgasms were over, well, I disappeared into the night."

I considered his response carefully—the flirty smile, the sexual overtones, and the flippant nonchalance—and while it was all very convincing, this was the first time I'd noticed a slight tension in his posture.

I'd hit a nerve, and I wanted to know what.

"Why do you disappear?"

"Hmm?"

"You said you disappeared into the night. Why?"

Benoit shrugged. "No one gave me a good reason to stay."

"No one since..."

He straightened then cocked his head. "What makes you think there's a 'since' in there?"

"Because I've been watching you very closely over the last two weeks, and this is the first time you've looked uncomfortable."

Benoit looked down at his hands, then licked his lower lip, and I knew I was right. Someone had hurt him in the past. Someone had made him avoid relationships, and I wanted to know who he was—and why he was still breathing.

"I had a bad breakup, that's all. I confided in him about

certain things, and when it was over, he used it against me. See, nothing that dramatic. Plus, it was years ago."

"He betrayed you."

Benoit nodded. "He did."

I shook my head and closed my eyes, my mentor's face flashing behind my lids in that final moment we shared when he flipped open his knife and lunged—

"Dimitri?"

My eyes snapped open and focused on Benoit, who reached over to place a hand on top of my fist.

"Are you okay?"

The concern in his voice told me I looked anything but. However, not about to bring up that bastard's name in Benoit's company, I merely nodded and drew my hand from his.

I reached for my wine glass. "There's nothing worse than a betrayal. If there's a snake in your life, you need to cut off its head."

Benoit stared at me for a long moment before nodding and reaching for his own glass. "I couldn't agree more."

8

BENOIT

FTER DINNER, WE lounged by the fireplace and opened up a second bottle of wine, but the constant interruptions from members of his team had us retreating to our bedroom for the night.

Finally.

I wasn't just curious about Dimitri's moves between the sheets—I was also horny beyond belief. I hadn't expected all the teasing and delayed gratification coming from the monster himself, not when that was *my* MO.

Before this went any further, though, there was something I needed to take care of.

When I entered the room, I picked up a small carry-on from my line of luggage and turned around, giving Dimitri a sensual smirk.

"I'm going to change into something more...enticing," I said, running my finger down the length of his chest. It was like steel to the touch, and my cock twitched impatiently.

Dark eyes stared down at me, deep and intense. "Or you could just take everything off."

"I could. But then you'd miss unwrapping the gift I brought to wear just for you."

When his gaze dropped further down my body, I knew I had him. He was curious and all in on drawn-out pleasure.

"Be right back," I sang, sashaying into the en suite and shutting the door behind me. Once I was alone, I reached for the lip gloss and unscrewed the bottom. A compartment opened up and I quickly unfastened the hidden cameras in my cuff links, my heartbeat picking up with Dimitri on the other side of the door. It was always a risk wearing any kind of recording device, since he and his team would no doubt be familiar with the usual tech. Thank God Alessio was always changing things up and creating new ways to keep our actions secret, or I would've been a lot more worried.

Hopefully the cameras had gotten a good view of the maps that had been laid out and marked up when I barged into the dining room. We needed to know the locations of his meetings and whom he was meeting with. That would go a long way in letting us know whether Dimitri Stavros's reign could be trusted.

I popped the tiny cameras into the compartment, twisted the bottom back on, and set the gloss back in my makeup bag. Then I listened at the door for any sound, but it was dead quiet in the bedroom. I was tempted to make a quick call, see if the videos went through okay, but that was pushing it too far. Besides, I had more pleasurable tasks to get to tonight.

Starting with this, I thought, pulling out the emerald-green thong I'd purchased specifically for Dimitri to enjoy. Green, the color of money and jealousy, something I figured a man like him would appreciate.

After stripping off my clothes, I put on the tiny scrap of material and admired myself in the mirror. This was the sort of thing I'd enjoyed wearing in my twenties during my performing years, when my body had been at its peak, with none of the effort it required now to look this good.

But I still had it. Thank God, or none of this would be working out to my advantage.

I gave myself another once-over, tousled my hair a bit, and then grinned. Damn right I still had it.

Wanting Dimitri to enjoy unwrapping his surprise, I reached for one of the plush navy robes hanging in the closet and slipped it on. It was much thicker than the usual hotel robes, probably to account for the weather here, but I wouldn't be keeping it on long.

I took in a deep breath, steadying my excitement, and opened the door—

Only to be greeted with an empty room.

What the hell? Didn't he know he was supposed to be naked and waiting for me?

Movement outside on the balcony caught my attention, and I slid my feet into a pair of slippers before opening the door. A blast of cold air stung my face, but Dimitri sat casually in one of the chairs with a cigar, like it wasn't below freezing.

He was silent and still, puffing on the cigar and holding the smoke in his mouth before looking up at me and blowing the stream in my direction.

"And here I was hoping we were going to *heat* up the night," I said, looking out at the snow lightly falling just beyond the balcony.

"If you're cold"—Dimitri ran his eyes over me, then looked to his lap—"I can think of a quick way to warm you up."

I liked where this was heading.

I stepped out onto the covered space and moved over to where he lounged back in his chair like some sort of king.

"Are you inviting me to take a seat?"

Dimitri brought the cigar back to his lips—and I'd be lying

if I said I didn't find the way they surrounded the end of it arousing as hell.

"I'm inviting you to do whatever will warm you up."

When I stopped in front of him and looked down at where his ankle was propped up on his knee, Dimitri lowered it, giving me full access to climb onto his lap.

Not about to waste the opportunity to give him a little payback for his earlier teasing, I reached for the sash of my robe and ran my fingers along the tie, giving it a little twirl for added effect. His attention shot to the move, just as I'd expected it to. Then I slowly untied the knot and let the robe part so it was hanging from my shoulders, showing a tantalizing glimpse at what lay underneath.

"Another for your collection," I said.

Dimitri cursed, and I reached for his cigar and brought it to my mouth. I took a puff then placed it in the ashtray beside him before I straightened and saw his eyes tracking over the strip of naked chest, abs, and the emerald thong doing its best to conceal me.

He reached down to adjust the erection pressing against the zipper of his pants.

"Uh-ah," I said, then reached for his hand and moved it aside as I lowered myself to straddle his lap. "If you want to touch something, touch me."

Dimitri's eyes flared as he slipped his hand under the lapel of my robe. He placed his palm on my bare skin, and despite the frigid air outside, that first touch was like being kissed by a flame.

Heat radiated from him and warmed every part of me. I arched into his touch as he started to slide it down my chest to my nipple.

"Mmm." The growl that rumbled through him made my

dick stiffen inside its tiny confines. "I've imagined this moment from the second I saw you step out on the stage."

"Me in your lap?" I reached for his shoulders, locking my fingers behind his neck, keeping me in place.

"You *naked* in my lap."

"I'm hardly naked, *mon monstre.*"

Dimitri slipped his other hand inside my robe and snaked it around my waist, tugging me even higher up his lap. I groaned as our covered cocks met and rubbed against each other. "You will be very soon."

"Is that right?" I teased, leaning back so I could watch his face as I ground myself over his thick erection. "Maybe you should've stayed inside where it was warm if *that* was what you were after."

Dimitri leaned in and scraped his teeth along my jaw, his wandering hand trailing up my spine, making me arch forward.

"If we'd stayed inside, I wouldn't have been patient enough to take a moment and enjoy you."

"Ah." I let my head fall back in pleasure. "Is that what you're doing?"

Dimitri kissed his way down my neck, and when he started to suck at the base of my throat, my fingers tightened in the back of his hair. I sighed as he raised his head and locked those dark eyes on mine.

"Yes." He slipped his fingers under the waist of the thong and grazed the sensitive head of my cock.

I sucked in a breath, catching my lower lip between my teeth, and Dimitri wrapped his hand around my dick. My eyes slammed shut as toe-curling pleasure flooded me.

"And I'm going to enjoy *fucking* you the rest of the night."

I thrust my hips forward, my thighs tightening around his as I propelled myself closer to him. Needing the friction on my dick more than my next breath. He left scorching kisses up the side of my neck, and the contrast of his heat and the cold at my back had a shiver rolling through me. I arched my neck to the side, wanting more of those kisses that told me just how much he wanted me.

I closed my eyes and smiled to myself as he nipped at my earlobe. "Maybe this is where payback happens. Wouldn't that be a shame?"

Dimitri drew back, and I reached down between us to stroke his dick.

"Maybe I should leave *you* like this," I said. "Wanting and hard for me. That would serve you right."

A growl ripped free of him before the words were even out of my mouth. He stopped massaging my cock and reached up to grip the back of my neck, hauling me in close.

"Don't even fucking *think* about it." His menacing timbre shot straight between my thighs, and before I could respond, he slammed his lips down on mine, ending the conversation.

Heat and arousal swirled as Dimitri took control, and this was what I'd been waiting for—for all that power he held to come bursting out. It had only been a matter of time before his carefully contained façade would crumble and I'd get to see the pent-up passion underneath.

He didn't give me even a second to get my bearings as he dominated the kiss, his tongue taking possession of mine and giving me my first taste of him.

And *fuck*—I'd known it would be good. I just didn't expect my whole body to be on fire. He was unrelenting, holding me tight to him as our mouths explored and we stole each other's breath.

This was exactly what I wanted, and what I'd needed after all this buildup.

As Dimitri stood up, I wrapped my legs around his waist,

my robe falling open but our connection never breaking. Not even when I rocked my hips to get that intense friction I sought when our cocks rubbed up against each other.

With a curse, he kept a tight hold on me with one arm, the other reaching behind himself to open the door. The second he pulled it wide, his hand was back on my ass, plumping and kneading, his fingers moving closer to exactly where I needed them to be.

Gone was any thought of my mission, and in its place was a singular focus:

Blow my fucking mind tonight, you beautiful monster.

9
DIMITRI

THE SECOND I stepped into the bedroom, I kicked the door shut and made a beeline to the bed. I'd waited weeks for this moment, where I'd finally have the seductive dancer in my arms, and now that I had him there, I wasn't wasting any more time.

Benoit's bare legs were wrapped tightly around my waist as his fingers tangled in my hair. His tongue was teasing and agile as it devoured every inch of my mouth, and his rock-hard dick was rubbing against me in a way that made it difficult to walk. But when I finally lowered him to the edge of the bed, Benoit released his hold and lay back on the mattress. His robe fell open to reveal the emerald G-string that had finally lost the battle to keep his cock concealed, and the sight of its shiny, plump head had me licking my lips.

Benoit spread his legs, planting his feet on the floor as he hooked his thumbs into the elastic at his waist and lowered it a fraction, giving me a tantalizing glimpse of the rest of him.

"Like what you see, *mon monstre?*"

Did I fucking ever. He'd teased me on stage like this twice now, and I'd be damned if that was all I got this time.

I moved between his legs and leaned down to plant a hand on either side of his head. Benoit arched up, about to wrap his arms around me, but there'd be time for that later. Right now I was focused on getting what I wanted.

His cock, in my mouth.

I placed a hand on his chest and urged him back to the mattress, then straightened and trailed my fingers down the center of his body, not stopping until I reached my target.

My fingertips grazed the sticky slit tempting me with his pre-cum, and with my eyes locked on his, I brought a finger to my mouth and sucked.

Fucking delicious...

Benoit's breathing came harder as he stared up at me, my silence making the sexual tension in the room crackle as he waited for my next move.

I reached for my belt and unbuckled it, then flicked open the button of my pants.

"Offer yourself to me."

Despite his vulnerable position, Benoit arched a brow. We both wanted this, that much was obvious, but where it'd all been about the tease before, now I wanted it to be about possession.

I wanted him to willingly give himself to me. I wanted him to understand what it meant. If he crossed this next line, if all of his teasing finally culminated in his offering his body to me, I was going to take him—and he would be mine for the next month.

Benoit licked his lip, then placed a palm on his stomach and slid it down toward his pelvis. His fingers slipped under the G-string, and I saw his fist grip the root of his dick under the tiny scrap of material.

A feral sound of desire rumbled through me as he stroked up his length, root to tip, revealing himself to my hungry gaze.

"Take it," Benoit said, sliding his hand back down and aiming his luscious cock my way. "It's yours." My jaw clenched at the explicit offer. It was exactly what I'd wanted to hear, and when he arched his body and whispered, "Take it, *mon monstre...*" I moved to my knees between his and put my hands on his thighs.

His dick was only inches away from my lips, and when I leaned forward and dragged my tongue along the underside of his erection, he groaned and fell back to the bed.

I moved up over him and flicked the glistening tip with my tongue, and when his flavor exploded on my taste buds, it was all over. I dug my fingers into the firm skin of his thighs, wrapped my hand over his at the base of his cock, then directed him to my greedy mouth.

The second he penetrated my lips, Benoit's hips jacked up off the mattress and he slid in deep. But I wasn't letting him run this show, not when I'd waited so long to finally get my hands and mouth on him.

I slid my palms up his torso and held him to the mattress as I drew my lips off him and stared up his body.

"Keep still."

Benoit lifted his head and gazed down at me, his cheeks flushed, eyes dark, pupils blown. "And if I don't?" He squeezed my sides with his thighs and writhed on the covers beneath him. But two could play this little game of one-upmanship.

I removed my hands and reached for the edge of the thong that was shoved down and under his balls and tore it apart, freeing his body of the material. Then I hooked each of his legs over my shoulders and opened him up nice and wide.

"Then you'll miss out on the best tongue fuck of your life." I smirked. "Your choice."

Benoit arched up again, and for a second I thought he was going to defy me—until he slipped his hands under his body.

"Feel free to bend me to your will. I'm *very* flexible."

I was going to take him up on that offer, but first things first—I lowered my head and sucked one of his balls between my lips, reveling in his pleasure-filled groan as I switched to the other, then teased and taunted both. I nuzzled into the root of Benoit's cock, the scent of his arousal filling my nostrils as I devoured the sensitive sacs. Then I licked my way up his throbbing dick, tracing the veins with the tip of my tongue.

I was ravenous, desperate to memorize the taste of this sensual man who'd danced his way into my every fantasy, and when I finally swallowed him down again, I took him all the way in.

"*Merde.*"

As he began to fuck my mouth, his pre-cum coated the back of my throat, and goddamn, he tasted better than he had any right to. With the fantasy I'd built of him in my head, no one could live up to the hype, but with every suck and swallow, I was beginning to think a month wasn't *nearly* long enough to satisfy my hunger.

When Benoit bucked up past my lips again, I couldn't deny how sexy it was to see him take his pleasure from me. But tonight I needed to establish some clear rules, and he'd been teasing my dick long enough. It was time to make him beg.

I licked up the underside of his length, all the way to the tip, where I flicked my tongue over his slit as I took in the way he was splayed out and flushed against the sheets.

"You have a very talented mouth, *mon monstre*," he said on a ragged breath, but I only cocked a brow at him before lowering my head again.

With his legs still over my shoulders, I shifted his hips up and spread those smooth, plump ass cheeks apart, getting him right where I wanted him. It was a good thing he was flexible, because I wasn't gentle as I dove in, swiping my tongue along his cleft.

He sucked in a breath, gripping the sheets. When I flattened my tongue and licked over his clenched hole, a string of curses left him, only about half making any sense to me.

That's what I want, I thought as I repeated the move and then gave his entrance several flicks. *Go wild for me.*

The only problem? He wasn't the only one losing it. As I speared my tongue and sank into the heat of him, pushing through the ring of muscle trying to keep me out, I got another addictive taste of him.

I tightened my fingers on his cheeks, keeping them wide open so I could tongue-fuck his ass, and Benoit raised his hips to meet my mouth, giving me a deeper dive inside. His legs began to tremble where they rested on my shoulders, but still I didn't give him even a second of reprieve.

As I pulled out and swirled my tongue along his pucker, he tangled his fingers through my hair, pulling tight like he couldn't decide if he wanted relief or wanted even more.

I didn't give him a choice.

Shifting my hands beneath him, I lifted him toward my face like he was my own personal buffet. I spat on his hole, lubing him up with the tip of my tongue, and then slid a finger inside.

"Yesss," he said, that greedy, perfect ass of his devouring my finger like it was desperate for another.

I added a second, shoving them both inside and lifting my head to watch his reaction.

I thought I'd find him with his head thrown back and reveling in what I was giving, but instead he had lifted up on his elbows, watching every move I made with intense focus. As my knuckles pressed up against his entrance, he moaned.

That moan was music to my ears, and I flicked my tongue around his hole while I scissored my fingers inside him, working him over, getting him stretched so he could take every inch of my cock.

I didn't plan to take it easy on him, and from the way he writhed beneath me, he was impatient for more than just my fingers. Or maybe that was my own erection talking, strangled behind my briefs.

Benoit's breathing turning ragged had me glancing up to see he'd taken hold of his dick and was getting himself off. His hand moved in time with the one I had deep inside him, and hell no that wasn't going to work for me.

Drawing my fingers out of him, I rose and grabbed hold of his wrist, stilling his movements.

"Did I *say* you could touch yourself?"

He panted. "I didn't know I needed your permission. Should I say please?"

"No." I lowered his legs to the mattress and stood up, hauling him up with me. He was unsteady on his feet, and as his robe hit the floor, I turned him around to face away from me.

Then I bent him over the edge of the bed and said, "You can fucking beg."

10

BENOIT

MY BODY THRUMMED with frustrated arousal as I stood, bent at the waist, over the edge of the bed. The covers were warm against my cheek from where I'd just been spread out at Dimitri's mercy, and my cock ached for the release he seemed hell-bent on making me wait for.

I tried to calm my breathing, tried to think of anything but how fucking talented that man's tongue was. But no matter how hard I tried, nothing could stop the fire licking through my veins.

My legs shook as I waited impatiently for Dimitri to make his next move, and when the rustle of material hit my ears, I knew it was time to make mine.

I grabbed hold of the covers and crawled up onto the bed. My goal was to make Dimitri wait for it...just as he did me.

My knees had just cleared the mattress, putting my ass front and center of his view, but just as I was halfway across the bed, a firm hand clamped around my ankle.

A loud gasp left me as strong fingers tugged me back to the

edge of the bed. Then that same hand moved to the center of my back and shoved me face down into the mattress.

My dick throbbed where it was trapped between my body and the covers, and when Dimitri moved in behind me this time, the heat of his naked skin scorched the back of my thighs.

"Running away so soon?"

Oh sweet Jesus. I wanted to see him so damn bad. But then again, it was probably better that I couldn't, because that gravel-rough voice coupled with what I could feel behind me would have me coming in seconds.

"Not running, just...prolonging the enjoyment."

Dimitri planted his hands by my head, then shifted down over me. The feel of his thick cock nudging up against my ass had me swallowing back a whimper. "I think you were running."

I wriggled back into him, wanting to impale myself on him. "Maybe I just wanted to be chased."

Dimitri's throaty chuckle by my ear sent a delicious shiver through my entire body.

"I'll have to remember that. But time's up for you tonight, I'm afraid." He reached down and slipped a hand between us, spreading my cheeks. "I want inside this exquisite body of yours."

I wanted that too, and just so there was no mistake, I widened my stance.

"Yes," Dimitri growled. "Show me that pretty hole. Show me where you want me to put my cock."

Putain. When was the last time I'd had someone talk to me like that? A long damn time. The men whose beds I usually visited were refined, sophisticated, gentlemanly types.

Dimitri was none of those things. He was rough, brash, and lethal, a combination that was turning out to be one hell of an aphrodisiac. I wanted to go wild with him. I wanted him to take me without constraint.

A hand at the nape of my neck held me in place as he nudged up against my back entrance, teasing me with the head of his dick. My fingers curled around the bedcovers, then he breached my stretched hole, and the burn of his intrusion—despite the thorough tongue lashing he'd given me—had my teeth gnashing together.

"I fucking knew it..." he said to himself as he slid into me, inch by tortuous inch.

His fingers tightened at the back of my neck, the one on my ass digging into my skin as he spread me even further apart, and I knew he was looking at us. The way his cock was now fully lodged inside me. The way my ass was stretched around his thickness.

My balls tingled at the visual I'd just painted for myself. Then Dimitri began to pull out of me, and I couldn't stop my cry.

The hand at my neck let go to reach for my other hip, and when he plowed forward this time, the entire bed shifted under the power of his thrust. The scrape of the legs on the wood floor was almost as satisfying as the grunt of pleasure from the man behind me.

Dimitri had lost his words, his ability to form coherent sentences, and I clenched my ass around the intruding length inside it.

"A tease even between the sheets..."

"Not. Between. Sheets," I panted as I pushed back onto him.

Dimitri moved down over me. "Gonna get so deep you forget what it's like *not* to have me in you."

I didn't have an answer for that—just a sound, one full of lustful yearning, because I wanted that. I wanted that so fucking bad I almost came from the mere promise of it. But when Dimitri gripped the covers by my head and started to rut me like an animal in heat, I closed my eyes and allowed all the sensations to flood through me, over me, inside me.

I was no longer in control. *He* controlled every nerve ending, every sensory hot spot on my body. I was his to use, to have. His to *take*. And my leaking cock could attest to that—it was making an absolute mess of the bed beneath me. The friction of the covers added a whole other sensation to go with the intense prostate massage Dimitri was administering.

"More," I begged, delirious with the kind of pleasure that led to obsession.

Dimitri seemed to understand, though. He stilled, deep inside me, let go of the covers, and slid an arm under me. Then he straightened and pulled me to my feet, his forearm firm against my collarbone.

Teeth sank into my shoulder, hard. "More?"

I nodded, and he slid his palm down the middle of my body and wrapped it around my erection. I cried out from the touch, the heat of his hand exactly what I wanted and needed to take this to the next level.

"That what you want?" he asked, and jutted his hips forward, nailing my P-spot.

"Yes. *Putain, oui.*"

He stroked up my shaft as he pulled from my body, swiping his thumb over the slit. Then he let go of me, brought his hand up, and said, "Lick it."

I swiped my tongue over his palm, tasting myself there, then spat in it.

"Let me fuck it," I said. "While you fuck me."

A harsh curse echoed around me as Dimitri once again took hold of my cock, and this time there was no teasing, no playing around. The second his fingers surrounded me, I shoved back on the dick inside me, then fucked forward into the fist waiting for me.

Dimitri gripped my hip and immediately picked up the pace.

It was only when his bare chest slapped against my back that I realized I hadn't gotten a chance to look at him, not the way I wanted to. But I couldn't focus on that right now, not when he was fucking me into oblivion. I'd get a chance to explore Dimitri's body the way I wanted to soon, and from the brief glimpse I got, it was rock hard with a dusting of dark hair covering his deeply tanned skin. God, he was delicious in a way I craved. Such a bad, bad boy, with the looks and power to match.

I shouldn't be as turned on about that as I was.

His thumb swiped over my slit on a stroke, just as he hit that sensitive bundle of nerves again, and it sent me gasping.

There was no way I should still be standing, not with the force with which he pounded into me, or the way my unsteady legs felt like they were sinking into quicksand. He seemed to understand I was seconds away from falling at his feet and flexed his hand on my hip to hold me tighter. I lifted my arm and gripped the back of his neck, drawing him closer, pressed up against my body and giving me something to hold on to.

"You're so fucking tight," he growled in my ear.

"You're so fucking *big*."

The way I felt him shudder ever so slightly, like he was close to losing control, had an arrogant sense of satisfaction rolling through me.

So much so, I deluded myself into doing something I really shouldn't do.

My hand joined his on my dick, and I gave a couple of strokes before pushing him away. At the same time, as his cock pulled out to the tip in my ass, I made my move. I turned around, wrapped my arms around his waist, and pushed him down onto the bed. Climbing on top of him to straddle his body took all the strength I had left, but I enjoyed this little game we were playing too much to not try to take control.

For a moment, I thought he'd let me, too. But the second I lifted up on my knees to sink down onto his massive erection, he flipped me so hard and fast to my back that my head spun.

"First you run. Then you try to dominate." His heavy body, all muscle, pinned me to the mattress. Then he reached down for the tie of my robe that was still lying on the end of the bed and pushed my arms up over my head.

"Ooh, kinky," I said, squirming beneath him, not from discomfort but just to rub my body all over his. From this position I could see him, *all* of him, and I had to admit—I liked his way of doing things.

He tied my wrists together with the material from the robe —a much more comfortable option than handcuffs—and then wrapped them around the wrought-iron headboard.

"Still saying *more*?" he asked.

"*Oui, mon monstre.* I want *everything.*"

His nostrils flared, and a heartbeat later he shoved my knees up to my chest. He didn't enter me slowly, but thrust himself back inside in a way that had me sucking in a breath at the bite of pain. It soon turned to pleasure as he began to rock inside me, moving his hips to nail the spot that had me nearly blacking out in ecstasy.

"There," I said, trying to buck up into him to keep him right where I wanted him, but it was impossible to do restrained. He had me incapacitated, had full control over my body so that all I could manage to do was watch him and take what he gave.

And fuck, that was an incredible view.

His black hair fell past his ears, strands sticking to the light sheen of sweat on his face. As he thrust into me, driving me closer to the edge and holding my calves to keep me in place, I let myself openly stare at him. Every muscle of his glorious body was flexed, giving me a view that had my mouth watering and my cock leaking with arousal. I couldn't even find it in me to care that he wasn't jacking me off anymore, not when I was so close to exploding that, had he been touching me, this would all be over with already.

Dimitri slammed into me, harder and faster, the headboard hitting the wall with every thrust. He ruled over my body, an unspoken warning vibrating between us that I wasn't allowed to come until he did. And *fuck* did I need this release, almost more than I needed to breathe. It was all I could do to keep my thinly held self-control intact.

"Will you come all over me?" I taunted him. "Or inside of me?"

That challenge had Dimitri's eyes narrowing, but his movements became erratic. His throat corded, his head fell back, and then he came inside me with a roar that echoed off the walls. A hot rush of cum filled my ass, and the sensation had my orgasm hitting so fast that I didn't have time to warn him before I detonated. Jets of cum burst out of me, coating my chest and abs as I cried out.

"*Merde*," I said, breathless and waiting for my vision to come back.

Dimitri was still inside me, and I was still coming when I felt him lean down and lick a path across my abs. I opened my eyes to see him watching me, that intense gaze on my face while he swallowed my cum.

It was so damn hot that I could've come again right then if he hadn't just drained me completely.

I let out a curse as he tasted me again.

"That's not fair." I pretended to pout as I lowered my

aching legs to the mattress and stretched them out on either side of him. "When do I get to taste you?"

Dimitri lifted up to his knees, his spent cock sliding out of me and leaving me far too empty except for the warmth flowing out of my ass and dripping onto the sheets.

He swiped his finger through the mess on my chest, keeping those dark eyes trained on me as he said, "When you earn it."

11

DIMITRI

A SOFT VIBRATION coming from the alarm I'd set had me opening my eyes, but I was already awake anyway. Sleep never came easy, and certainly not with a meeting taking place in the early hours of the morning.

The room was nearly pitch black, and I could only just make out Benoit sleeping beside me. His breathing was soft and steady, and for a moment I watched him, jealous of how peaceful he seemed. Life seemed full of joy for him—he was able to indulge in men and drinking and dancing, whatever he wanted, to his heart's content. What would that be like? To sleep through the night or make my way in the world without the weight and the worry and the constant looking over my shoulder?

That was a luxury for softer men, but I wouldn't begrudge Benoit for enjoying life's pleasures. After all, there was nothing soft about the body I'd used to its limit all night. He'd been as insatiable as I was, and had my presence not been required at this ungodly hour, I would've been tempted to wake him with my mouth around his cock.

Fuck. I couldn't think about that now. Couldn't think about the chaos he could bring to my life over the next month or how intriguing it was to have him around. Right now I needed to focus on what was about to go down.

With my suit already pressed and in the closet, I dressed quietly in the en suite, making sure I looked the part of the menacing arms dealer. Not that it was a difficult feat. I was barely forty-five and the lines between my brows were etched there permanently, whether I was scowling or not. The scar that ran down my left cheek was a jagged, ugly thing, still red and raised, but it no doubt added a layer of intimidation to my appearance.

I flicked off the light and stepped out of the en suite, pausing for a moment to make sure Benoit was still asleep, and then slipped out into the hallway.

My team was already waiting in the foyer, all of them silent and dressed in black—the ones going with me in suits, the others in tactical gear.

I ran my eyes over each of them, counting them up, making sure we were all set. Omar moved in beside me and handed me a gun, and I pulled back the slide, checked the chamber was full of lead, and then slid the weapon into the holster beneath my jacket.

"Let's go."

They all filed out in silence behind me, snow crunching under our footsteps as each team member made their way to the waiting cars that would drop us off several blocks from our destination. With our plans already set, nothing needed to be said outside of each person testing their mics as we traveled just outside the city center.

Though I'd heard Prague had a thriving nightlife, the scene obviously wasn't happening on the side of town we were on.

Everything was quiet as we exited the cars and started down the cobblestone streets.

Too quiet.

If I wasn't here for business, I liked to think I would've taken more time to appreciate the medieval architecture and the beauty of the place, but if I were honest, we could've been anywhere. If I'd seen one city, I'd seen them all, though I could confidently say I was partial to the ones that stayed over eighty degrees on the regular.

We continued down the winding roads, all senses on alert. A block away from the flower shop, Hugo gave me a nod and then team two veered off to take up their positions at the back. I glanced over my shoulder, making sure Omar, the bodyguards, and I were alone, then continued on, slipping my hands into my pockets to ward off the frigid bite in the air.

It was just coming up on three a.m. and I couldn't help but think of the words of my mentor—*There are only ever two kinds of people up at this time of the morning, Dimitri: cops and criminals.* I didn't want any unexpected interruptions from either. I'd be dealing with the latter soon enough, but on my terms, the way I liked it.

We reached the flower shop, and the door was shut. A *Closed* sign hung inside the glass, and the shades were drawn on the windows. But that was to be expected. This wasn't where we'd be entering. Instead, we headed to the side alley where they received their deliveries.

Omar took the lead, checking for any hostile bystanders before giving me the all-clear. I made my way down to where a lone light shone over a thick wooden door. Omar took position, facing the street as I knocked. Seconds later, a slat slid open and narrow eyes met mine.

"Turn around, face the opposite wall," he ordered me, his voice gruff, his accent thick.

I wasn't one to usually follow orders, but if I were sitting inside a flower shop at three in the morning waiting to meet up with the most lethal weapons dealer in the world, I'd want to see his face too.

I pivoted and stared at the bricks opposite me, and it wasn't until I looked closer at the mortar in line with my eyes that I saw it. A tiny camera, no doubt scanning my face.

Done playing exhibitionist, I turned back to face the door. "Either tell your boss I'm here and open the fucking door or tell them you let me leave and—"

I didn't even get to finish my threat before the sound of bolts echoed around us and the door yawned open. Apparently the idea of my leaving without seeing his boss would lead to consequences he clearly didn't want to incur.

"Follow me," he said. I stepped inside, Omar following, leaving the bodyguards outside to keep watch on the alley.

We made our way down a narrow hall, the old brick of the building's façade having made its way to the interior as well. Then the gatekeeper opened a second bolted door and pulled it wide.

"She's waiting for you downstairs."

I eyed the stone steps that seemed to lead into a black void, then Omar moved ahead of me and we began our descent. Three steps down and the door shut behind us, and had I not been accustomed to such clandestine meetings, I might've thought something nefarious was about to take place.

As it was, a flickering torch blazed to life at the bottom of the stairs and Josefina Nováková appeared.

"*Zdravím vás, pane Stavrosi.* I trust you found my little flower shop easy enough."

Her thick, chestnut-colored hair cascaded in waves over delicate shoulders as she angled her flawless face up toward us. She had a slender build but was taller than average for a woman, at around five eleven.

But what Josefina might lack in physical strength, she made up for with smart, cunning defenses. Something that came in handy when one's field was political espionage.

"I did. Though I have to say, the greeting was much cooler than I expected."

She laughed as we reached the bottom of the stairs, her painted lips curving into a crimson smile. "Why? Because I'm a woman?"

"No." I stepped around Omar and leaned down over her, my face drawn tight. "Because you want something only I can get you."

She shrugged a shoulder, trying for nonchalance, but I didn't miss the way she swallowed or glanced at my scar.

"I can't risk my cover being blown. Not even for you, Mr. Stavros. But if you don't want my money—"

Quick as a lightning bolt—and just as deadly—I snatched the torch from her hand and grabbed her wrist with the other, yanking her in close. I held it up by the side of her beautiful face, and as the shadows of the flames flickered over the sharp angles of her smooth skin, I said, "Then what? I don't usually like to start my meetings off with threats, but if that's the tone you'd like to set, I'm happy to play."

I shifted the torch a little closer and she reared back, clenching her teeth.

"Nothing to add?" I asked.

When she shook her head, I released her with a gentle shove and handed the torch to Omar.

Straightening her shoulders, she led us into the small, circular room that was barely big enough for the five of us— which included both male and female guards standing behind a table for two. Josefina gestured for me to take a seat before doing the same, and I could feel Omar's tensed form beside me. It was a dangerous situation to put ourselves in without knowing ever-changing motivations and loyalty. Trust wasn't something you could give in this line of work, not even to those around you.

"What can I do for you?" I said, keeping my gaze steady on her, giving her all my attention and ignoring her backup. I didn't give a shit about the guards. Omar would be trained on them, and giving even a glance in their direction would make me look like I was worried. Fuck that.

"You are aware that I don't know you."

It was a bold way for her to start the conversation, especially when we'd met before. I wasn't going to bring that up, though, not when I'd been an inconsequential second-in-command.

"You've had a long working relationship with my mentor, Giorgos. There's no reason we can't continue to be of service to each other."

She scoffed. "You say that and yet you have my building surrounded."

I glanced pointedly up at her guards. "Safety precautions are necessary, don't you agree?" When she didn't answer, just continued to stare at me, I added, "So again I'll ask, what can I do for you?"

I hadn't come all this way not to make a deal, but if she wanted to sit here and have a staring contest before putting in an order, I wouldn't blink.

"Guns," she finally said, drumming her long red fingernails on the table. "I want the latest and greatest. Combat knives. Chemical and explosive grenades."

I nodded, took the tablet Omar offered, and flicked through until a selection of grenades came up, then handed it over.

"Take a look at the inventory, make a selection, and I'll get it for you."

Josefina took the tablet. "Just like that?"

"Yes. After you transfer the funds, of course."

"Of course. You have something of everything in stock, then?"

"I have ways of *getting* something of everything." I slipped my hands into my pockets. "You want to test me? Go ahead. I'm not going to stop you from buying one of everything."

She grunted but then shifted her attention to the tablet, punching in the quantities she wanted before flipping through to the next section—semiautomatic rifles and pistols. It was your one-stop online shop for black market weapons. Click and add to cart—it was that easy.

"There, you get those to me within the month and you can consider my business yours."

"You get me your money by the end of the *week* and I might consider keeping you on the books."

Josefina gave a clipped nod. "Fair enough. But you fuck with me, I won't take it lying down."

I scoffed and gave her a slow once-over. "Don't worry, Miss Nováková, you're not my type."

She bristled under my intense gaze, probably used to seducing men into doing whatever she wanted. But unfortunately for her, my interests lay warm and naked back in my bed.

A place I was ready to return to—now.

"If we're done here, I have some other pressing matters I must attend to tonight."

She gestured to the stairs. "I trust you won't be offended if I don't see you out?"

"Not at all." I headed toward the stone steps, Omar following, his gun still trained on the three at the table in case anyone got any stupid ideas. Before we disappeared out the door at the top, I called back, "I'll be in touch."

12

BENOIT

I'D GLIMPSED THE maps oh so casually last night, so when I woke in the early hours and Dimitri wasn't there, I knew exactly where he'd gone.

And when he wasn't back in bed by the time the sun came up, that told me all I needed to know about his sleeping habits. He *didn't* sleep, not more than three or four hours, and that tracked with many of the powerful men I knew.

Me, on the other hand? I slept like a perfectly swaddled baby. A full night's beauty sleep *was* of the utmost importance, after all.

After a day of exploring the grounds, I joined Dimitri for dinner, separate from his team, which I found interesting. Would he dine alone if I weren't around? Or did he just prefer not to bring me around his work?

So many questions about the man I'd be spending the next few weeks with.

I set my bishop in its new position on the chessboard and then reached for my wine. "Your move."

Dimitri took his time, weighing every option like it was a

life-or-death situation. Maybe for him it was. I got the feeling he didn't like to lose.

When he finally made his move, his dark eyes flicked up to mine, challenging me.

He was so damn sexy sitting in a cozy leather chair by a roaring fire, its flames casting shadows across his face. It made him look even more dark and dangerous, which, apparently, was exactly the kind of man my dick was into, judging by the way I'd had a semi since we started this game.

Last night was an epic sex marathon, and I shouldn't have even had the energy to look at him that way, but damn. Tall, intimidating, and Greek apparently did it for me. Who knew?

I focused back on the board, contemplating my move. He'd just put me in a tough position, but if there was one thing I knew how to do, it was wiggling my way out of a seemingly impossible situation. Usually that meant using every ounce of sex appeal I had, and while that didn't help in a game like this, I *could* distract him a bit.

I made a show of slipping off my jacket, revealing a sleeveless amethyst silk top that showcased my arms and shoulders. Then, deciding that wasn't enough, I unfastened a couple more buttons so he had a good look down my chest.

As I lifted one of my pawns, I swirled my finger over its rounded tip, keeping my gaze down at the board like I didn't know what effect I was giving off.

"Hmm. This is so...*hard*," I said, bringing the pawn up to tap against my lips as I contemplated my next move.

"That's not going to work." When I looked up in question, Dimitri shook his head. "I see what you're doing."

"Oh? What am I doing?"

"You have a hot-as-fuck body—"

"Why, thank you for noticing."

"—but using it to distract me won't work."

I gave a shocked gasp. "Are you suggesting I'd *cheat*?"

"Are you saying you wouldn't?"

"Maybe the fire has me feeling a little...warm."

"I could put it out."

"Or I could just take off my clothes if I get too hot." I dropped my pawn into position.

Dimitri's eyes shifted to the move, his lips curled, and a second later he swiped my piece off the board, replacing it with one of his. "Told you it wouldn't work."

"Well, you don't have to look so smug about it."

"Maybe I'm just happy I can actually resist you when I put my mind to it."

"Wait." I lounged back in my chair and crossed one leg over the other. "Did you just admit to being...happy?"

Dimitri took a sip of his whiskey. "Now who's being smug?"

"Me. But it's well earned. You're a tough nut to crack."

"And is that what you're trying to do? Crack me?"

I swirled the wine around the bottom of my glass and eyed the flickering shadows dancing across his face. "Just trying to get to know the man I'm—"

"Sleeping with?"

"There wasn't all that much sleeping going on last night. Before or after we tested out the mattress."

Dimitri's eyes narrowed. "You didn't sleep well?"

"I don't mean me, *mon monstre*. You're the one who slipped out in the early morning."

"I told you, I don't like to stay in the same place for too long."

"Even a night?" I finished off my wine with a final sip and placed the glass down. "I think there's more to it than that."

"And I think *you're* overthinking it." Dimitri eyed the board. "It's your turn."

I let out a sigh and sat forward, trying to determine what countermove he'd make depending on each of the moves open to me, but it wasn't easy. Compared to Dimitri, I was a novice at playing this game. So much so I almost second-guessed the *other* game I was playing with him—almost.

I picked up my rook and moved it into the spot left open by the pawn he'd just knocked off the table. When he chuckled, I realized my mistake and went to pick it back up.

Faster than I could blink, Dimitri reached across the board and took hold of my wrist.

"What do you think you're doing?"

I raised my eyes to his and almost melted on the spot under his incendiary stare. "I thought of a better move."

"Too bad. Once you relinquish your grip on the piece, your turn is over."

"You're making that up."

"Am I?"

"Yes. Everyone knows there's a clock that you push when you finish your move."

"And when there's no clock," he said, drawing me around the board until I stood in front of him, "your move is over when you stop *touching* your piece."

"Says you."

"Says me." Dimitri tugged me down onto his lap. "And I haven't stopped touching you yet, so it's still my move."

He slid his hand up my arm and then drew the tip of his finger down the V of the neckline.

"So I'm your 'piece,' then?" I whispered, my dick apparently not having an issue with that at all. Play piece, piece of ass, piece on the side—okay, I kind of had a problem with the last one. But I already knew there wasn't anyone else warming his bed, so for now I was okay with this scenario.

Especially when Dimitri dipped his head and put his lips to the side of my neck.

"For the purpose of this game?" He smoothed his hand down to my waist and pulled me higher on his lap, sucking on the sweet spot just behind my ear. "Definitely."

I hummed and wriggled in his lap, wrapping my arm around his neck. "And are we going to stay in this musty old castle and play games for the rest of our stay? Or are you going to take me out to explore?"

Dimitri flicked his tongue over my lobe, then moved the hand at my waist down to my thighs and urged them apart. Never once did he lift his palm, relinquishing his move.

"I'm having a good time exploring right here. Aren't you?"

God yes, I was. If I had my way, I'd rip all my clothes off and let him explore me all night, naked. But I needed something else from him right now. Something other than multiple orgasms.

"I am." I sighed, rolling my hips up into the hand now massaging my cock. "But you know something I'd really like to do?"

Dimitri kissed his way across my cheek to the corner of my lips. "What's that?"

"See the Christmas markets."

The hand covering me froze as Dimitri raised his head, and I put on my most dazzling smile.

"Not really my thing," he said, and leaned in, about to take my lips with his, effectively ending the conversation. But that wouldn't do. I had to get to those markets, and I would do— and *not* do—whatever I must to get there.

"Oh no you don't," I said, putting a hand to his chest and craning back to look him in the eyes. "You think you can keep me all locked up and naked in your bed the whole time I'm here?"

"That was the idea."

I dropped my mouth open, feigning shock. "What kind of man do you think I am?"

Dimitri was about to answer when I put a finger to his lips. "Nope, don't answer. Just say you'll take me. *Please.*" I batted my lashes for added effect. "Prague's famous for them."

"Is that right?"

"It is." I could see I was breaking through his stoic wall, and I was hoping one more little push would get him there. "How about this? You take me to the Christmas markets and indulge me in some glühwein, and when we get home, I'll indulge *you* in anything your heart desires."

"Anything?"

I leaned in, took his lip between my teeth, and bit down. "*Anything.*"

Dimitri raised a brow but then lifted his hands. "Then what are we waiting for? It's your move."

13
BENOIT

THE AMOUNT OF clothes I was wearing was criminal, but so was being out in temperatures lower than my morals.

Lucky for me, I had a hot man to nuzzle into.

With my hand tucked into Dimitri's arm, we strolled through the Christmas markets at Old Town Square, and it was exactly the winter wonderland I'd always heard about. The enormous tree that lit up the night was even larger than the one at the Wenceslas Square market, and the sound of a choral group singing holiday songs filtered through the air. It was even more beautiful than I'd expected, with red-roofed little huts filled with crafts being sold by local artists, decorations and lights everywhere.

This had been a spectacularly good idea.

As we passed one of the food huts, I breathed in deep. I didn't know what it was they were making, but it was a savory delight that made my mouth water.

"Whatever that is, I need it," I said, and Dimitri stopped

and looking over at what was on the grill—barbecued sausages that had no right to look as delicious as they did, and in the display were meat dumplings that made my stomach growl.

There was no way he could've heard it over the music, but he lifted a brow in my direction before ordering two of everything.

"What about them?" I nodded at the two bodyguards who trailed several feet behind us. Their presence was putting a definite kink in my plans, but I'd figure out how to get around it. It wasn't the first time I'd had to come up with a plan B on the fly.

Dimitri handed me a plate of food before diving into his own, starting with the sausage. "They don't need distractions."

"No? Watching you eat that sausage is pretty distracting."

That garnered me half a smirk, but I wasn't lying. Seeing a huge piece of meat slip past his lips had me hungry for something entirely inappropriate for where we currently stood.

"They're not watching me."

"I thought that was their job."

"They're watching everyone else."

And that was a problem. I was part of the "everyone else."

I shrugged that off and bit into the meat dumpling, moaning as the exquisite flavor hit my tongue. Dimitri's eyes dropped to my mouth and he licked his lips. I wasn't sure if that had to do with the sausage he'd just finished or my moan, but the combination was a hot one. It definitely took the edge off the winter chill.

A flash of long hair out of the corner of my eye had me jerking my head in that direction, but it wasn't the man I was looking out for. I casually perused the crowd like I was taking everything in, searching out the familiar face I needed to somehow give the recordings I'd gotten from my cuff-link cameras.

One good thing about Alessio was that he wasn't someone Dimitri would know. He preferred his tech cave the vast majority of the time, and he wasn't a famous face, unlike some of my other Libertine brothers.

He was nowhere to be seen, not yet, though I had no doubt he'd be here eventually. I just hoped I didn't freeze my ass off before he decided to make an appearance.

Actually, that sounded more like something Alessio *would* do.

"Everything okay?"

I turned back to see Dimitri studying me with an unreadable expression.

"Of course." I flashed what I hoped was a convincing grin. "Why do you ask?"

"You stopped talking."

"I have been known to do that on occasion, you know. Like when my mouth's full, for example." I winked at him, but he wasn't buying it.

"Maybe so, but there's nothing in your mouth right now. Did something else catch your attention?"

Putain. *Think fast, Benoit...*

I'd clearly underestimated how closely he was watching me.

"Actually, I saw someone across the way making some blown glass ornaments. Would you mind if we double back and check them out?"

Dimitri looked across at the stalls we'd wandered by earlier. "You didn't see them before?"

"I must've missed them with all the other things

distracting me. Delicious food. Sparkling lights. Happy people." I hooked my arm back through his and looked up at him. "A sexy man keeping me warm."

Dimitri lowered his head and brushed his lips across mine. "We'll circle back. Just this once."

"Well, thank you for accommodating me."

"You know how I feel about staying in one spot."

"*Oui*, but we're at a Christmas market. What could possibly happen out here?" As we started down the aisle, I glanced over my shoulder at the men trailing us. "Plus, we have your men watching out for you."

"And you."

"Me?"

"Yes. It's not just me I have them protecting."

That was going to make this even more difficult. But I'd been in tricky situations before, and no matter what, I always managed to find a way out of them.

Like that time I got trapped in a duke's walk-in closet and had to shimmy through his air duct to get out. It'd been years since I'd been *in* the closet, and I did not enjoy the return.

We passed by a little wooden toy shop and a puppet maker who was demonstrating his puppeteering skills. I would've loved to stop and enjoy the show, but it was in that exact moment I spotted a tall, broad-shouldered man in a wool coat, with a black beanie over long hair. It was time to get moving.

I slid my hand down Dimitri's arm and linked our fingers, turning to face him.

"Come on," I said, tugging him along faster. "For someone who doesn't want to stand in one place too long, you sure know how to dilly-dally."

"I didn't realize we were in such a rush."

"We're not, but I don't want all the pretty ornaments to be gone before I get there."

Dimitri arched a brow, and just as he was about to say something, flakes started to fall down around us. I looked up to see snow falling over the twinkling lights, and it was such a magical sight that I forgot all about Alessio.

"It's snowing," I said, moving in close to Dimitri.

"That it is."

I let out a dreamy sigh, closed my eyes, then held my face up to the soft, falling flakes. "Isn't it magical?"

Dimitri didn't immediately answer, and when I opened my eyes I saw him looking down at me, not the snow. His eyes twinkled from the reflection of the lights around us as he brought a hand up to my face and took hold of my chin.

He brushed a thumb over my lips. "I thought you were in a hurry."

"And I thought you didn't like to stand still?"

"Do you have an answer for everything?"

"Only if it gets me what I want."

When Dimitri's eyes dropped to my mouth, a shiver ran through me. From the cold? Or from the spark of desire when he looked at me? There was no denying the way my body reacted to him, which was both a good yet very dangerous thing. On one hand, our attraction made my time away from home more enjoyable. On the other, I couldn't lose focus over why I was really here.

Wait, *why* was I here again?

"I know what you want," he said.

"You think so?"

He nodded and leaned in, angling his head and bringing that sinful mouth closer to mine. "You wanted..." His lips grazed over mine, but the second I parted them, hungry for that kiss, Dimitri stepped back and gestured toward one of the stalls. "...a pretty ornament."

I blinked and almost stumbled forward, the spell broken, but I refused to show that he'd just thrown me off my game.

Instead, I smiled and headed for the gorgeous decorations, keeping an eye out for where Alessio had gone. The artist behind the table welcomed us in, and though I knew exactly what she said and how to converse in Czech, I kept to a simple "*Dobrý den*"—good day.

Along with the glass-blown ornaments were vintage pieces and hand-carved wooden designs, and I admired several of the reindeer before moving on.

Alessio needed to hurry the hell up or he was going to miss the drop. I doubted Dimitri would be down to spend another night here, though he'd done a good job of humoring me so far. This was so not his scene, but getting him here in the first place had been a win.

Now if only Alessio would—

Awareness prickled the back of my neck, the feeling of eyes on me, and I instinctively knew they weren't Dimitri's. Or his bodyguards'.

To confirm my suspicions, I casually picked up one of the vintage handheld mirrors. My cheeks were a perfectly flushed pink, though I would've preferred my nose be a shade lighter, but all in all I looked fucking gorgeous. As I ran my fingers through my hair, I saw Alessio.

About damn time.

He strolled up to the stall as if he didn't have a care in the world and began to check out the items on display. Just another man minding his own business and enjoying the festivities.

My heart started to beat faster, as it always did in these situations. Even as confident as I was, there was always a chance of getting caught, and it was going to be tricky to make the drop with Dimitri and his bodyguards *right* there.

"No need to check yourself out. That's my job," came Dimitri's low voice behind me, and I caught his eyes in the mirror. His hands moved to my hips, his fingers dangerously close to sliding into the pockets and ruining this whole charade.

Merde.

Thinking fast, I set down the mirror and put my hands over his, sliding them down to my ass instead as I turned around to face him.

"Oh yeah?" I said, leaning in to nip at his lower lip. "Do you prefer to check me out from the front or the back?"

"Yes." He said it with such a serious expression that it took me off guard and a burst of laughter rumbled out of my chest.

"Perfect answer." I kissed the tip of his nose and went back to browsing, looking for something with any hidden crevices I could use. The tiny metal tube was burning a hole in my pants pocket, and I needed to find a way to get it to my brother even with a stall full of people and watchful eyes.

My adrenaline kicked up a notch as I spotted a hand-carved nativity scene. It was an elaborate piece with several nooks and crannies. I could definitely hide the tube in that without anyone being the wiser.

Now to let Alessio know.

Feigning a gasp, I reached for the carving and spun around, making sure to be loud and excited while showing Dimitri my find.

"Look at this," I said, holding it up for him, but at an angle I knew Alessio could see. "I can't imagine how much time it took to create something so exquisite."

"Two months," the artist said from behind the table, smiling proudly.

Dimitri raised a brow at me as if to say, *Really?* Because

clearly he wasn't interested at all, but he said, "Nice," for the artist's benefit.

I made up for his lack of enthusiasm by covering my heart with my hand. "Two *months*? *Mon Dieu.* What a true *artiste.* So much time on all of these hidden details..." I ran my finger over one of the wise men bearing gifts and decided the open cove behind him would be the perfect hiding spot. Out of the corner of my eye I saw Alessio glance my way and shake his head, and I knew he'd gotten the message.

Now to drop the package.

I gave the nativity a last little pat, and as I turned away from Dimitri, I slid my hand into my pants pocket, letting my coat act as a shield. I grabbed the tube with nimble fingers, leaned forward to set the piece down, and quickly nestled the tube into the cove of the carving.

Bam. Done. Stress level diminished.

Time for a celebratory—

"Give it to me." Dimitri held his hand out. "The piece."

My entire body went still. Perhaps my heart even stopped. Had he seen...? No. There was no way. Unless he could quite literally see right through me, there was no reason to panic.

Or was there?

Still facing away from him, I managed to force a breath through my nose.

"What?" I asked.

Dimitri didn't bother answering, moving past me and reaching for the carving.

I stepped forward, using my body to block the nativity. "Wait, what are you—"

"You want it." It wasn't a question.

"I..."

He cocked his head to the side as those dark eyes landed on mine. "You always get what you want. You want the piece."

Holy shit. The sigh of relief I wanted to let out was over-whelming. He thought I wanted to buy it. *Of course.*

I forced one of my teasing smiles and stepped in close, letting my hand wander down his chest. "There's something I want a helluva lot more than that carving," I said, low enough that only he could hear.

"You can have both."

"I'm greedy, but not *that* greedy."

Dimitri didn't look convinced. As a matter of fact, he looked like he was about to grab the damn carving to buy it for me himself, and that just couldn't happen. Alessio was burning a hole in my forehead with his stare, and I had to move fast.

"If you really want to encourage my bad habits, you could get me something that would be put to far greater use," I said, and reached behind me for the item.

"And what's that?"

I held up the vintage mirror with a "Voila!" and the smirk he gave me was as close to a grin as I was going to get.

I'd take it.

Without a word, Dimitri snapped his fingers, and one of his guards stepped forward and handed the artist a thick wad of cash. Her eyes widened in surprise, as did mine, and then Dimitri snatched up the mirror and my hand and led us out of the tent.

Alessio caught my eyes briefly as I passed, but anything more than a quick look was too risky. It was in his hands now, and it was up to him whether he took the nativity home with him or just fished it out.

It'd look kinda cute on his desk.

The second we exited the covered stall, I sucked in a huge lungful of air. I hadn't realized I'd been holding it while I was in there, but the threat of getting caught was real.

But it was done. Too close for my liking, but I'd had closer calls and lived to tell the tale.

I reached for the mirror in Dimitri's hand and took it, lifting it up to our faces.

"Oh my," I said. "Look at the state of these two gorgeous but frozen sex gods. Looks like they need some glühwein to warm right up, stat—what do you say?"

14

DIMITRI

ANOTHER NIGHT, ANOTHER bedroom, but this time it came with a private performance.

I no longer had to share Benoit with other leering eyes and stiff cocks in a room full of people. This one-on-one attention he'd promised was the only reason I'd agreed to spend a few hours wandering around Prague's Christmas markets in the cold. It wasn't my thing, but the festivities seemed to please Benoit, and since he'd already proven he was worth every penny, I would make sure to keep him happy.

Give him what he wants, take what I want.

"Now this is more like it," Benoit said as he stepped into the room and let his coat drop from his shoulders and down his arms. He still had a few layers to go after our time outside, and I was going to enjoy the show.

"This room is more to your liking?"

"I'm sure any room in this castle is *acceptable*, but this one's a step above, wouldn't you say?"

"Perhaps. Bigger is better for you?"

As he walked toward me, he lowered his eyes below my hips. "Bigger is *definitely* my type." Then he pushed me back onto the bed and began to pull his gloves free, one finger at a time. "Make yourself comfortable."

I spread my hands behind me, resting back on them. This was what I enjoyed, the tease that followed through.

Benoit took his phone out of his pocket, hit a couple of buttons, a sultry song started to play, and the striptease began.

As he swayed his hips, he reached up for the scarf artfully wound around his neck and slowly pulled it down.

He wasn't even showing any skin yet and already my dick was stirring to life. It was in the way Benoit moved his body, the way his hazel eyes penetrated mine. Being the sole subject of his attention had my adrenaline pumping in the same way as the many dangerous positions I'd put myself in. This man was every bit as high risk, but it was a risk I was more than willing to take.

"Take your sweater off," I said.

Benoit gave a low chuckle and shook his head. "You're not the one in charge here, *mon monstre*." He kicked his winter boots off, one after the other, both of them landing clear on the other side of the room. "This is my show."

"I thought it was my show?"

"And I thought I told you to sit back and relax?"

I narrowed my eyes, but I'd let him have control in this instance. When I complied, the bossy bottom continued.

Those hips moved in an indecent way as he stepped between my spread legs and wrapped the scarf behind my neck, pulling me toward him. I sat up and went to touch him, only for him to slap my hands away.

"I'm sorry, sir, but putting your hands on the performers is against the rules."

I grabbed a fistful of his sweater and jerked him toward me, grazing our mouths together. "I make the rules."

Benoit hummed, the sound vibrating against my lips, and he nipped at them before shimmying out of my hold.

His fingers flirted with the edge of his sweater, lifting it a few inches to give me a peek of his taut stomach and then lowering it again.

He was drawing this out on purpose now. If I'd kept my mouth shut, he'd be naked already, but the tease was emerging, and it was all I could do to lie there and watch. I reached down to where my cock was straining against my zipper and rubbed the heel of my hand over it.

Benoit's eyes dropped to the move, and that was when it occurred to me that two could play at this particular game.

I stroked myself once, twice, and then a third time, and when Benoit merely stood there and licked at his lips, I smirked.

"What happened to my show?"

Benoit's eyes flicked up to mine, and the teasing glint from seconds ago had turned downright scorching. But he'd started this and I wasn't about to let him off the hook until he finished it...naked.

"The sweater, Benoit. Take it off."

My first order had fallen on teasing ears, but this time it seemed he had a little more incentive to lose his clothing. He pulled it up and over his head and tossed it at me, before turning his back and aiming a sultry gaze over his shoulder.

"Now you. Unzip your pants."

So that was how this was going to go. A little quid pro quo. I could get on board with that.

I reached for the button of my pants, flicked it open, and slowly drew down the zipper, then tugged them open, revealing my tight briefs that were molded to my cock.

Benoit's nostrils flared as I thrust my hips up into my hand, and he cursed in French and looked away. But then, not about to be rushed, he made a show of *slowly* bending at the waist, smoothing his hands down one leg in a tantalizing move that showed off just how flexible he was. Then he switched sides and ran them back up the other.

My dick ached at the way his pants stretched taut over his fabulous ass, and reminded me just how good it had looked naked and bent over my bed the night before. If he wanted to drive me crazy, mission accomplished.

The sound of his belt buckle hit my ears, followed by his zipper, then he hooked his fingers into the sides of his pants and inched them down his hips.

My breath caught in the back of my throat, the anticipation of all his smooth skin coming into view making it difficult not to get to my feet and end this little game now. But I would wait. I wanted to see what was coming next. I wanted to see what *he* would do to make *me* come next.

Benoit began to sway to the dick-throbbing tune that began to play, and as he turned to face me, his erection was clear to see, outlined behind a sheer thong that left nothing to the imagination. He ran his hands down over his body and into the barely there material, and I did the same.

Benoit drew his bottom lip behind his teeth, his hooded eyes watching my hand disappear into my briefs, and we both gripped our cocks at the same moment. My low growl mingled with his groan as the sexual tension between us built with every stroke.

I hadn't meant things to get off track this way. I really had wanted my dance, but as he stood before me stroking that luscious cock, I realized I wanted something more.

I sat up and whipped my sweater off so I was as naked as

he was. Benoit's eyes trailed up to the light smattering of dark hair that covered my pecs, and as his hand began to move a little faster, I lay back down.

"Take off the rest of your clothes."

Benoit blinked lust-hazed eyes at me but didn't argue, releasing his hold on himself and shoving his remaining items to the floor.

When he straightened, his gorgeous body—including that delectable dick—was on full display to my greedy eyes, and I knew I'd made the right decision.

I crooked a finger at him. He stepped between my thighs, and I took hold of his shaft and gave him a firm squeeze.

"As tantalizing as this little show has been," I said, my voice rough as sandpaper, "I find I'm out of patience."

"Oh?" Benoit let out a shaky breath and thrust forward into my fist. "Then what is it you want?"

I ran my eyes up over all that smooth skin, to his sinfully gorgeous face. "For you to finish off this dance all over me."

A seductive chuckle slipped out of Benoit as he reached for my shoulders. "I've never known you to be subtle, *mon monstre.* But just so we're clear—you want to watch *me*"—he leaned in and brushed his lips over mine—"come all over *you.*"

"From my mouth to my cock." I bit down on his lip—hard. "Think you can do that?"

He shoved my shoulder back to the bed.

"*Oui,* it'll be my pleasure."

And mine, I thought as he climbed up on the bed and straddled my thighs. I went to direct my cock up, for him to lower himself on, but Benoit swatted my hand away and shook his head.

"Oh no you don't." He shifted further up my body, past my aching erection, and settled on my abs. "There was no mention of *you* doing anything. So for now, I think you can just lie there and enjoy the show."

He started to roll his body over the top of mine in a way that should be fucking illegal.

"In fact," Benoit crooned as he walked his fingers up my chest, "why don't you slip your hands behind your head?"

My body vibrated with restrained power as I allowed him to pin me to the mattress. But we both knew one surge of adrenaline would be all I needed to have him laid out flat. So for now I would indulge him, knowing that *he* was about to indulge *me*.

"I love your body," Benoit said, more to himself than to me, as he put his palms on my chest and began to rock over me. I could feel his thighs tighten at my waist as he dragged his hot balls over me. "So strong," he continued. "So hard." His fingers dug into my skin, his short nails biting in a way that would likely leave blood. "So *powerful*."

Benoit let out a low moan as he reached down and took hold his cock, then he tipped his head back and closed his eyes, and with his body braced for maximum movement, he *really* began to dance for me.

His fingers flexed, his hand stroked, his hips swayed, and his entire body rolled in time to the provocative beat throbbing all around us. He was magnificent to watch, his movements so fluid even as he pleasured himself. It was like a well-choreographed dance he'd done a hundred times before, and judging by the masterful way he worked his shaft, that was likely accurate.

My hands itched to touch, grab, pleasure the man, destroying every thought I had. But, not wanting to deprive myself of what I knew would be one hell of a finale, I gripped my hair and pulled the strands tight, in an effort not to come before he did.

"Jesus, Benoit..."

He moaned, and those hazel eyes opened and locked on mine.

"You look and *feel* unreal."

Benoit bit into his lower lip as he swiped the head of his cock with his thumb. Then he reached down and held it out to me.

I craned up, sucked it between my lips, and groaned as his flavor hit my tongue. As I lay back down, Benoit started to move a little faster.

"You're so fucking sexy."

"Mmm..."

"Sensual."

"Tell me more," he panted, and dug those nails hard into my chest.

"The most gorgeous thing I've ever set my fucking eyes on." My breathing was ragged now, my dick aching for release as I watched him get himself off. "The second I saw you, I knew I was going to do *anything* to have you."

Benoit cried out then, my words spurring on his climax as he bowed forward and tipped his head back. His cock jerked in his fist as hot jets of cum sprayed out over my chest and hit my chin and face.

He was a feast for the eyes—and tongue—as I licked his arousal from the corner of my lips, his flavor exploding in my mouth like a potent aphrodisiac, as my own orgasm raced down my spine.

I gritted my teeth and reached for his hips, ready to flip him to his back and take him like the starving man he'd turned me into. Then Benoit's eyes opened and he flashed me a sly smile.

"So...did *that* earn me a taste of you?"

My words from last night wound tight around my frustrated cock like a lover's fist—or better yet, Benoit's mouth

—as he climbed off my lap and planted his hands by my hips.

"You earned more than a taste." I looked down at him and directed my dick to his mouth. "You earned a whole fucking mouthful."

15
BENOIT

Location: Luxury Train, Prague to Destination Unknown

I'D DONE MANY things in my life. Gone everywhere. Seduced many a man. Been accustomed to more private jets and chauffeured cars than I could count. But Dimitri was giving me a first I'd never even considered: traveling across Europe on a luxury train.

I took to exploring while Dimitri met with Omar in the back lounge. Always private business with those two, and Omar had stared me down until I finally left the room.

No matter. That was what the recording device I'd planted in the lounge was for.

I strolled toward the bar and ordered a cognac, then scanned the occupants of the car as I waited. There were a few unfamiliar faces, but others I'd seen around the castle in Prague briefly. From what I could tell, Dimitri's entourage took up the majority of the train's accommodations, and though I was tempted to ask one of them where we were heading, I'd wait to pry that info from the man himself.

"Your cognac, sir." The bartender set the snifter in front of me, and though it was still relatively early in the day, I took a long gulp of the good stuff. Hell, time didn't matter on vacation—

I stopped short, drink halfway to my mouth, and set it back on the bar top.

I wasn't *on* fucking vacation. Though everything about this trip so far had felt like it, I was here for a reason. The job was the most important thing.

"Is Hennessy not to your preference, sir?" the bartender said. "We also have a stellar Courvoisier I recommend that—"

Shaking my head, I waved him off and took another sip for his benefit. "This is perfect. *Merci.*"

He nodded and moved on to the next guest as I felt someone come to stand on the other side of me.

"You are French?"

I glanced at the man who had a good twenty years on me, but the twinkle in his eyes gave him an attractive edge.

With the alcohol encouraging my playful side, I grinned. "I am. Though I could be a good many things for the right man."

He threw his head back, laughing. "Definitely a Frenchman."

"Benoit Olivier," I said, holding my hand out for him. He obliged by planting a kiss there. "And you are?"

"Oskar Krüger. It's very nice to meet you, Benoit."

"It is, isn't it?"

That earned me another laugh, along with a round of drinks, courtesy of my new friend.

I didn't necessarily need another glass, but then again, my mission was accomplished for the day, or at least until I needed to remove the device I'd planted, so what could it hurt?

"Is it too bold to ask where you're heading?" he said, and then added, a little hopefully, "Maybe we're getting off at the same stop."

"Now that's a great question, Oskar. I'm not actually sure."

He looked puzzled at that, and I couldn't blame him. How many people boarded a train with no known destination? I wasn't even sure of the stops along the way, given the way my cell service kept cutting out every time I did a search for the itinerary.

I leaned in close, as if to impart a secret. "Apparently it's a surprise. Romantic, isn't it?"

"Oh, I see." The disappointment in Oskar's tone was clear, but he gave me a small smile anyway. *"Warum sind die schönen Männer immer vergeben?"*

Without thinking twice, I responded in fluent German, *"Keine Sorge, auch du wirst dein Glück finden, Hübscher."*

Oskar had started to reply when his gaze traveled over my shoulder and his smile fell.

I turned to see who had interrupted our little tête-à-tête and was surprised to find Dimitri standing there, an unreadable expression stamped across his face. That was nothing new, though, and if there was one thing I was becoming good at, it was distracting Dimitri from whatever was on his mind.

"Well, would you look who finally stopped doing business long enough to indulge in something a little more pleasurable." I held up my glass and dangled it between my fingers. "Can I tempt you into joining me, *mon monstre?*"

Dimitri's sharp eyes shifted over my shoulder to where Oskar stood, then back to me, as he slipped a hand in his pocket and moved to stand beside me at the bar.

"I didn't realize you spoke German."

A frown pulled between my brows at his response, until I realized my mistake. I'd gotten so comfortable with Oskar that

I'd naturally slipped into speaking one of the many languages I knew well.

Putain.

I laughed and placed a hand on Dimitri's arm as I made a quick pivot. "Not fluent. Just enough to get by."

Dimitri's brow rose as he looked to where Oskar had disappeared back into the crowd. "Enough to flirt with the other passengers, don't you mean?"

Oh thank God. He was just *jealous*, not suspicious of the fact I knew the language. I could work with that. A jealous beast was much easier to tame than a betrayed one.

"Aww." I smoothed a hand up his arm and squeezed his bicep. "There's no need to be worried. I know where I'm laying my head tonight."

Dimitri's eyes fell to my lips, and I licked them, just to make sure he was thinking about kissing me.

"You better. I don't take kindly to others touching what's mine."

I sidled in close enough that my body was flush against his side, then whispered by his ear, "Then perhaps you should stop working so hard so I don't go off wandering..."

Dimitri took hold of my chin between strong fingers, then leaned in until his lips brushed over the top of mine. "Or maybe I should just put a leash on you and keep you close."

"Kneeling at your feet?" I asked, and batted my lashes. "Only if you promise to pet me and treat me like a good boy. Maybe even throw me a bone...er."

Dimitri growled and took my lip between his teeth, snaking a hand around my waist.

Mission accomplished—beast tamed. Or at least distracted.

"So." I put a hand to his chest and gently pushed him back. "You never did say—would you like a drink?"

Dimitri's fingers brushed over my ass as he shook his head. "No. I wanted to come and see if you'd like to get something to eat with me before our next stop. After that I have business to attend to and will be otherwise occupied."

I feigned a pout and ran my hand down his chest. "All work and no pleasure makes one a grumpy boy."

Dimitri took my hand and drew it further down his body. "Does this feel like I'm not taking time for pleasure?"

I curled my fingers around him and groaned. "Not when you're going to make me wait."

"But good things come for those who wait."

I chuckled but released him before draining my drink. "Then alas, I will wait. Because I definitely want you to come for me."

Dimitri smirked. "Good boy." My mouth fell open at this glimpse of playfulness from him, then he took a step back and said, "Join me for lunch?"

And I knew I would've said yes, job or not.

FINE FOOD, FINE wine, and an even finer man to share them with made for a delicious meal, so I tried not to be offended that our time together didn't last long. The meeting was more important, and getting a direct account of what went down during those talks, and whom they were with, was far more important than leaving me to my lonesome.

I could definitely find ways to fill my time.

I walked Dimitri back to the lounge, relieved that he was using the same location for this meeting that he had for the one with Omar. Otherwise, I'd have to fish the recording device out of the flowers and get it to the next location somehow, and honestly, what a pain. I liked my missions with as few obstacles as possible, thank you very much.

Omar was already in the lounge, as was one of the body-guards. The other had been silently trailing us, as was always the case whenever I was near Dimitri, and it was something I had to keep top of mind.

Dimitri cracked his neck from side to side and peered out the window.

"ETA five minutes," Omar said without looking up, his attention on the screen of his tablet. "Client is there and waiting to board."

"Good." Dimitri turned away from the window. "Let's get this deal done."

Omar lifted his head, looked pointedly at me, and said to Dimitri, "Boss."

Clearly, he didn't want me in the room, or even hearing a whisper about any deal, which made the satisfaction I felt at getting his real opinions on the record even better. I couldn't *wait* to hear what that guy said when he thought no one was listening.

Dimitri drew me in for a kiss that made me want to linger, but then he pulled back and said, "I'll find you later."

The dismissal was clear, and I gave him a cheeky smile as I backed away. "Don't take too long, or someone might scoop me up."

He growled in the back of his throat and started toward me, but I laughed.

"No need to worry, *mon monstre*. Enjoy your meeting."

Dimitri narrowed his eyes, but unbuttoned his suit jacket and took a seat in one of the lounge chairs by Omar. His second-in-command sneezed twice and then cursed under his breath.

"There a problem?" Dimitri said.

"These fucking flowers."

"Well, get rid of them."

My hand was already on the door, and their words had me pausing. Surely they didn't mean get rid of *my* flowers, because...*merde.*

I whirled back around to see Omar reaching for the bouquet on the table, and *no, no, no,* he couldn't get rid of those. He'd ruin the whole damn plan.

Panic kick-started my heart as I strolled casually back toward them.

"Oh, darling, let me," I said before Omar got his hands on the vase. "If you're allergic, you really shouldn't touch them."

He glanced up at me, the first eye contact he'd made with me for days, and gave a curt nod before sitting back.

"He can do it," Dimitri said.

I waved him off. "It's no problem at all. Truly." Inside I was screaming, because this was giving me nothing *but* problems. I needed a reason to come back here after I fished the damn device out of these flowers so I could plant it somewhere else before their client boarded. Which, judging by the way the train was already beginning to slow, would be happening any minute now.

A litany of curses erupted in my head as I reached for the vase. I needed to leave something to come back for. What the hell could it be?

My ring tapped against the vase, and that was it. I quickly shimmied it down my finger with my thumb as I lifted the flowers, and as I turned away, I let it fall to the rug. It didn't make a sound, and I thought I was good to go until Dimitri spoke up behind me.

"Benoit. You forgot something."

Putain. Scheiße! Fuck.

I turned back around. "Did I?"

"Yes." Dimitri gestured toward Omar, who stared at his

boss for a long moment before swallowing a sigh and looking at me.

"Thank you."

"Oh. You're very welcome. You boys behave yourselves." I shot them a wink and then left the room, bypassing the guard stationed outside the door.

Moving fast, but not enough to attract attention, I headed down the hall and beelined into our suite for the night, shutting the door behind me. As I rummaged through the stalks to find the device, I tried to remember everything I'd seen in the lounge, any easy-to-access places I could use. There would be several pairs of eyes on me, so any move I made would be seen.

Nowhere to hide.

With the tiny piece of hardware in hand, the backing still sticky, I placed it on the backside of my belt end, somewhere I'd have easy access to when I was in the room. Then I took a deep breath, threw my shoulders back, and headed back down the hall.

On my approach, the guard stepped out in front of me, blocking the door.

"I know they're about to have a meeting, but I accidentally left something of value inside." I gave him an apologetic smile. "I'll make it super quick, promise."

He narrowed his eyes, and just when I thought he'd tell me to get lost, he knocked on the door. At Dimitri's "Enter," he opened the door, and I slipped inside, holding my hands up.

"I'm so sorry, but my ring must've fallen off in here. Have either of you seen it?"

"We're about to—" Omar started, but Dimitri put his hand up.

"What does it look like?" he asked.

"It's a gold onyx, and it's been in my family for generations." I sounded on the verge of tears, and that prompted Dimitri to get up and start looking.

"Are you sure you had it when you came in? It might've been lost at the bar." Dimitri paused. "Perhaps your German friend had slippery fingers."

"I'm positive I had it. Maybe if I retrace my steps..." I walked over to the window as they searched the table—well, Dimitri did. Omar glanced at it briefly until Dimitri gave him a death glare anyone would wilt from, and both he and the guard jumped up to help.

Keeping them in my periphery, I reached for my belt end, peeled off the recorder, and then grabbed the curtains with both hands. I shook them out so I could check the floor beneath them, but all the while I was attaching the device to the back middle panel of the curtain. When I was sure it was fastened well, I let go and shook my head.

"I don't see it anywhere."

"Boss, we don't have time for this," Omar said.

"That's up to me," Dimitri snapped. "We'll find it faster if you get on your knees and crawl."

Now *that* I would pay good money to see.

The guard was inching closer to the spot I'd dropped the ring, and hopefully he'd find it soon, because the train was pulling into the station—Linz Central Station in Austria, as a matter of fact.

I filed that information away and gave a little sniffle for their sake. I was devastated, after all.

The guard stopped suddenly and picked something up off the rug. He studied it before holding it out to me. "This it?"

I gasped and reached for the ring. "Yes! *Oh dieu merci!*" I gazed down at the piece of jewelry I really wouldn't have been heartbroken to lose. It wasn't a family heirloom, and it definitely wasn't the half-a-mil monstrosity a sheikh who was obsessed with me had gifted me after a night together. Or, as he'd said, "Go into my jewelry collection and pick one."

No, this was part of the costume. A nice enough vintage piece that fit a dancer's lifestyle, not one from my own, very extensive, collection.

"You're an absolute lifesaver," I said, smiling at the guard and curling my hand shut around the ring.

"That is part of his job description," Dimitri said. "Saving lives."

"Well, I guess that means I have eight left, right? Better use them wisely."

Dimitri reached for my hand and uncurled my fist, revealing the simple black-and-gold piece. "Which finger?"

"Considering it slipped off my ring finger before, let's go with the middle this time."

He held my hand and slid it up halfway, but it was too tight of a fit.

"You know what? I think I'll just keep this one safely tucked into my bag instead."

"A good idea," he agreed, handing me the ring back before lowering his mouth onto mine. I knew the clock was ticking from the way the train had come to a stop, but he kissed me leisurely, sweeping his tongue inside my mouth. He was so damn good at it, like *brain-meltingly* good. So good I was making up terms, because *delicious* wasn't covering it. It was all I could do to hold on while he took control of the kiss.

He pulled back suddenly, leaving me breathless, and opened the door. Those dark eyes were flashing with desire, but he had enough self-restraint to not walk me to our room himself.

As I brushed by him, I started to remind him not to take all day, but he beat me to the punch.

"I'll be quick," he said, voice low. "Be ready for me."

16

DIMITRI

WITH BUSINESS CONCLUDED, I was ready to get back to the pleasure side this trip had unexpectedly delivered during my downtime.

Yes, I'd paid for Benoit to accompany me on the trip, to be at my beck and call. But I was starting to find myself wanting to be at his. Leaving him after lunch had been more difficult than it should've been, considering what the meeting was for —establishing my position as the head of our arms organization after Giorgos's demise had been my priority since his fall. But ever since Benoit had come along, I'd found my focus divided. Something I was aware I needed to conceal around my men.

Weaknesses weren't something I could afford, and caring for someone in any capacity—sexual or otherwise—was a weakness.

But I could do it. I prided myself on my poker face and ruthless nature, and just because I had a hot body waiting for me during my downtime, that didn't mean I was weak. It meant I was a man with needs, wants, and desires, and I just so happened to have a sexy-as-sin man waiting to fulfill every one of them whenever I wanted him to.

My cock stirred at the thought. Benoit naked and waiting for me every night. That sounded like something I could get used to. But I was aware our time together had a time limit, not to mention a price tag.

I walked through the train carriages, heading back toward our suite. I'd already checked the bar and restaurant cars and Benoit was nowhere to be found. Maybe he'd decided to indulge in a little afternoon nap before this evening.

Now that's something I wouldn't mind interrupting. Perhaps even turn it into some afternoon delight?

With my mind focused on getting to Benoit and waking him with my hands, mouth, and body, no one was more shocked than I when I slid open the door to our sleeper suite and found him standing half-dressed at the bar cart in our living area.

With his tailored pants pulled snug over his backside, it appeared I'd interrupted him mid-dressing as he poured himself a glass of bourbon. His hair was wet and slicked back from his shower, and as I stood there staring at him, a wayward drop of water slid down the back of his neck and between his shoulder blades.

Benoit placed the crystal stopper back in the decanter and lifted his glass, and when he turned to continue getting dressed for dinner, he spotted me. His face was completely devoid of makeup, but that didn't take away from his appeal. His lashes were full and dark, and the stubble around his lips and lining his jaw was so fucking sexy he made every other man I'd ever been with fade to nothing more than a dull echo.

Clearly aware of his effect on me, Benoit leaned back against the cart and brought the glass to his lips.

The room suited Benoit with its Art Deco style and intricate wood paneling. The soft decorative lighting and muted tones gave off a sexy but relaxed atmosphere, one that I enjoyed coming back to after a stressful meeting. But nothing about the room and the long chaise longue and queen bed had me feeling relaxed right now. If anything, they had me more revved up.

"*Bonsoir*," Benoit finally said, his tone so close to a purr that I was tempted to do what he'd suggested earlier at the bar and pet him.

"Afternoon."

Benoit pushed off the door and slinked his way over to me, his bare feet somehow even sexier than when they were in five-inch heels.

Maybe it was that he was half dressed? All the better to get him fully naked.

"If you're here," he said, taking another sip of his drink, "can I assume you're now mine for the rest of the night?"

I was starting to think I would be his *any* fucking time of the day. But I took the glass from his fingers, drained it, and tossed it on the chaise. Then I grabbed the back of his neck and pulled him in so I could share the final sip with him.

My tongue and the bourbon swirled between our mouths, and as we swallowed it down, some of it slipped from the corner of his lips. I followed the liquor with kisses along his jawline and down his neck, and when I reached his shoulder and sucked, Benoit moaned.

"Don't you mean that you're *mine*?" I said, kissing my way back up to his slick mouth.

Benoit gripped my hips and moved in to grind his body all over me, and when his erection grazed against mine, I knew we weren't leaving this suite for dinner anytime soon.

I glanced at the chaise, but it was way too short and narrow for the two of us, and the bed was too far away for my impatient cock, so instead I settled on something much closer and quicker.

I slid a hand around his waist and walked him backward toward the large viewing window in our suite. "How do you feel about a little exhibitionism?" I asked, nipping at his lips, which curved into an immoral smile.

"What do *you* think?"

I trailed my fingers down the center of his naked body to his pants and undid the button.

"I think you'd fucking get off to being in front of others. Or should I say"—I unzipped him and slipped my hand inside to find him naked underneath—"I think you'd get off *fucking* in front of others."

Benoit's head fell back on the glass pane as I wrapped my hand around him. A sensual moan slipped free of those talented lips, and I couldn't help but lean in and take another taste. I speared my tongue deep inside his mouth, the lingering taste of bourbon an intoxicating mix with his own flavor, as I swiped my thumb over the head of his cock and began to work him.

"I can't promise you an audience," I whispered over his lips. "But I can promise I'm about to turn you around and fuck you right here, in front of this window. And if anyone is out there to see, then they'll be the luckiest person to ever live."

I let him go and took a step back, and holy shit was he a sight: lounging back against the window with his kiss-swollen lips, a red mark forming on his neck, and his thick erection jutting from his pants. He was the very picture of sex and debauchery, and by the time I got through with him, we'd add satisfied to the mix.

"Show me what I want to see, Benoit."

Without a word, he slipped his thumbs into his pants and

shoved them down his legs, then he kicked them out of his way.

"Good. Now turn around."

Benoit did as he was told, placing his hands on the window and bracing his feet apart before canting his hips back and showing off that perfect ass.

"This what you want, *mon monstre?*"

I reached for my pants and tore them open, then moved up behind him, took hold of each ass cheek in my hands, and squeezed.

"I'm going to fuck you so hard you leave a mess all over this window."

Benoit leaned back into me. "If that's supposed to be a threat, I'm afraid you've misunderstood my turn-ons and turn-offs."

"Not a threat," I said by his ear, and felt him shiver. "A goddamn promise."

I muscled him back into position and then looked down at where he was squirming into my hands. I plumped his cheeks together and then apart, then slapped the tight, bouncy skin.

Benoit sucked in a gasp of air but angled himself better for me, clearly wanting more, and several harder, faster slaps later to each cheek, he was whimpering. I spread his ass cheeks apart, spat on the top of the narrow strip of skin that led to his hole, then slicked it down over his eager pucker.

"Dimitri," Benoit panted as I pushed against the tight ring of muscle.

I wanted in there, and I wanted it now. But I knew the way I was feeling, and if I went at him with no kind of prep, I would tear him the fuck apart.

"Not yet," I grunted, and spat on the same spot, letting it run down to where my thumb was pressing for entry.

Benoit's body immediately sucked me inside, and it was me catching my breath this time as I watched it disappear.

God, the things I could do to this man. The things I *wanted* to do to him. I could only imagine how experimental Benoit would be. He was such a sensual creature by nature, and as I removed my thumb and he whimpered, my cock lurched.

"So needy. Don't worry, I'm going to fill you up real good, soon. I'm just getting you ready for me."

"I'm ready," Benoit said, and gave his dick a rough pull.

I pushed two fingers in him, making him gasp. "Not for what I want to do, you're not."

"Am so," he insisted between choppy breaths as I scissored my fingers in and out of him, finding and rubbing up against his prostate.

"I'm not feeling gentle. It'll hurt," I told him, digging my other fingers into his supple skin hard enough to bruise. I wanted to split him in half, spread him wide—and I wanted to see how far I could push him.

How much pain did he like—want?

"I want that," he finally said. "I like the burn. The stretch. I want it all. I want to feel you for *days*."

He was delirious with pleasure as he writhed on my fingers and pumped his cock. But I'd warned him. I'd given him the chance to say no. And that was about all the goodness I had left to give.

"Well then." I leaned down and bit into his shoulder—hard. "Who the hell am I to deny you?"

17
BENOIT

THE MOMENT I told Dimitri what I wanted, his fingers left my body and he backed away. This time, I didn't focus on the loss of him, not when I knew what I had to look forward to.

He knew how to work his massive cock in a way that had mine already leaking, the evidence of my arousal coating my hand on every stroke of my dick.

Anticipation curled low in my stomach, and it was a struggle not to turn around and beg him to hurry up. Patience wasn't my middle name.

Lucky for me, it wasn't Dimitri's either.

He grabbed my wrist, halting my movements, and the next thing I knew, his thick erection was in my hand, smearing my pre-cum on his cock to use as lube.

That was so damn hot I could only watch, especially when I knew it wasn't nearly enough cum to make it a smooth slide inside me. He wanted things rough, and I was ready to take what he would give.

"You have an audience." Dimitri nodded at the window.

The first things I noticed were the snow-covered mountains, and then I realized we were passing through a town, with several residents milling around the streets. Many glanced up at the train, and I could only imagine what they were seeing right now.

Me. Gloriously naked in the window and wearing only a provocative smile. *You're welcome.*

"We can't give them a good show if you don't fuck me," I said, taunting Dimitri.

It worked.

With his fingers wrapped around my wrists, he slapped both of my hands up against the window pane, followed by my chest, and then kicked my legs open wider. My breath fogged up the glass on every exhale as he pressed up against me from behind.

"Never had anyone talk to me the way you do..." he said by my ear.

"All too scared of the big, bad *monstre?*"

"Or smart." He removed one of his hands from over the top of mine, and I trembled.

My arousal was at the very brink as I waited for him to unleash all the power I could feel vibrating behind me, and when he grabbed the back of my thigh and raised it at a forty-five degree angle, I sucked in a breath.

"They knew if they mouthed off," he said, "they'd risk getting *this.*"

One forceful thrust later, and he was lodged as deep inside of me as he could be. I shouted out at the intrusion, the bite of pain making my toes curl on the floor of the train carriage as it sped along the tracks. My eyes slammed shut as my body desperately tried to reconcile how good it felt despite the burn licking through my veins.

"Not so mouthy now, are you?" Dimitri said.

"Hard to speak, darling, when your *monster* dick is coming up the back of my throat."

He chuckled, a sound that was both sinister but also damn sexy. It stroked me in all the right places and had me trying to push back to take even *more* of him. But Dimitri had me split and pinned, my front against the window, my leg hiked up to give him access, and my body impaled on the biggest, thickest cock I'd ever taken.

"Don't act like you don't like it—your ass is like a fucking steel trap around me."

I moaned and squirmed against him. "No escaping me now."

I meant it in a sexual capacity, of course, but when Dimitri grunted and his fingers tightened around my thigh, I knew I was in much deeper with him than I cared to admit.

I'd been sent in to gather intel, to get information using any means necessary and within my comfort level, and as Dimitri began to pull out of me, I realized that maybe the problem was that I was *too* comfortable.

I was willing to do anything and everything with him—not for intel, but because I wanted to, and that was starting to alarm me.

Not enough to *stop*, mind you.

Dimitri tunneled forward again, the sting and burn still there but easing a little now as my body got used to the intruder taking it over. I could feel his warm breath on my neck as he plowed into me several times over, his guttural groans making my dick pulse against the window pane every time he bottomed out.

I couldn't remember a time I'd been so *manhandled*, taken so roughly, and it was both exhilarating and arousing. Dimitri took what he wanted with brute strength and no apologies, and right now he wanted me.

"Coming up on another stop," he said, stilling his hips so that his cock throbbed, trapped inside me. "The last one for miles. Open your eyes, see the people as they watch you get good and fucked."

Mon Dieu. My entire body tensed at his words. I was on full display here. Dimitri was balls deep inside me, and every inch of my front, including my stiff, leaking dick, was captured like we were in a window in Amsterdam's Red Light District.

I opened my eyes and focused on the snow-covered trees as the train began to slow. As a platform filled with people came into view, Dimitri started to move again.

My breath was coming hard and fast now. I had no doubt Dimitri had paid handsomely for our end of the train, and that would include a certain amount of discretion. But would it also include dismissal of complaints of public indecency?

We weren't *technically* in public, but as the train came to a full stop and people looked up at the passenger cars, as they tended to do, I saw several sets of eyes lock on me and widen.

But there was no stopping the man behind me, nor did I want him to. So I plastered my body to that window and gave them one hell of a show. If I was going to go to jail for indecent exposure, might as well make it a good fucking story.

Hah, now there was a pun my brothers would love to get behind. Literally.

I licked my lips and started to rub myself against the window pane. I was making a mess of the glass, my pre-cum allowing my dick to slip and slide with ease as I stared down at the gaping onlookers. I probably should've been ashamed or embarrassed, but I couldn't find it in me to care. I was a performer at heart, a man who loved being the center of attention, and I definitely had their attention right now.

Why wouldn't I? My body was fucking *spectacular.*

"Well, would you look at that," Dimitri rasped by my ear. "You've drawn quite the crowd."

"*Oui.* So why don't we give them that show you promised?"

"My fucking pleasure." Dimitri kissed under my ear and started to suck as his hips picked up a frantic rhythm. He kept me in place, nailed to the glass, balanced on one leg, as he went at me like a madman.

I slid up and down against the glass, my cries loud enough in the car now that we'd stopped that I was sure other guests could hear—but I didn't care. I wouldn't have cared if people stormed into our suite and took a seat to watch the way Dimitri was pounding me like I was here for his pleasure and his pleasure only. My mind was gone—it had left along with my morals and common sense as I let pleasure and sensory overload take over.

Dimitri yanked my head back as he slammed his hips hard up against me, and my cry of pleasure was intense. Every nerve ending was tingling, every sense I had overwhelmed, as he rutted against my prostate in a way that had me close to collapse. It was like I was having an out-of-body experience as he scraped his teeth along my jaw and growled, "Come." I panted once, twice, then he rammed into me again and demanded, "Come for *me*...and them."

And that did it.

With Dimitri so deep inside me I didn't know if I'd ever feel complete again without him, I jerked, tensed, and then came like a fucking geyser all up the window for the gathering of people below.

Black spots clouded my vision, blocking out the stunned expressions, but I didn't care, not when I could hear and feel the roar of Dimitri exploding like a powder keg behind me. His shout was so loud that I knew people *had* to hear, as he flooded my hole with his hot cum.

I dropped my forehead to the glass, giving myself a minute to catch my breath and lean into all the sensations flowing through—and out of—my body.

Sex with Dimitri was... Well, there weren't words. It was wild and untamed, the best I'd ever had, and that was saying something. There was a reason I preferred to keep my entanglements to a one-and-done, because a high like this was addictive.

Good thing I had my head on straight.

Dimitri's dark chuckle sounded behind me, and then his fingers were lifting my chin, forcing me to look out the window. Shocked faces stared up at us, but a few looked intrigued. No doubt this wasn't something they were used to seeing on the trains passing by, but this was their lucky day.

Dimitri drew his spent cock out of me and then turned me around, pushing me back into the cum-covered glass and giving the voyeurs outside a prime view of my ass. His lips slammed down on mine, rough and possessive, and when he ripped his mouth free, he said, "You're worth every fucking penny."

18

DIMITRI

BENOIT WASN'T IN the bed when I woke up the following morning. It was rare I slept more than a handful of hours, but I was finding I fell into a deeper, longer sleep the more time with him passed. It was unnerving, especially considering I hadn't heard him leave the room. I was usually so hypervigilant that any shift, any movement, should've alerted me.

Where had he ventured off to?

I checked the time and tossed my bag on the bed before packing up the clothes we'd left strewn all over the floor. We'd be arriving in Venice soon, and I wanted eyes on Benoit before the doors opened.

Not that I was worried about his slipping away. Though it wasn't like he was chained here. I was positive he was enjoying his time with me so far, and I'd definitely made it worth his while.

Ignoring the niggling thought in the back of my mind, I zipped the bag shut, leaving it with the many others Benoit had brought for the trip. He wasn't a man who went anywhere without ten pieces of luggage at the very least, so the idea of his vanishing was laughable.

Although I wouldn't put it past any other passengers who caught a good look at Benoit to shoot their shot with him. The man from the bar had certainly been keen to take him somewhere alone.

Fuck, that had pissed me off. Not the fact that anyone else would be tempted by Benoit, but because I was annoyed by it. The sliver of jealousy making its way through me tasted bitter on my tongue, and that was it.

I'd started for the door when it opened suddenly. Benoit swept into the room, grinning broadly when he saw me, and then called out to the guards over his shoulder, "No need to worry, boys—the sleeping *monstre* has awoken from his slumber."

He gave them a little wave before shutting the door, and I narrowed my eyes.

"Where have you been?"

"Oh, you know. Making my rounds with all the men over twenty-one before we leave." He paused, waiting for me to respond, maybe laugh, but I only scowled.

Shaking his head, he moved in close, curling his finger into the waist of my pants and tugging me in. He brushed his lips against mine and said, "I'm only teasing, *mon monstre*. You were sleeping so hard I thought I'd grab us a bit of breakfast to go."

He held up the paper bag with a flourish, grinning proudly. I hadn't even noticed he'd been carrying anything, which was another mark on my get-it-the-fuck-together list.

I must've still been glaring, because Benoit's smile faltered a little. It was so brief that I thought I'd imagined it, because then he reached into the bag and held up a pastry.

"I thought a delicious *pain au chocolat* would put at least a hint of a smile on your face. Are you trying to prove me wrong this morning?"

The flicker of jealousy that had ignited my temper burned out at his offering, followed by a feeling I wasn't used to: guilt.

I was so quick to jump to conclusions. To believe the worst. But that was my way, how I'd grown up and been trained. Strike first, ask questions later.

Benoit wasn't the enemy, though.

So calm the fuck down and eat the damn pastry.

I lowered my head and took a bite of the croissant he held, keeping my eyes on his as the chocolate melted in my mouth. It was still hot, like it'd just come out of the oven, and perfectly crisp on the outside.

"Almost as delicious as me," Benoit said with a smirk.

"Not even close."

As I lifted my head, he ran his finger along the edge of my mouth, where a bit of chocolate had escaped, and then painted his lips with it.

"Care for another taste?"

Wrapping my arm around his waist, I hauled him against my body, a surge of possessiveness overtaking all rational thought, licking and sucking, diving into that delicious mouth that had no business being as sweet as it was with such a sinful tongue.

Benoit's hum of approval vibrated against my lips as he wrapped his arms around my neck, our bodies pressed so close together that nothing could get through.

"Now this is a much better greeting," he murmured. "Next time I'll paint my whole body in chocolate so you can go wild."

"Why do I have a feeling you'd actually do that?"

"Because you know I would." Benoit nipped along my jaw as I lowered him back down to the ground. "And you'd enjoy every single inch."

"I look forward to it. But it's going to have to wait," I said, as the train eased to a stop and a voice came over the loudspeaker, announcing our arrival at a station. "We've got somewhere to be."

THAT "SOMEWHERE TO be" was Venice, Italy, a city I'd traveled to for work on several occasions. While I'd never gotten a chance to fully enjoy all it had to offer, with Benoit maybe I'd at least dip a toe in.

But as we stepped off the train, it wasn't a mild, sunny day that greeted us, but a thick fog along with a chill coming off the Grand Canal. While it wasn't the several feet of snow we'd left in Prague, it was still a gloomier welcome than I'd anticipated.

Benoit lifted his sunglasses and squinted. "*Are* we in Venice? I can't tell."

He wasn't wrong about that. With the view obscured past the few feet in front of us, we could've been anywhere.

I didn't like not being able to see. It made my hackles rise, my defenses go up as I scanned the perimeter. My guards moved in front of us, keeping the train at my back, and directed the staff to load our bags into the private water taxi we'd hired.

The taxi I couldn't even fucking see.

"I suppose I'll have to put away my skimpy little swimsuit," Benoit said with a pout, sliding the sunglasses back down onto his face. "What a shame."

"You'll do no such thing."

"You think you deserve another show, huh? Want to take my briefs off with your teeth this time? I won't complain."

As stoic as my guards usually were, that comment had one of them pressing their lips together to keep from reacting.

"There goes that mouth again."

"Want to shut it up?"

"I *want* you to get in the taxi so we can get moving." I glanced around us, checking all sides before returning my attention to Benoit. "We've been stationary too long."

He gave a nod and moved to take the hand of the taxi driver waiting to help him on. Minutes later we were off, after being informed it would take a half-hour or so to get to our hotel— something that would've been enjoyable if I could see more than a couple of feet on either side of me. As it was I was struggling to see the driver, so the quicker this trip up the canals was over, the better.

For the first time since I'd met him, Benoit sat quietly beside me, my mood clearly projecting the seriousness of the situation I found myself in. It was times like this that I often wondered what it might be like to have a normal job, like...a teacher.

"Five minutes out, boss." Omar's voice cut through my concentration as the taxi turned and started to slow, making its way under a bridge and finally pulling up at the dock of the St. Regis Hotel.

My men jumped out first and started to help unload the baggage, as my guards walked up the dock and made sure everything was secure. The second I got the signal, I turned to Benoit, who remained unusually quiet.

"Time to go," I said, and gestured to the steps that led off the taxi.

Benoit got to his feet, but put a hand on my arm, his eyes locking on mine. "Do you ever just sit back and...relax?"

"No."

His lips twisted. "Because?"

I looked over my shoulder, my paranoia kicking into high gear as we stood there. "Because people like me can't afford to."

"People like you?"

Not about to stand here a minute longer, I led Benoit over to the waiting driver to exit the boat. "Bad people."

Benoit's feet faltered, and then he stopped and turned to look up at me.

God. Why won't he just get off the damn boat?

"You think you're bad?"

"You don't?" Jesus, I must be going fucking soft if that was the case. "Are you forgetting why you're here?"

"*Non.* I'm here because I want to be."

"You're here because I paid you to be." My response was more curt than I would've liked, but I was tense, and flirting with Benoit wasn't at the top of my agenda right now.

Benoit gave a sugary-sweet smile as he patted my arm. "Believe what you like, *mon monstre*. But I don't do anything unless I want to."

He let go of me and turned to the driver, then took the man's hand and went to climb out of the boat. But as he lifted his foot, the toe of his boot got caught on the edge and he stumbled into the man's arms instead.

The two fell back several steps, until the driver finally caught his feet, and when Benoit righted himself on the dock, a litany of apologies flowed from his lips—in Italian.

"*Mi dispiace tanto, signore. Le mie scuse. Il mio piede è rimasto incastrato e ho perso l'equilibrio. Non sono mai così sbadato. Sono così imbarazzato.*"

Just how many languages did Benoit know?

"*Non c'è problema, signore. Stai bene?*"

"Yes, yes. I'm all right. Just slightly mortified." Benoit swallowed, and forced a small smile as he looked at me. "You weren't supposed to see that."

"Yet I clearly did. How is it you can manage to walk in five-inch heels but trip off a dock in flats?"

"Umm, it's foggy. I didn't see—"

"The boat?"

"Okay." Benoit put his hands on his hips. "Do you think you could maybe take a little less joy in making fun of me, and maybe be a gentleman and help me the rest of the way up the dock?"

I reached for his arm and slipped it through the crook of my elbow. "Better?"

"Much."

"Very good. Then let's go." We started up toward the hotel where my guards waited. "Tell me, how is it you know so many languages?"

Benoit's feet faltered slightly and he grabbed my arm a little tighter. "Sorry, still a little unsteady on my feet."

"No problem," I said, and stopped, turning to face him. "But you didn't answer my question."

Benoit raised a brow, the clueless persona not suiting him one little bit.

"The languages. Where did you learn to speak them? And how many do you actually know? I've counted five now."

Benoit licked his lips, then grinned. "I see you're keeping a close eye on me."

And he was still evading my question.

"Of course." I took his chin in hand. "Why would I look anywhere else if you are in the room?"

"True enough." Benoit closed the gap and pressed a kiss to my lips, the flirt in him re-emerging. "And to answer your question, I know a little bit of *many* languages. Enough to get by, anyway. I started picking them up whenever I went to a new country to dance. It's much easier to fit in when you can speak a little of the native tongue. Plus, I found I had an aptitude for it."

The response came easily off his tongue, and it definitely

made sense. But as we stood there on the dock staring at one another, it was the first time I felt unease swirl in the pit of my stomach.

Maybe it was the fog. Maybe it was the fact I'd been standing on this fucking dock for about five minutes longer than I wanted to. But something didn't feel right.

Or maybe some*one*.

19
BENOIT

THE SATIN SHEETS were cool against my skin as I stretched out on the bed, content as a kitten after Dimitri had used my body for his pleasure for the last hour. It was late, but he didn't climb in beside me, instead crossing the room to grab his shirt from where I'd thrown it over a lampshade in the midst of...well, *my* pleasure.

"Just what do you think you're doing putting clothes on?" I rolled onto my side and ran my hand over the empty spot where he should be.

"I've got to work."

It was a damn shame that he punctuated those words by pulling his briefs up over that gorgeous ass, blocking my view.

"You can't work in bed?"

Dimitri looked at me over his shoulder, and I stretched again, showing off my long, lean, naked body to its full advantage. His gaze roamed over me, from the tips of my toes all the way up my thighs, over my spent cock.

"I could," he said carefully. "But I wouldn't get anything done with you looking like that."

With a loud sigh, I plumped the pillow beneath my head and got comfortable. "You're right. I wouldn't be able to resist distracting you, and then I'd never get any beauty sleep."

Dimitri smirked. "You'll get plenty tonight, not that you need it."

"Why do you say that? Do you not plan on joining me?"

"It might be a while, is all."

"Is everything okay?"

He pocketed his phone. "Fine. Just a busy time right now. Get some sleep."

Curiosity at what was happening behind the scenes niggled in the back of my mind, but I nodded and faked a yawn. "Don't be too long."

He stared at me for a long moment before nodding once, and then he was gone.

I lay there for a few more minutes, waiting to see if he'd come back, but when he didn't I sat up, watching the door.

I'd need to be quick.

I was a little surprised that Dimitri had chosen to stay at the St. Regis instead of a more private home, but it would make it much easier for me to slip out for a few minutes than if he were just down the hall in another room. I had a drop to make to my brothers, all the audio from the train meetings safely tucked away after I'd secured the device before disembarking. It'd been a close call in the lounge when I went to grab it from where I'd hidden it in the curtain. Just my luck that Omar and several others from Dimitri's crew had been in there having coffee when I walked in. Even better luck that they seemingly couldn't stand me, or didn't trust me, and scattered like roaches when the lights came on.

Worked for me. Somehow the device had slid down from where I'd stuck it, and it took me a hot minute to find it.

That wasted time was also why I'd had to grab croissants. Dimitri would've been suspicious of why I'd been gone so long if I hadn't, and I was grateful he'd leaned into the jealous side of his nature rather than the paranoid one.

I quickly threw on some nondescript dark pants and a sweater, not wanting to call attention to myself. It was out of my nature for sure, but necessary tonight. After loading my pants pockets with what I needed—including an unopened pack of cigarettes and a lighter, should any unwanted attention find me—I slipped out of the room and took the stairs instead of the elevator. Though we were staying in a suite on the top floor of the hotel, there were only six floors, so schlepping it down didn't require any effort at all, unlike the time I'd spent several days with a billionaire banker on the seventy-second floor of a hotel in Singapore. I hadn't thought my thighs would ever recover after such a burn coming back up.

When I got to the ground floor, I took my time peering out through the exit door, keeping it open only a sliver in case Dimitri and his guys had chosen to do business down here. There were plenty of people milling around, but the weather seemed to be keeping them all indoors instead of wandering out to the garden area on the canal.

Parfait. Then that was where I'd go.

I slipped out of the stairwell and kept to the perimeter of the room, then stepped out into the cold night air.

Merde, no wonder everyone was still inside. It'd gotten even colder as night fell, the breeze off the water making it intolerable.

Just find a hiding spot, make the call, and get back upstairs before your dick freezes off.

I scanned the courtyard, looking for an ideal spot to make the drop so Alessio or one of the others could make the pickup, but it was going to be tricky. All three sides backed up to a building, and directly in front of me was the canal.

Eh, they'd figure it out. If I was an asshole I'd give them a hard time and place it somewhere damn near impossible to get to, just for fun. It was too cold for those shenanigans, though, so I made my way toward the canal, where a row of tables and chairs backed up against the meticulously manicured garden. The trees there were tall enough to block me from view if anyone inside was watching, and I chose a seat in front of them facing the canal.

Crossing my foot over my knee, I drew the compact out of my boot, dialed a number into the hidden phone, and brought it to my ear.

"'Bout time you checked in. We were about to send out a search party."

I smirked at Alessio's put-out tone. "Aren't *you* the search party?"

"Yeah, so let's not make it for your body."

"I mean, many would love to search for my body—"

"If it's alive."

"Okay, way to get morbid."

Alessio sighed, clearly trying for patience. "The drop?"

Right. That's why I was calling. "In the courtyard, head toward the canal—"

"If you put it out on the water..."

I chuckled and looked around to make sure no one had come across my hidden spot. "I thought about it, but no. There's a set of tables and chairs backed up against a fancy little garden. Head to the one that has the three taller trees hiding it. You'll find it in the middle pot."

"Got it." I was about to hang up and hightail it back inside, out of the cold, when I heard, "Everything okay with you?"

The question was unexpected, especially from our tech

genius cave dweller, but I appreciated the thought. "Every-thing's great."

There was a pause. "Great? You're hanging out with one of the most dangerous men in the world. How is that great?"

"Have you *seen* the man?"

"Aaand that's my cue to end this conversation. If things start to be *not* so great, remember we can always find you an out."

"Got it. But all's good. Tell King to stop feeling guilty about sending me in. I'm rather enjoying myself."

"Yeah, I'll do that. Now get the fuck out of there—I've got something to pick up."

"*Au revoir,*" I told him before ending the call and slipping my compact back into place, then I headed back up to the suite and, quiet as a church mouse, slipped into bed, undetected.

A HAND WHIPPING back the bedcovers later that night had my eyes popping open and searching for my intruder. I scram-bled up the bed, rubbing at my eyes, remembering Dimitri had said he wouldn't be back until late. So when strong fingers grabbed at my wrist and pulled me upright, my heart thundered.

The dark room made it difficult to immediately place my late-night visitor, but with all the concern and threats Dimitri had talked of, I wondered if someone had come for him.

It wasn't until I heard, "Get up," in his familiar deep voice, that I realized Dimitri must've gotten his business over and done with early.

"*Mon Dieu,*" I said with a small laugh, my heart starting to finally calm. "Is that any way to wake a man from his slumber?"

A firm hand at my chin had me looking up into Dimitri's

face, and now that my eyes had adjusted I could see his stern expression.

"It is when I want you up and ready in the next two minutes. Get moving."

Wait. Had something happened? Dimitri was acting much more brusque than when he'd left. Was there some kind of threat going on that had him on edge?

"Is everything okay?" I asked.

But Dimitri didn't respond, merely shifted off the bed and tugged me to my feet.

Putain. What was going on right now? He never acted this way. Or, at least, he hadn't with me since we first met.

"Dimitri?" I tried again. "Is everything okay?"

He ran his eyes down over me, then looked to our bags. "Get dressed. You've got two minutes. Don't make me wait longer or I'm coming in to get you."

Fair enough. I knew when and when not to push this man, but as I pulled an outfit from my bag and hurried into the en suite, I couldn't help the knot forming in the pit of my stomach.

Had I messed up tonight? Had one of his men seen me?

I didn't think so. I'd been careful on my way out, careful when I called Alessio, but I couldn't stop the paranoia from creeping in. Because what would a man like Dimitri do to someone who betrayed him?

Well, the scar on his face was a stark reminder that he wasn't exactly into "talking things through." So the sudden shiver of fear now racing down my spine felt appropriate.

A knock on the bathroom door had me jumping.

"You ready?"

Ready for what? But, not about to keep him waiting, I pulled open the door, draped myself against it, and played the part I was there to play.

"Don't you know you can't hurry perfection, *mon monstre?*"

Dimitri gave my outfit a thorough once-over, but when he said nothing, just walked to the door and opened it, I swallowed the lump forming in the back of my throat.

"Time to go."

Right. But where?

I followed him out into the hall and into the elevator, deciding to keep my mouth shut since he wasn't in the mood to talk. When his guards accompanied us, the hair on the back of my neck stood on end.

I didn't have a good feeling about this, and the fact that Dimitri hadn't touched me sent all kinds of worst-case scenarios creeping through my mind.

The elevator doors swept open as we reached the lobby, and he directed me toward the doors we'd entered upon our arrival. When we stepped outside and I saw a man standing at the top of the dock waiting on us, my feet froze.

A gondola floated on the canal below, the lights flickering on it making it easier to see, and when Dimitri noticed I'd stopped, he turned to face me.

"Is there a problem?"

I didn't have a goddamn clue. If he'd brought me out here several hours ago, I would've said no in an instant. But with his mood, the time of night, and the fact we had several heavily armed men around us, I was suddenly thinking that *I* might have a very big problem.

At the bottom of a Venice canal.

"Benoit?"

"Uh, *non*, no problem. You just surprised me, that's all."

Dimitri arched a brow but turned and gestured toward the dock. "After you."

I swallowed and chanced a quick look behind me,

wondering if this would be the last time I saw solid ground, then headed toward the waiting gondola.

I took a seat, and as the gondoliers pushed the boat away from the dock, all I could think was, *Thank God for Alessio and his fancy tech shit, because his chip in my arm might be my only way out of this.*

20

DIMITRI

MY ENTIRE BODY remained tense as the gondolier navigated the narrow passage that led to our final destination. The only light came from the lanterns hung sporadically along the walls, but they didn't pierce far enough into the fog to do much good.

None of this made for an ideal situation, but it had to be done, and it had to be now.

Benoit was quieter than usual, not a cheeky remark to be heard as he sat beside me, my guards positioned at our backs. I wondered if he had any clue what was about to happen next.

He was smart, though, and he'd been to Venice before. No doubt he knew exactly where we were headed, which would piss me off to no end. I wanted the element of surprise when it came to him. He deserved that much.

"Up ahead, sir," the gondolier said, but as I peered through the darkness, I couldn't see a thing. Guess I'd have to take his word for it, something I didn't fucking like. At all.

Benoit cleared his throat. "And just what, exactly, is up ahead?"

"A surprise," I said, but didn't elaborate. The less I said, the better this would go for him.

My hands curled into fists where they rested on my thighs as blue lights up ahead did their best to shine through the fog, lighting our way. Before every meeting with buyers, the potential for danger made my adrenaline spike, but tonight my heart hammered louder and faster than on any of those nights.

Because the man sitting beside me was more of a threat to me than any of those armed, paranoid clients.

The loading dock came into view only as we pulled up alongside it, several men in suits standing there silently, staring down at us. The blue lights we'd seen lined the doorway behind them.

"Don't move," one of my guards said gruffly behind us, before stepping up onto the landing, his hand staying close to the gun tucked into his side.

"Dimitri." Benoit kept his voice low, and it didn't escape my notice that he called me by my name and not the nickname he preferred to use. "What is this?"

After a brief talk with the men on the dock, my guard looked back at me and nodded.

"Let's go." I stood up, offering my hand to Benoit, who looked at it with a puzzled expression, like he didn't know whether he should take it.

Good. He didn't have a clue where we were or what we were doing. Or, apparently, if he should even trust my intentions.

That was a first. It also proved he was sharp enough to sense danger, and that wasn't something he needed to forget with me. I wasn't a good man. I wasn't safe. Which meant he wasn't either.

Benoit took my hand, rose to his feet, and threw his shoulders back, almost like he was steeling himself for whatever was ahead. He stepped up onto the dock and I followed behind, grabbing hold of his hand again as we were led to the entry.

I side-eyed him and arched a brow. "Ready?"

"I don't know what I'm supposed to be ready for, *mon monstre.*"

Ah, there it was. Even if there were nerves overriding him, that confidence was there, back to taking the lead. It was one of the things that had attracted me to him in the first place, and why I'd arranged this late-night escapade.

The second the massive doors yawned open, we walked slowly into the darkness, a guard in front of us and one behind. Once we were inside what felt like a small room, the doors were slammed shut, and only once they were secured did the ones in front of us open.

Benoit squeezed my hand at the ear-piercing techno remix that filtered out, along with the blinding beams of multicolored lights flashing in every direction.

All I could see were multitudes of writhing bodies, sweat-soaked and heads lolled back in ecstasy as they danced to what the DJ played.

Instantly, my stomach clenched, this scene not at all what I was comfortable with. But then I glanced down at Benoit to see his reaction, and the surprise on his face made it all worth it.

"*This* is what you got me out of bed for?"

I glanced around at the gyrating bodies then back to him. "You don't like it?"

Benoit laughed and then stretched up to put his lips by my ear. "Like it? I *love* it. But if you'd told me where we were going, I would've dressed more appropriately."

I leaned back and ran my eyes down over his black cowl-neck sweater and pants. "What's wrong with what you're wearing?"

"For this place? Everything. But mainly the fact there's too much of it. Why didn't you just tell me where we were going?"

I grinned at his put-out expression and drew him into my arms. "I wanted to surprise you. Are you?"

"Surprised?" Benoit looped his arms around the back of my neck and shifted in close. "*Oui*, very. But can I give you a tiny pointer?"

"You may."

"Maybe smile a little next time. You know, when you're ordering me out of bed after midnight. It might help ease the sheer panic that something terrible is about to happen."

A frown pulled between my brows. "What did you think was going to happen?"

Benoit patted my chest and let out a trilling laugh. "My mind was full of wild scenarios. But I have to admit that this was not one of them. Do you frequent dance clubs often, *mon monstre?*"

"Never."

"Oh…" Benoit slid his hand down my shirt to the hem. "So this is all for me?"

I took his wandering hand, brought it to my lips, and kissed his palm. "For the most part, but selfishly, I want to watch you dance for me."

"Oh no you don't. You brought me here," he said, and interlaced his fingers with mine. "So you're going to dance *with* me."

"I don't dance."

My words were clear, so I wasn't sure why he kept on pulling me toward the crowd of people.

"Benoit," I growled, looking over my shoulder to my guards, who had their eyes glued on the two of us.

"I'm not taking no for an answer. You dragged me out of bed and ordered me here, so *you* are going to dance with me."

He stopped on the edge of the other dancers and turned, then started to slink his way back into my arms. "Don't act like you don't want to."

Fuck, he wasn't wrong. The idea of him moving in my arms was tempting. But I was well aware how unsecured the area was and just how easy it would be for someone to get to me if they wanted to.

"Dimitri..." Benoit purred as he swayed away from me, his fingers going to the edge of his sweater. Then he slipped them under the wool and the material was gone, leaving him in nothing but his black pants. "Don't walk away from me. Not yet."

And *that* was the fucking problem. I wasn't sure I could walk away from him, ever.

"I *don't* dance," I reiterated with a lot less determination.

"Fine," he teased with a sexy smirk, then slinked up to me again, looping his sweater around the back of my neck and pulling my face in close to his. "Then how about you just stand there and I'll grind all over you."

How in the hell was I supposed to say no to that? Instead, I sent up a prayer that my guards had eyes in the front *and* back of their heads, because there was no way I was walking away from this man. Not tonight.

I reached for Benoit's hips, and the second I got a hold and pulled him in, he flashed a triumphant smile and tipped his head back.

"Yesss," he moaned, before taking hold of my shoulders and running a leg up the side of mine to my hip. Then he leaned back and rocked his erection up against mine, and I struggled to hold him upright.

The music throbbed all around us, and as Benoit moved that sinful body against me, my cock became as hard as a steel pipe. Damn, this just might've been the best idea I'd had this entire trip. It was one of the most reckless, but I couldn't find it in me to care with Benoit so close.

"Can't dance, huh?" he shouted as I began to move with him to the music.

"I'm just following your lead," I said, holding on to him, my only movements a direct response to the feel of his grinding against my dick.

"Well, I'll take it. You *move* very well, *mon monstre*." He grabbed hold of the sweater and pulled himself up until our lips were inches apart. "Now stick your tongue in my mouth, would you, since I can't very well have your cock out here on the dance floor."

"Says who?" I growled, thinking about our exploits on the train.

I could shut this place down in less than ten minutes, but maybe the excitement from the train had been the audience, in which case...

I dug my fingers into his ass and hauled him up my body. "I can have it in you in seconds—just say the word."

Benoit crossed his ankles at my lower back and rolled his hips forward. "I don't think so. You dragged me out here, so before you get *that*, I get *this*."

He crushed his mouth to mine. I wanted any part of him I could get, and if this taste was all I would get, then I was going to take it.

I tangled my tongue with his, teasing and tasting every inch of him—and judging by his harder, faster thrusts, he was enjoying me as much as I was him. I nipped at his lower lip and started to kiss my way down his neck, uncaring of the people around us, oblivious to any kind of danger that might be near. In that moment, if someone had taken me out, I would've gone with a smile.

Benoit slowly leaned backward, letting his hold on the

ends of the sweater slip until he was leaning back from me at a horizontal angle, showing off the strength in his abs and that spectacular fucking body.

Jesus Christ. What was he *doing* to me?

I wasn't the kind to grind on a dance floor, and I certainly wasn't the kind to let someone grind all over me. But as he righted himself and then slid those long legs down my body, I knew I'd dance with him here until the sun came up if that was what he wanted.

"You're so damn sexy," I said, and reached for the back of his neck, dragging him forward. Then I leaned in and licked a path from his neck up to his ear. "Sweaty, sexy, and all fucking mine."

Benoit turned his head and bit at my bottom lip, tugging on it as he slipped his hands under my shirt. "Undo this."

With my eyes on his I unbuttoned the material, but with his sweater around my shoulders, the shirt stayed in place. That didn't seem to bother Benoit, though, as he slid his hands up my body and pushed it out of his way. Then he dipped his head and dragged his tongue over my nipple.

"Fuck," I said as he aimed his eyes up at me and I grabbed the back of his hair. "Don't be a tease."

Benoit licked his lips and then went back to doing just that. He flicked that nimble tongue over the tip and then took it between his teeth and bit down hard.

I twisted my fingers in his hair and dragged that tortuous mouth away from me.

"Careful," I warned, but he merely smiled and moved to my other side, giving that nipple the same treatment, all the while making my dick jealous of the attention. I tipped my head back as the blue lights flashed around us, letting him kiss his way further down my body.

I knew we should stop. The train was one thing—a

controlled environment where I could see my surroundings and had a door between us and the rest of the world, and any potential threats. But out here there was no divide, and when his hand went to the button of my pants, I stopped him.

I glanced down and saw the question in his eyes. "Not here."

Benoit pouted but nodded, and when he spun around to back up into me, a dancer from the crowd stopped moving and started to stare...at Benoit.

What the fuck?

I was about to muscle past him and tell the gawking creep to keep moving, but then a smile split his lips and he walked right up to Benoit and said, "Gabriele?"

Gabriele? My entire body froze, including my feet, as Benoit looked up. Who the hell was this guy, and why was he calling Benoit *Gabriele?*

As the strange man opened his arms and pulled Benoit into an embrace, Benoit's entire body tensed and he reared back. Every thought about who this guy was and what was going on left my brain in that instant and was replaced with a possessiveness I had no right feeling.

"Let him go," I barked, and shoved the stranger back from Benoit.

He reached for his shoulder and rubbed it, a frown forming between his brows before he looked back to Benoit, who stood silent beside me.

"Gabriele, it's me, Enzo. You don't remember?"

I glared down at Benoit and waited for him to respond, but when he said nothing and the other man took a step forward, I moved between them.

"I wouldn't do that if I were you."

"We're friends." He went to step around me, and that was it.

I reached out, took the guy's wrist, and twisted it at an unnatural angle. He cursed, but the beat of the music turned loud and hard at just the right moment, as I moved in until our toes were touching.

"You are not friends. You don't even know his name. So how about you turn the fuck around and walk away?"

"But I—"

"Turn. The. Fuck. Around. *Now*." I added more pressure to my hold, and finally he nodded.

"Okay, okay."

I let him go with a shove, and he quickly disappeared into the crowd as I turned back to Benoit.

Gone was the sexual high he'd been floating on minutes ago, and in its place was a look of shock that he quickly hid.

He placed a hand to his chest and let out a small laugh as he moved up on his toes and said by my ear, "My hero."

But that wasn't enough. I wanted more. I wanted to know who the fuck that was, and why he was calling Benoit that name. "Who was that?"

Benoit shrugged and went to walk away from me, but I reached out and took hold of his arm, spinning him back to face me.

"He clearly knew you. Or thought he did. Gabriele?"

"No." Benoit laughed and waved a hand through the air. "It's dark, and he's probably been drinking. He got me confused with someone else, that's all."

I narrowed my eyes as Benoit brushed a kiss over my lips.

"Come on, don't let some stranger ruin our night."

I stared down into his hazel eyes, that gnawing in the pit of my stomach back from earlier, when we'd gotten off the water taxi.

I wanted to believe Benoit that the man was nothing but a confused drunk, but it sure hadn't seemed that way. In fact, he'd been pretty damn positive that Benoit was this Gabriele, almost looked *hurt* when Benoit responded the way he did.

"Dimitri?" Benoit held his hand out to me, and as I took hold of it, he gave a sensual smile. "You want to get out of here?"

Yes. Yes, I did.

Then I was going to work out why and what else Benoit was lying to me about.

21

BENOIT

I'D DODGED A bullet last night, there was no doubt about it. In all the years I'd spent going undercover and pulling missions, I'd never actually been as close to getting busted as I thought I was last night when Dimitri rudely awakened me. My heart had actually stopped at one point, but then the fog of sleep disappeared and I remembered that should anything happen, my brothers would show up in a flash.

If I wasn't taken out before then. But no matter. Dimitri's prickly demeanor had only stemmed from being uncomfortable, because last night was so *not* his scene. But he'd done that for me, gone out of his way to surprise me with a night out dancing, and that had me feeling some type of way deep down.

With my toes, I flipped the hot water back on and relaxed into the tub. Sure, I'd been lounging in the bath for a half-hour already, but my sore muscles deserved a good soak. Dimitri was just the right kind of rough in bed, and I enjoyed the fact that I could still feel him the next day. I really shouldn't be enjoying my time with him as much as I was, but I couldn't seem to stop myself. I didn't really *need* to—I mean, I knew my limits. Just because the man was hot and fucked like it was his last night on earth didn't mean I wasn't fully aware of who he was or that danger lurked around every corner. That *was* the reason I was here—to figure out whether Dimitri could be trusted.

I closed my eyes, turned the water off, and tried to clear my mind long enough to enjoy the amber-scented oil I'd poured into the bath with a heavy hand. But every time I tried, all I could see was his face, and all I could feel were his hands stroking over every inch of me.

Fuck it.

It wasn't like anyone knew my thoughts or that I wasn't allowed to enjoy my time here. If it turned out Dimitri wasn't a guy we wanted to be dealing with, well, then I'd cut ties and disappear back to Manhattan once the mission was over.

Unfortunately, my brain wasn't quite thinking that way. It was on the what-if-he's-a-good-guy-who-does-bad-things train of thought. I didn't want to admit to myself that there was some minuscule bit of hope inside that Dimitri wasn't a man I'd have to avoid in the future...or be on the opposite side of. That never boded well for those caught in the Libertine cross-hairs.

And speaking of cross-hairs... What were the odds that I would've run into someone I knew at a club in Venice in the middle of winter? Especially Enzo, of all people.

I cringed thinking back to the way he'd called me Gabriele in front of Dimitri, something that should've really set off alarms in *mon monstre*'s head. I'd played it off, but I had to admit that seeing Enzo had rattled me.

It'd been at least a decade since I'd gone undercover as "Gabriele," befriending Enzo so I could secretly gather information about his tech billionaire father. He'd been part of a group that'd been too close to uncovering King's private business, TerraKohr, and my efforts had managed to throw them off the scent. Enzo had never known about my involvement. Which was why he'd been so friendly last night—but damn if he hadn't almost blown my cover.

A knock sounded on the bathroom door, but Dimitri didn't wait for me to answer before walking inside.

"Just checking you haven't turned into a prune," he said, coming over to sit on the edge of the tub. He was wearing more clothes than he had been earlier, down to the buttoned suit jacket, and I arched a brow.

"Why don't you join me and see for yourself?"

Dimitri ran his eyes over my body, but didn't make a move to undress. "Tempting," he said, "but I have somewhere to be."

"Yes, you do." I pointed to the other side of the bath, where my feet barely touched with all the extra room, and made a little splash with my toes. "You belong right there, so get naked and get in. Please and thank you."

"Not sure if you've forgotten, but this is a business trip for me. That means I actually have to go and conduct some."

Oh, I hadn't forgotten. His business was always on my mind. But I feigned my best pout and batted my lashes. "Fine. I won't stop you. But it's such a shame to waste a good bath."

"I would agree," he said, and trailed his fingers down the side of my face. "But I'm sure there'll be other times."

Dimitri straightened and headed to the door. "I won't be long—it's just a quick walk to St. Mark's Basilica."

Wait. Did he just tell me where he was conducting his business tonight?

"I'll get in, do what I need to, and be back in less than half an hour." He glanced at me, and I quickly schooled my features into a relaxed smile, not the shocked expression I knew had just crossed my face.

"Wonderful. Do you think you'll want to eat in tonight, or—"

"Eating in sounds like a good plan. I want tonight to just be about us."

I licked my lips, excited by his promise. But in the back of my mind I couldn't help but wonder if I'd be able to sneak out of here, follow him to St. Mark's, and get back in time to meet him without his knowledge.

It was a risky move, but one that could give me some important intel. King would love to know who Dimitri was meeting up with here, and since he'd practically given me his meeting place and time, surely it was a sign I should use it.

"I love the way your mind works, *mon monstre.*"

With a final nod, Dimitri slipped out of the en suite and seconds later the penthouse door, and that was my cue to get my ass out of this tub.

It really was a shame to waste the bath, but business called, and if I didn't hurry up and get into some clothes, Dimitri would get to the church before I even got out the front door.

I pulled on a pair of black slacks and a sweater and, after grabbing my compact phone and slipping it in one of my boots, headed for the door of the suite. I put my eye to the peephole to see if anyone was in the hall and, seeing it was clear, gently pulled open the door.

I stuck my head outside to make sure no one was posted on our floor, but it seemed Dimitri had taken his guards with him tonight.

That made sense, especially if he was walking. It just meant I needed to be extra vigilant when following, keep enough distance that no one spotted me.

I took the stairs down to the main floor and headed out of the lobby and through the courtyard. It was another cool night, but not half as bad as the night before. That meant there were a lot of people out and about, which worked in my favor. The more people milling around, the more I could blend in.

I always was good at working a crowd.

A quick word with the concierge provided the direction I needed to go to get to Dimitri's meeting place, and I headed in the direction of St. Mark's Basilica, ready to see who my favorite arms dealer was meeting up with tonight.

22

DIMITRI

THE SECOND I shut the bedroom door behind me, my face fell. I glanced at where my guards lingered in the hallway, raised a finger to my lips, and shook my head. They fell back, not following after me as I bypassed the elevator and took the stairs instead, giving Benoit enough time to dress and follow me.

Because he *would* be following, if my hunch was right. I'd given him just enough information regarding my destination without showing my entire hand, which meant if Benoit was doing what I thought he was, he'd be too curious to resist trailing me.

Part of me hoped I was wrong about him, that my paranoia had gone off the rails this time. But too much was adding up, and I didn't like the sum of those parts.

Once I got to the ground floor, I paused in the lobby and pulled the leather gloves from my coat pocket. I scanned the room as I put them on, memorizing the faces of those lingering in case any of them were Benoit's co-conspirators.

Then I pulled the hood of my jacket over my head and

headed out into the cold night. It was strange not to feel the eyes of my guards watching me, but this was something I needed to do on my own. No interference, just the two of us— Benoit and me.

The night was relatively quiet as I made my way through the streets of Venice, walking purposefully but not as quickly as I normally would. I kept my hands in the pockets of my coat, not wanting my balled fists to tip anyone off to my mood.

It wasn't long before I felt it. A stare. Someone behind me watching, following, keeping far enough back that I couldn't see their reflection in the windows or catch them out of my periphery.

God fucking dammit.

I should've seen it sooner, but Benoit—or Gabriele, or whatever his real name was—was so thoroughly believable: charming, handsome, seemingly carefree, but just oblivious enough not to sound any alarms. Add in an undeniably sexy body and it was easy to see why anyone would fall under his spell.

Hell, some dumb bastard would even shell out millions for the fucking privilege.

I clenched my teeth so hard pain shot through my jaw, but I kept the domes of St. Mark's Basilica in my sights.

All day I'd had niggling thoughts, stirred up after the stranger in the club insisted that Benoit was Gabriele. It brought up other times I'd pushed his behavior to the back of my mind. The different languages, explained in such a flippant way. That he was a dancer. He had to know how to charm his way around in different countries.

Bullshit.

God, I felt like such a fucking idiot, one blinded by a pretty face and a spectacular ass. That was so not me, but apparently when it came to Benoit I'd let down more than my damn pants.

I'd let down every guard I kept in place, and all because he showed some interest.

It was pathetic. *I* was pathetic, apparently so hard up that I'd paid for a literal spy to sleep beside me.

At least, that was what I suspected Benoit to be. He hadn't killed me yet, so that ruled out his being an assassin—and he'd had several opportunities to put a knife to my throat when I'd passed out beside him after using his body all night.

So he was here to collect something. Information on me, my meetings, my organization? He'd been particularly curious about our itinerary that first night in Prague, looking over the map, brushing off Omar's concerns and even convincing me to brush them off too. But he'd clearly been looking for more than the next stop on his paid vacation—he'd been looking for intel, and I'd given it to him.

So how had he pulled it off? Secret cameras? Mics? I'd had his luggage thoroughly checked and been sure to check *him* myself, so he must've been working with some pretty high-end tech. That led me to believe there was someone bigger behind this. Someone providing the latest and greatest equipment.

But who? Maybe the Redwater Syndicate?

A red haze of fury clouded my vision as I turned onto a narrow street and headed toward a set of stairs, the feeling of someone watching and following me ever present.

What a fool I'd been. If this had been anyone else, any of my men, who'd brought a spy into our midst, there'd be dire consequences.

But it hadn't been. It'd been me, *the boss*, and no matter how much I'd enjoyed Benoit, it had to come to an end—and so did he.

I sidestepped a couple with their arms entwined, out on a nightly stroll, and thought of the night Benoit had cuddled up to me at the Christmas markets. It felt like months ago, not days, standing in the snow and watching his face light up when I bought him that vintage mirror—

My feet faltered as that night came back to me in vivid clarity—more specifically, the lead-up to that night. Benoit had been *so* adamant we go, almost pushy, betting me over a game of chess, and damn if that beautiful distractor hadn't gotten his way.

So who had he really been there for? Certainly not me.

And that made my anger boil up all over again. Because while I was furious he'd lied to me, the idea he'd been fucking me and then meeting up with someone else right under my nose made me close to psychotic.

I wanted to strangle him *and* demand answers.

The closer I got to what I'd told him was my destination, the quicker my pace. It was a good thing I'd told my guards to hang back at the hotel, because I wasn't giving them the satisfaction of getting their hands on Benoit, and I sure as hell didn't need witnesses to the fact he'd pulled one over on me.

I crossed the courtyard, heading to the side of St. Mark's, and then looked for somewhere deep in the shadows to prowl. A narrow walkway with branches leading off it was the perfect spot, and I took the path to the right and waited.

He'd follow me down, I was sure of that. Whatever he was after, he needed to be close enough to get the intel he wanted, so even though my rage vibrated off me in palpable waves, I kept still against the stone wall.

Here, kitty, kitty...

The silence was ominous as I listened for footsteps. When several minutes went by with nothing, I briefly considered that maybe I'd been wrong.

But then one of shadows on the wall moved. Just the slightest bit, but enough to catch my attention. I didn't breathe as I watched it move another inch...and then another. Testing the waters, seeing if it was safe to dive in.

My gloved hands curled by my sides, itching to grab him, but I waited for him to move a little closer. He wouldn't be escaping me, and I wasn't about to jump the gun and let him slip from my grasp.

He was so damn quiet, his shoes not making a sound. His breath didn't even make puffs of air. I'd pulled my scarf up over my mouth, and no doubt he'd done the same, but the shadow still moved in my direction, and then...the toes of his boots inched past the opening in the wall.

In the blink of an eye I moved, snatching him up so fast that he didn't have a chance to utter a sound before I shoved him hard up against the wall and pressed my gun into the side of his throat.

Benoit's eyes flared with surprise for only a second before he schooled his expression into something more neutral. Something that pissed me off even more.

But what had I expected to see? Hurt? Concern? An apology?

Get your fucking head out of the clouds, Dimitri. He betrayed you.

And that was all the reminder I needed to demand, "Who the *fuck* are you?"

23

BENOIT

I WAS IN deep shit.

I should've known better than to follow Dimitri tonight. He'd never let slip his intended location before, but I'd been getting too comfortable, thinking that after last night he'd never suspect me. I was too in my element, too charming for him to possibly think I was anyone other than the dancer I claimed to be.

How wrong was I?

Dimitri pressed his gun against my neck deeper, making it difficult to breathe. But if I didn't say something and soon, I might not get the chance again.

"Now, now, *mon monstre*. No need to be so rough." I winked, still playing my part just in case. "Although we both know I like it that way."

"Don't fuck around with me—"

"Why?" I asked, batting my lashes. "If I recall, you rather liked when I did that."

Dimitri gritted his teeth, his dark eyes close to black now. "Who. The. Fuck. Are. You?"

Merde. It was clear my ruse was up, and all I could hope for was to keep him talking long enough that Alessio found me and Dimitri didn't, oh, I don't know, pull the trigger.

"What do you mean? I'm Benoit. You know that—"

"I know you're lying to me."

"*Non,*" I said, then shrugged the best I could. "Well, not about that, anyway."

Dimitri's nostrils flared as he shoved a leg between mine and leaned into me, crushing me to the wall. It was a move I would've enjoyed had the barrel of a gun not been kissing my jaw.

"You think I'm playing here? That this isn't loaded?"

No, I definitely didn't think that. Dimitri had set this trap well for me. For weeks now we'd been playing a dangerous game of chess, from the second I stepped on the stage of his club back in Dubai. So there was no way I believed he'd set this up without having an end game in mind. And the fact he was an arms dealer led me to believe that game ended with him taking this queen off the chessboard.

"I'm pretty, not stupid. You'd never put a gun to anyone's head without having a bullet in it. But really, *mon monstre,* do you want to mess up such perfection?"

"So that mouth really is yours, not part of an act?"

"I told you—you know me."

"I know who you *want* me to know." Dimitri's jaw clenched, and it made the jagged scar on his cheek even more pronounced. Or maybe that was just the fact it was a glaring reminder of how brutal he could be. "Who you were *sent* to be."

"And who is that?"

"The perfect distraction."

I preened a little despite my completely fucked situation. "Why thank—"

"That wasn't a fucking compliment," Dimitri growled, and slowly cocked his head. "Who do you work for?"

A bunch of assholes who are late to the party, that's who.

But I wasn't about to say *that.*

"You. Really, Dimitri. You've got this all wrong."

"I don't think so," he said, his voice lowering several menacing octaves as he leaned in and put his mouth by my ear. "I think I've finally got this right. All the languages. The casual way you show up at the exact right time to see information you shouldn't. The man at the club calling you a different name... I think you're working for someone, and you're going to tell me who before—"

"You what?" I said, and turned my head so we were eye to eye with the gun between us. "You put that in my mouth? Come now. You might want me dead, but we both know you'd rather put something else in my mouth than that gun."

A flare of something—could've been arousal *or* rage—flashed in his eyes before he lowered the gun and yanked me in so our mouths were a whisper apart.

"I don't like traitors."

"So why haven't you pulled the trigger yet?"

His eyes narrowed a fraction. "I'm waiting for an answer."

"Maybe." I lowered my eyes to his mouth. "But I don't think that's all. You could've sent anyone out here tonight to get answers. Instead you came alone. Why?"

Dimitri jammed the gun back under my chin, his eyes blazing. "You're not the one asking the fucking questions here. Tell me who sent you, or the next thing I do *will* be pulling the trigger."

The sound of a gun cocking had Dimitri freezing, and I looked past his shoulder to where Lachlan stood, looking far too trigger happy with his weapon pointed at Dimitri's head.

"I wouldn't do that if I were you," he said. "But if you'd like to try, it'd give me an excuse to blow your skull clean off your shoulders. Your choice."

A second gun was cocked, this time from Dimitri's other side, and Alessio smirked.

"Now, Lachlan, maybe we should hear the guy out. Ask him why he thinks it's a good idea to threaten Benny boy."

Dimitri turned his head slowly toward Alessio, the gun at his forehead, and recognition dawned. "I've seen you. The Christmas markets."

"Not as stealthy as you thought," I said to Alessio, my breath coming out on a gasp. I tried moving my neck to the side to get some air, but Dimitri jerked his attention back to me and didn't give an inch. Even with the guns pointed at his head.

The man had no fear. It was as impressive as it was terrifying.

"What gave it away?" I said. "The hair, right? So long and luscious—"

"Shut the fuck up," Dimitri snapped, my sweater still tangled in his fist. "What have you done?"

Alessio moved in closer. "You're not the one asking the questions anymore. Drop the gun."

Conflict warred in Dimitri's eyes, and though he didn't show it, I knew he was regretting his choice to lure me here without backup. He was in a shit position now, but a man like him wouldn't go down without a fight.

"And if I do?" he bit out, his stare locked on me. "What happens then? You dump my body in the canals and steal my business?"

"Sounds familiar," Alessio mused. "Isn't that what you did to your mentor?"

Lachlan snorted, his focus on Dimitri never wavering. "I

heard he was chopped into so many pieces that they'll never find them all. Sounds like the work of a psychopath to me."

Lachlan didn't have room to talk, but that was still news I hadn't heard before. It was not like I wasn't *aware* I'd been sleeping with a dangerous man, but we'd never gone into specifics about his work or his mentor. That'd been part of the plan, but one wrong move and here we were.

The fact that everyone still had guns drawn didn't bode well for whatever they'd seen and heard on the recordings.

My stomach sank at that realization, a reaction I hadn't expected. Somewhere in the back of my mind I'd hoped we wouldn't end this month together on bad terms, but now it seemed the time I'd spent with Dimitri would be all I got.

Mission completed.

So why did my chest feel tight?

"Here's what's gonna happen," Alessio said. "You'll drop your weapon and come with us. As long as you don't pull any bullshit, you'll end up in one piece when we get there."

"I don't believe you," Dimitri said.

"That's your choice. Bossman wants to see you. We have our orders, and they don't include bringing in your lifeless body."

"But we'll do it," Lachlan's words were a dark promise he wouldn't hesitate to act on. "And don't think I won't enjoy the hell out of making you suffer."

"With an offer like that, who could say no?" Dimitri narrowed his eyes on mine, searching, and I could see the moment he made his decision.

He lowered his gun from my neck, but instead of tossing it on the ground, he shocked all three of us by putting it in my hands.

"If you're going to threaten me, then you be the one to pull the trigger," he said, stepping back from me, his powerful body vibrating with unleashed fury.

Lachlan searched him for other weapons, finding several more and pocketing them all.

The weight of his gun was too heavy in my hands, the feel of it unfamiliar—and unwanted. Violence wasn't my scene, and I knew there was no way in hell I'd ever shoot Dimitri.

Well...if there were a threat to my brothers I would, but it wouldn't be a fatal shot. Maybe in the leg or something to have him incapacitated for a few minutes, but not dead on the ground.

I shuddered at the thought and wondered why I didn't feel more relief at my brothers showing up when they did. Dimitri had been ready to kill me. He'd hesitated, sure, but that didn't mean he wouldn't have followed through. I'd lied, broken his trust, and was now a traitor in his eyes. In his world, there was nothing worse.

"Benoit." Alessio jerked his head to the side for me to join him, and then we followed behind Dimitri and Lachlan and began the walk to wherever King had set up camp.

There was no telling what version of King we'd face when we arrived, but one thing I did know: this version of Dimitri somehow felt more lethal than he had with his gun in hand.

And that was something that should've scared us all.

24

DIMITRI

IF I'D THOUGHT I was pissed before when I was luring Benoit into a trap, it had nothing on the pure, violent rage coursing through me now. Three guns were trained on me, but that did little to keep me from attacking. I wanted the big boss. I wanted the head of that snake on a fucking platter, and that was the only reason the men walking beside and behind me were safe for now.

Benoit included. The goddamn traitor.

At least I didn't have to look at him right now. His betrayal burned through my veins, but why was I surprised? Because I'd thought he was different? I wasn't delusional enough to think he was with me for any other reason than I was paying him to be. This was the way of the world. Money and power, seduction and double crossing. It was par for the fucking course.

It didn't take us more than five minutes to get to the nondescript house they'd commandeered. Of course they'd been close. They'd want to get to Benoit—or me—as fast as they could if something went down. The question was, how had they been watching? Or tracking? No doubt they'd been following us since the moment Benoit arrived at the castle in Prague—

Shit. No. They'd been watching long before that. Benoit had been a trap in Dubai, one I'd fallen for hook, line, and sinker. Was he really even a dancer? He had to be. No one moved their body the way he did. No one captivated with just a look like he could. But there was more to the man I'd let into my bed than he let on.

Who the fuck was Benoit Olivier, really?

A sharp shove to my shoulder came from behind. "Keep moving," Alessio said, forcing me to keep walking down the dark hall of the house. There was nothing on the walls, not a personal item in sight that would tell me anything about the people it belonged to. It had a vacant feel, like its purpose was for this meeting only.

I took note of my surroundings, the exits, every window we passed, the stairs to the left. Listened for every breath, every creak, any indication of how many others were in the house with us.

The room I was brought to had no windows, and no other doors besides the one we came in through, but it wasn't as sterile as the others. A roaring fire in the fireplace joined the overhead chandelier in lighting up the space, and there were a couple of cream couches and leather chairs set up that gave the impression that this was a far cozier meeting than it was.

As we drew closer, the lone figure in the room rose from one of the chairs, tall and dark-skinned, with a powerful set to his shoulders that told me without words he was the man in charge.

My fingers twitched at the savage urge inside, the one that said to hell with the consequences and to take every one of them down. If they thought they had me trapped in a cage, they should think again. All it would take was a spark and I'd burn their world down.

I narrowed my eyes at the man as he turned to face us. *And just who are you, motherfucker?*

"Dimitri Stavros," the man said, stepping into the light so I could see his face.

And right there was my second surprise of the night—the big boss, the one orchestrating this whole thing...was Tyrone Kingston? One of my high-profile clients? Or, rather, my mentor's client. He'd been on my list to contact when I headed to the States, but it seemed he'd grown impatient.

"No shit. And you're Tyrone Kingston."

"Indeed." Tyrone moved closer, his eyes shifting to the others in the room. "You can leave us."

"Boss?" The one who'd threatened to blow my head off my skull stepped up beside me. "I don't think—"

"I *said*, leave us, Lachlan." Tyrone's eyes came back to mine. "I don't think Dimitri here wants any trouble. We'll be just fine."

If *fine* meant the second they were out the door I'd have him incapacitated, then yes, we'd be just fucking peachy.

Lachlan looked unconvinced. "He seemed to want plenty of trouble earlier."

"Is that true?" Tyrone asked, his stare unwavering as he took my measure.

"What do you think? I had two guns pointed at my head."

"Only because you pulled a weapon on Benoit."

"And what would *you* have done if you found out you were fucking a traitor?"

"The same thing."

"Yet you sent him in anyway."

Tyrone shrugged. "I sent him to watch you, not—"

"Fuck me?"

"Correct. That was"—Tyrone looked to Benoit, who had been silent longer than I could ever remember him being— "his decision. Lachlan, Alessio, out."

The two muttered something, then reluctantly turned to leave, and Benoit backed up a step, about to follow.

"If it's all right with you, King," he said in that lyrical voice that was so familiar, "I think I might go with—"

"*You* stay right where you are."

"*Oui*, okay. I wasn't sure what you wanted."

My ass he wasn't sure. Benoit wanted to make a quick getaway, that much was clear. He'd done what he'd been sent in to do: seduce the schmuck, fuck his brains out, then leave once he was finally caught. It made sense he'd want to cut and run now.

As the muscle exited the room, and the door clicked shut behind me, I looked at Benoit. He still held my gun in his hand, but that would be easy enough to wrestle back. I had him by a good couple of inches—and I had a feeling that if he were to shoot, it wouldn't be to kill. When I'd mentioned doing just that earlier, he'd practically turned green.

"Now, where were we?" Tyrone said. "Ah yes, introductions. You are correct, my name is Tyrone Kingston. But most call me King. Business associates included."

"And why the fuck would I care about that?"

"Because that's what I'm hoping we will be."

I narrowed my eyes. "Business associates."

"Yes."

"So you sent in a spy?"

Benoit stepped forward, holding up a finger. "I don't really like the term *spy*, per se. I like to look at myself as a social chameleon. Someone who can fit into any situation and—"

"Get information for their bosses using underhanded, traitorous moves?"

Benoit opened his mouth to retaliate when King held up his hand. "That's enough, Benoit. I understand this is not how you like to conduct business, Mr. Stavros, but we needed to know if we could trust you."

"And this is the way you decided to go about it?"

"Yes. We needed more information. All we knew about you was that you were Giorgos's second-in-command. After his untimely demise, I'm sure you can understand how we might have questions for his successor."

"Which you could've had answered if you'd set up a fucking meeting. How am I supposed to trust you now?"

King slipped his hands into his pockets, his outward appearance all calm and patient despite my obvious agitation. I, on the other hand, was fucking livid. Not only had I been lied to, but all my previous business dealings had now been compromised. All because this fucker wanted to make sure I passed the Q&A portion of his little interview.

Fuck. That.

I wasn't some employee of his, and it wasn't up to *him* whether I decided to take him on. So he could take whatever intel he'd gathered and shove it up his—

"I'm not sure how you're going to be able to trust me. But if you want access to the U.S. market, you're going to have to work it out."

Okay, so maybe *some* of it was up to him. The U.S. market was one of the biggest for me, and if this asshole was who people listened to then I was going to have to work shit out with him—despite wanting to go postal on his ass.

"This wasn't the way to gain my trust."

"Maybe not, but it *was* the way to find out what kind of person we'd be getting into bed with."

"Why not just ask Benoit?" I turned my attention to Benoit, who was watching our exchange in silence. "Isn't that why he was there?"

"Technically I was in your bed for the orgasms, *mon monstre*. But—"

"Benoit," King growled, "you're not helping."

"I'm just making sure he knows I was there because I wanted to be. Not in the hopes he'd scream out his business partners' names mid-climax. The only name I wanted coming off his lips then was mine. Which, by the way, you can now see really *is* Benoit."

"Can we please get back to the point?" King pulled an envelope out of his jacket pocket and tapped it. "The direction your previous leader was headed was one we don't want any part of. Supplying terrorist groups. Traffickers."

"Because *your* hands are so clean?" I said.

"Not at all. But intentions matter. We needed to see what yours are."

I let out a humorless laugh and crossed my arms. "Please, do tell me what mine are. I'd love to know."

Instead of answering, King held out the envelope.

"The hell is that?" I said, staying right where I was.

"An offer."

"You could just speak. Use your words."

A slow, dangerous smile curved King's lips as he continued to hold out the offer, not giving an inch. And neither did I.

"You're going to want to take that," Benoit said, but I didn't look his way. I didn't need him to give me his opinions. He'd done enough.

"It's interesting to me that you'd assume I want anything to do with you after this," I said. "I have more than enough to keep me completely occupied without you."

"I believe it." King nodded. "We've heard your meetings—"

"*Private* meetings."

"—and you've been successful at maintaining your alliances, as well as cutting ties with those who don't serve your interests, and negotiating better terms. I'm impressed."

"I don't give a shit."

"Clearly. But since you're still here," he said, holding out the envelope again, "why don't you consider taking me up on this?"

"If you've been following me so closely, you'd know I require more information about the people I'm working with than the previous regime."

"I'm aware. That's why I'm giving it to you."

Annoyed and completely over this, I snatched the envelope out of his hands and tore it open. Inside was a flash drive and a check that had more zeroes than I'd ever seen, and that was saying something, considering I was a multimillionaire.

I narrowed my eyes on King. "What the fuck is this?"

"All the information you need. You can access it here and now or walk away. Your choice."

I looked at the check again, one that would cement my spot as the new leader of my operation, no questions asked, then turned my attention back to King.

"Lemme see it."

King gestured to Benoit, who moved across the room, retrieved a laptop, and opened it in front of me. He smirked.

"Slide it in—you're good at that."

I scowled at the flirt, that mouth of his never seeming to stop, but inserted the flash drive.

The screen filled in an instant—window after window of names, companies, and faces that were known to the entire world. Some of the most powerful, influential *people* on the planet. Ones who wouldn't want their business becoming public.

My eyes shot up to King. "This is quite the list."

"Now you see why we needed to know if we could trust you."

"Who's to say you can?"

Benoit slapped the laptop closed, pulled out the drive, and tossed it in the fire.

"If I can't, then I guess we'll have another meeting," King said. "I won't promise it'll be as pleasant as this one."

King had my attention. I was intrigued by his offer; I couldn't deny that. The sheer amount of power on that list was something I didn't want going to another dealer. At the same time, I was still pissed with the way things had gone down.

I looked down at the check in my hands, contemplating the best way to go. "If I agree to this—"

"If?" King shook his head. "No ifs. I need an answer."

"And you'll get one if you stop interrupting me. Remember, *you* want what *I* have. What *I* can get you."

"But can you get it, in that amount?" King said, the uncertainty in his voice pissing me off to no end. "That's the real question."

I took a step forward and was shocked not to see musclemen one and two come racing in to protect their "king," because there was no way they weren't monitoring my every move.

"I can get it. Anything and everything you want. But not for"—I glanced at Benoit, who seemed pleased by my answer, and *that* just wouldn't do—"at least two weeks."

"Two weeks?"

"Yes. In case you've forgotten, this little trip you sent your minion on is a business trip. One I plan to continue."

"Fair enough." King nodded as though agreeing with me.

But newsflash: I wasn't asking for his fucking permission, and nothing about my next condition was going to be fair.

"I think so, and *he*"—I pointed at Benoit—"is going to continue with me."

"Wait, what?" Benoit stepped up beside King. "Why would you— Why would *I* do that? There's no need now."

"For you, maybe." I narrowed my gaze on him as all of his lies, his betrayals, came rushing back in. "But I paid a hefty price for your company, and if I recall, you have at least two weeks until that deal is complete."

Benoit let out a laugh. "That's funny, *mon monstre*. But you only paid me half. I'm happy to let you keep the rest. You know, to wipe away your tears over our lost moments together."

My hands clenched by my side. My desire to grab Benoit, haul him in close, and teach him a lesson ran a tight race with my desire to throttle him.

Instead, I turned my attention to King. "He comes with me or the deal is off."

King opened his mouth to refute me, judging by the stony expression on his face, when Benoit touched his arm and said, "I'll go."

"Benoit, you—"

"I'll go." Benoit looked at me. "Dimitri knows you're watching me now. That you're watching him. He won't hurt me."

"I don't like this," King said. But, not about to let this opportunity slip away, for Benoit to slip away without answering for his transgressions, I spoke up.

"He's right. I won't hurt him. Plus, you've just offered me something I want more than him." Insult flashed in Benoit's eyes. "I'm not about to jeopardize that. I am, however, going to take him with me as a sign of good faith and trust. After all, isn't that what we all want here?"

I could see King thinking over my offer, then he turned to Benoit. "Are you sure you want to do this?"

"*Oui*. I'll be fine."

King looked back at me. "You hurt him and you'll regret it."

"Fair enough," I said as Benoit handed him my gun. "But if I catch you following me again, the deal is off...both of them."

25
BENOIT

THIS ENTIRE NIGHT had taken one unexpected turn after another. Getting busted. Making deals. Heading back to the St. Regis *with* Dimitri...

That was the most surprising part of it all, that he'd wanted me to go back with him.

Perhaps *want* was too strong a word. More like wanted to punish me for my betrayal, so even though he'd promised not to hurt me, I had no doubt he was going to take pleasure in making my life miserable for the rest of our time together.

One thing I wouldn't do was give him the satisfaction of letting him know I was bothered by this little arrangement or the consequences I'd be subjected to. I'd be my usual flirty self, the one he knew and enjoyed.

Just maybe not right at this moment. The silence between us was so tense as we walked through the streets of Venice that I wasn't sure he wouldn't toss me in the water the second I opened my mouth. Not that I could blame him, because if the roles were reversed, I wouldn't be giving second chances.

Not that this was a second chance. It was just fulfilling the deal. He'd made that abundantly clear. Dimitri wanted Libertine's offer more than he wanted me. I didn't know why that stung, since getting him onboard had been the whole reason I was here, but I wasn't in the most rational mood at the moment. No, I was on high alert and would be for the next two weeks.

I started to turn left toward the hotel, but Dimitri grabbed my jacket and yanked me back. He walked in the opposite direction, and I frowned before jogging to catch up.

"Are you lost? The hotel is that way," I said.

"We aren't going back there."

"Right now or at all?"

He didn't answer, just kept moving.

Damn Dimitri and his penchant for switching rooms nightly. Now it had extended to changing hotels too? Or was this move directly tied to me?

As we approached a three-story terra-cotta house on the canal, an uneasy feeling settled in the pit of my stomach, and I stopped in my tracks.

"What is this?"

Dimitri turned around, a dangerous glint in his eyes. "This?" he said, walking slowly toward me. "This is a place you and your colleagues haven't been able to infiltrate."

He moved in so close that I had to arch my neck to look up at him, and then he grabbed my chin roughly.

"You asked me once why I change sleeping arrangements so often. The answer is you. You're the reason."

It wasn't the wind chill coming off the water that froze me to my core right then. It was the pure loathing in Dimitri's stare.

"No more spying." He jerked his hand away from my face, turned on his heel, and opened the door.

I could choose to follow or I could renege on the deal and

head back to my brothers. I knew which was the safer option, but that would mean breaking the deal and letting down my chosen family. I wouldn't do that. I could handle Dimitri and whatever he decided to throw my way, no problem.

Throwing my shoulders back, I sauntered into the house but was immediately blocked by Omar and his security guards in the foyer. They, along with Dimitri, circled me, and while it was an intimidating sight, I wouldn't be rattled.

"Here to escort me to dinner? Or am I on the menu this evening?" I said with a smirk.

None of them cracked a smile, because of course not.

"Make sure we weren't followed," Dimitri instructed Omar, who immediately headed outside with one of the guards, while the other guard left the room. "Take your clothes off," he said to me.

"*Pardon?*"

"Take. Your clothes. Off. I won't ask again."

"Oh? Don't you want to do the honors yourself? Give me a pat-down?" I gave a little shimmy, but all I got back was a pissed-off stare. "All right, then." I let my coat fall down my arms to the floor, kicked out of my boots, and then pulled my sweater over my head. I kept my eyes locked on Dimitri's face as I tucked my thumbs into my pants and briefs and slid them down my legs to the floor.

I stepped out of them, removed my socks, and did a twirl.

"Completely naked, as you wish," I said. "Going to search me now?"

"Yes." He ran his hands over me in a methodical, almost robotic way. There was no funny business this time, no lingering touches. Just a thorough once-over that made me feel like I should be bending over and coughing for him.

"Happy?" I said, when he finally took a step back.

"Far fucking from it." He bent and gathered my clothes then headed to the door his guard had left through.

"Um, hello, I need my clothes."

"No, you need whatever I choose to put you in for the next two weeks," he said, opening the door and handing my clothes off to someone who passed him a robe. "As of now, you will wear what I want and do what I tell you. Your belongings are gone, along with any devices or special little tech items you had stashed away in there. As far as you're concerned, you are mine to dress, feed, and do whatever I please with for the time we have left together."

Of all the ways Dimitri could've picked to hurt me, destroying my belongings might've been close to the top.

"I can't believe you took my things."

"And I can't believe you fucked me for your leader." Dimitri shoved the robe into my hands. "That's what you call dedicated."

"I didn't do that for anyone other than myself."

"More deception, more lies."

"*Non*, I—"

"Get dressed. Dinner is waiting for us, and when we step out of this room I expect you to look and act natural. In other words, do what you're fucking told."

I angled my chin up as I shrugged into the robe. "Yes, sir."

Dimitri's jaw bunched, but he said nothing as he turned and marched over to the door, which he pulled open so hard that I was surprised it didn't fly off the hinges.

Refusing to show any sign of intimidation, I sashayed by him and into the hall, where the remaining guard stood watch. "Which way, gentlemen?"

A firm hand at my elbow shoved me to the right.

"This way," Dimitri growled. "And keep your mouth shut."

I glanced at the fuming man beside me. "You told me to look and act natural."

"And flirting with anything that breathes is natural?"

"You should know, *mon monstre*. Up until today, you *loved* the way I flirted."

Dimitri threw open a large door. "Get in."

"Ooh, I do love this strongman thing you have going on. So alpha," I said, running a hand up his arm, playing my part. "So domineering."

Dimitri directed me to a long table and pulled out a seat at the head. "Then you're *really* going to love this."

He was right, I did like that. The gesture felt considerate, gentlemanly, and for a second I almost forgot we were at odds —until he grabbed my wrist and slapped a cuff around it.

"What are you—"

He hooked the other side of the cuff to the arm of the chair and leaned down behind me.

"I'm securing you. But as far as my staff is concerned, you are to play the part of my love slave. Got it?"

I pulled my arm up, testing the restraint. The metal rattled against the wood. "This is a little excessive, don't you think?"

"Not at all," Dimitri said by my ear. "You're a traitor, and I'm going to do whatever I have to in order to make sure you don't *steal* from me again."

I turned my head until we were practically nose to nose. "Aw, you admit it, then. I stole your heart."

Dimitri scanned my face, his expression cold as he straightened to his full height. "I don't have a heart."

He moved around to the other end of the table and took his seat, and my chest tightened at the distance. It was only feet, but it suddenly felt like there were miles between us.

"I don't believe that. I think I even caught a glimpse of it the night we went dancing. You know, the night you did something for me because you wanted to."

"Don't you mean for Gabriele?"

"Aw, don't be like that." I leaned across the table and lowered my voice. "If you think about it, the fact I used my real name with you is a compliment."

Dimitri arched a brow. "I can't wait to hear your reasoning behind this."

"Why, it was the orgasms, of course. I didn't want you to be shouting someone else's name." I shuddered at the idea. "Even *I* have my limits."

I shut my mouth as a man in a chef's outfit brought in two bowls on a plate and set them down in front of us. Dimitri thanked him, and as the man disappeared out the door, I noticed the soup spoon sitting on the table.

"Minestrone," Dimitri said, as if I couldn't tell from looking at it. "Get used to it. The likelihood I ever give you a meal requiring a knife and fork again is miniscule."

"Really? Someone like *you* is afraid of little old me?" I asked, picking up my spoon. "Next thing you're going to tell me is you're going to handcuff me to the bed."

"Cut it out, no one is here to see you."

"See me what?" I scooped up some soup and brought it to my mouth.

"Playing this ridiculous game you're playing. We both know why you're here, and it's not to cozy up to me. So unless someone else is in the room with us, I expect you to keep your mouth shut."

"First off," I said after swallowing down a delicious mouthful of vegetables, potatoes, and pasta, "I was told to gather intel with you, not sleep with you. I did *that* because I wanted to. Despite what you might think, no amount of money could get me on my back. I have money, lots of it. But apparently, a hot body, prickly demeanor, and dangerous asshole personality seem to be what's making my cock hard these days. So I slept with you because, quite honestly, I couldn't say no. And second"—I jabbed my spoon at him—"it's kind of hard to eat with my mouth shut. So if you don't mind, I'm going to just keep on opening it for life's little pleasures."

My eyes wandered down his body, and I smirked. "Should you want to give me one of life's *bigger* pleasures again, I'd also be willing to open it for that."

Dimitri said nothing to that, just went back to eating his meal, so I did the same.

Let him digest what I'd just told him—let it sink in that I'd slept with him for me, not the mission. Then maybe we could find some kind of common ground for these last two weeks.

When he was finally finished, Dimitri picked up his napkin and cleaned off his mouth. Seconds later he was walking past me, toward the door.

Okay, so much for finding a truce.

"Darling Dimitri, you've forgotten to uncuff me," I sing-songed, trying to lift my arm and getting caught by the chain.

He paused with his hand on the doorknob and looked at me over his shoulder. "No. I haven't."

Then he walked out, leaving me alone in the room with what was left of my minestrone.

My mouth fell open at the audacity.

"Hello?" I called out, and pounded my fist on the table. "I'm still tied to a chair in here. Hellooooo?"

26

DIMITRI

Location: Dimitri's Hidden Compound, Arabian Desert

OUR STOPS THROUGHOUT the rest of Europe were successful, if still a bit precarious in these early stages of a new working relationship...and so was trying to keep Benoit on his leash.

Even now, sitting beside me in the helicopter taking us to my desert compound, he snuggled in close, his hand inching toward my thigh as he did everything in his power to get under my skin. It was infuriating. I was the one who'd told him to act natural and not let on that we were at odds. But damn, did he have to be so fucking good at it?

I knocked away his hand, keeping my focus on the never-ending dunes awash in orange, red, and purple as the sun set behind us.

"You're missing out on what could be an incredibly

romantic moment, you know," Benoit said loudly into his headset.

"I didn't bring you here for romance."

"No, you brought me here to fuck, and you won't even do that anymore."

I glanced at the pilot and then shot a warning look at Benoit. This wasn't a private conversation; the line of communication was open between everyone on this chopper.

But Benoit already knew that, judging by the amused tilt to his lips. I should've known better than to think my glare would stop his mouth.

"All that sand..." he mused, leaning over me even though he had a perfectly good window on his side to stare out of. "I have a feeling I'll need some help getting it out of places it shouldn't be. Think you could give me a hand? Maybe even two?"

"No."

"Not even if I beg? It's been a while, but I remember how much you like me to do that with my mouth."

The fucked-up part of all this was I remembered that too, but the hot rage inside me still simmered, threatening to boil over. Maybe it'd been a mistake not to cut ties completely.

"Approaching the landing pad," the pilot said just as the testing field came into view. That was where all of our newly acquired weapons went through rigorous checks before they were posted for sale. Beside that was the hangar that housed everything from our helicopters and plane to the all-terrain vehicles that could navigate the desert. Beyond that, our weapons lab and operation headquarters, and on the far end of the compound, my private residence.

"Is all of this yours, *mon monstre*, or is this yet another stop on our trek?"

Considering I'd brought him here, there was no point in lying now. The compound was hidden in a desert no-man's land, where not even his high-tech bullshit could easily track movement. Only a select few knew about it. It was isolated, guarded, a veritable fortress for testing all the weapons for the governments, rogue agents, and private organizations I sold to.

I nodded as we began the bumpy descent to the landing pad. "Yes. It's mine."

Benoit's hum buzzed in my ear before he said, "Well, we won't have to wear nearly as many layers here. Things are looking up."

I didn't bother responding to that as the helicopter's skids finally touched down and the engine was cut. I unbuckled and wrapped my scarf around my face, then turned to Benoit.

"You might want to cover that mouth of yours—if the wind picks up, you'll get a mouthful."

He smiled, and I shook my head.

"Don't even."

"What? I didn't say anything."

He didn't have to. The filthy comment was written all over his handsome face.

Damn him.

I shoved open the door and climbed out, and once we were both free of the bird I saw one of my men exiting the main compound and heading our way.

"So what exactly are we doing here?" Benoit asked as we walked over the barren sands.

"You're doing exactly what I tell you."

"Ugh, why couldn't you have played this controlling role *this* hard when I would've enjoyed it?"

I thought I had, but apparently I'd been nothing but a big fucking pussycat to Benoit. One he just had to stroke the right way to get him to purr, and didn't that chafe?

"Here." I handed him a pair of glasses and earplugs, though it would serve him right if I left him to fend for himself. "You're going to want those where we're going."

"And that would be...?"

"Boss," my man greeted me, coming to a stop in front of us. "I trust you had a smooth trip in."

"We did. But it looks like the makings of a sandstorm soon, so let's make this quick, yes?"

"Of course." He turned and led us toward our main headquarters, then around to the testing field. "The shipment arrived last night. They're set up and waiting for you."

"Very good. I'll be there in just a minute," I said, and as he disappeared behind the wire fence, I turned to Benoit. "Have you ever been to a firing range?"

"You met my boss. What do *you* think?"

"I think you looked like holding a gun made you want to vomit. So, I'll ask you again, have you ever been to a firing range?"

"*Oui.* All of us know how to shoot."

"But you don't like to."

"Of course not. Why? Do you?"

"Yes."

Benoit let out a sigh. "Of course you do. So is that why we're here? For you to practice? Am I going to be your target?"

My lip curled. "Don't tempt me."

"If only I could. But alas, I think you're now immune to my charm. And personally, if you plan to tie me up to some kind of post, I'd rather it be for a flogging."

My cock jerked despite myself. *Fucking traitorous appendage.*

"You have an answer for everything."

"And you have none."

I gestured to the protective glasses and earplugs. "Put them on. The last thing I need is you getting hurt and your boss accusing me of reneging on our deal."

To my surprise, Benoit slipped the glasses on and pushed the earplugs into place. "I know, somehow I even manage to make these look good."

He did. But I wasn't about to let him know that. Instead, I headed behind the gate and let him follow.

Once inside, I spotted my man standing over by the table where several of the new weapons we'd acquired sat—the latest semiautomatics, sub-machine guns, grenades, night-vision and thermal devices, and predator drones. "This is the first order that came in," he said. "The second is due next week."

I nodded and went straight for the MP5K sub-machine gun. I'd been waiting on this piece of equipment in particular. As I picked it up, I noticed Benoit move as far away from the table as he could, so much so his back almost hit the fence.

So it was true, he wasn't a lover of weaponry, and didn't seem to like violence of any kind. That was interesting, considering the line of work he was in. I couldn't imagine his two friends having the same aversion. Not with the way that Lachlan guy had cradled his weapon like a lover.

I moved away from the table and into position in front of the target range, then positioned the gun so I could get a feel for the weight of it. It felt good, lightweight compared to a normal machine gun. A fact my customers would enjoy.

I checked that the magazine was loaded then lined it up with the target and let it rip.

Pop. Pop. Pop. The piece was easy to control as I fired, the accuracy unparalleled for close-quarters encounters, and it had a setting for longer distances. It was easy to see why it was in such high demand.

After firing several rounds at the target, I engaged the

safety and turned back to where my man stood, arms crossed, a smile on his face.

"Feels good, doesn't it?"

"Very." I nodded and headed back to the table, putting it down next to the others. "You got the numbers I'd need. Is it possible?"

"Definitely. Will take a little time, but we should be able to have it within a couple of weeks."

"Good. That's good." I was about to reach for the night-vision goggles when a radio crackled on the table. I scooped it up and barked, "Stavros. Go ahead. Over."

"Boss, there's some disturbance on the outer perimeter of the compound. Over."

"Define disturbance. Over."

"Three vehicles with stolen plates closing in fast. Over."

"How'd they get past the checkpoint? Over."

Static was all that answered for a long moment before he was back, his voice cutting in and out. "...refusing to stop... armed..."

My guards poured out from the headquarters, weapons in hand, and into armored off-road SUVs. The vehicles kicked up sprays of sand as they hauled ass out of the compound, and my jaw clenched tight.

"Find out who the fuck it is," I said into the radio, but in the back of my mind I already had a name. If this was an attack, it had to be the Redwater Syndicate. We'd already heard rumblings that they were considering moving in on our territory, but since our strained meeting the night of my gala, they'd ghosted.

The radio crackled again, and this time, there was an edge of alarm in his voice.

"Boss... advise... take shelter—"

The line died and I growled in frustration, thrusting the

radio into the chest of my weapons man. "Get a good line open and track them."

"Boss, maybe you should go underground."

"I don't run from terrorists."

"Understood, but..." His gaze landed on Benoit standing just behind me, and I cursed.

Benoit in a shootout would be the worst-case scenario, and I couldn't trust him to be alone. He'd only end up escaping, tracking down the action, and getting himself killed.

"Fuck." It only took a split second for me to make my decision, though it wasn't the one I'd make if I had any other choice.

I took a couple of semiautomatics from the table, shoved one into the holster at my waist while keeping the other in hand, and then grabbed Benoit by the arm.

"Let's go," I said roughly, leading him toward the entrance to the underground bunker.

"Wait, what's happening?" He tried to pull out of my grasp, but I only held him tighter as I spun to face him.

"What's happening is I need to get you somewhere safe, so do us both a favor and do what the fuck I say for once."

Benoit blinked but nodded, though it didn't escape my notice that he swiped a weapon of his own off the table as I dragged him away. I didn't care to fight it, not when it was possible we'd end up needing it.

A shot was fired in the distance and I moved faster, Benoit keeping pace with me. Bypassing the main house, we headed toward a small shed designated for the purpose of storing dust shields, though it really contained something far more important—and something that would come into use tonight:

The tunnel to my underground bunker.

27
BENOIT

MY ADRENALINE SPIKED at the sound of the gunshot, and I hurried down the ladder after Dimitri and landed in darkness.

It was pitch black and suffocating underground, but I supposed it was better than getting shot, though Dimitri had so many weapons on him and was in such a mood that I didn't put it past him to not use them on me.

"Keep moving," he snapped, grabbing hold of my arm again and pulling me along behind him.

"This would be a lot easier if there were lights."

"It's a tunnel."

"Exactly. Our tunnel at home has a lighted path, so maybe you should get with the times." When he grunted in response, I added, "Aw, you didn't think you were the only one with an underground lair, did you?"

All of a sudden my back hit the wall hard and Dimitri's forearm was pressed up against my neck, making it hard to breathe.

"I'm going to ask you this once, and don't even fucking think about lying to me," he said. That dark, deep voice did things to me, things completely at odds with my current situation. I should've been terrified. Alone, unable to see my surroundings, with a man who hated me now and had an arsenal.

I was so incredibly fucked up.

"The men outside. Are they yours?"

The question was so unexpected that I could only blink. "What?"

But the anger I could feel vibrating off him only grew, and this time when he spoke, his voice echoed off the walls. "Did you bring these men to my door, Benoit? Answer wisely, or I won't give a fuck about any promises I made to get you back to them in one piece."

Appalled and offended, I shoved him away from me enough that I managed to take in a gulp of air. "I have nothing to do with whatever's happening here. We don't attack unprovoked."

The silence that followed was deafening. I couldn't see his face to know what he was thinking, if he believed me or not. I may have still had a tracker in my arm, but my brothers weren't *this* reckless. King and Dimitri had come to an agreement, and that would be honored. Whoever was knocking on Dimitri's door wasn't anyone I knew about.

When he didn't put a bullet through my skull and towed me along behind him instead, I figured my answer had been accepted. The lack of apology, though, rubbed me the wrong way.

There was a beep and then a door opened to my right and I was shoved inside, stumbling into something that sent pain shooting through my knees.

I let out a string of curses and had to steady myself, my hands landing on something a lot softer.

Huh. Was that a mattress?

I pushed down on it again, and yep, it was definitely a mattress.

"Seriously, what in the primitive hell?" I said when the room remained dark. It made me claustrophobic—the air was heavy and sweltering. "Millions of dollars and you can't manage to turn on a light? Invest in some A/C? You're in a desert, for crying out loud."

"You can fucking leave."

"And risk getting shot? Those are my choices? Get killed or suffocate to death down here?"

"Shutting up is also an option."

"Wow, you know what? I've just about had enough of this bullshit." I spun around, ready to give him a piece of my mind, and ran right into him. Dimitri gripped my shoulders to steady me, but I jerked free of him. "Don't touch me."

"Oh, *now* you have boundaries."

"You mean when I'm locked in a pitch-dark room after someone just shot at us and you had the gall to accuse *me*?" I seethed. "Yeah, consider this the moment I decided I don't want your fucking hands on me."

I could feel the bed pressing up against the backs of my knees as I stared into the dark void where I assumed Dimitri's face was. It was probably a good thing I couldn't see it, though. At least this way I could actually pretend I didn't want him to touch me.

"Keep telling yourself that."

"I don't need to. All I have to do is remind myself what a gigantic *ass* you've been these last couple of days, and trust me, the revulsion is real."

"Which is why you've done everything in your power to seduce your way back into my good graces?"

I took a step forward, and was shocked when I ran into the equivalent of a brick wall.

Apparently this room was no bigger than a closet. Something I'd strutted out of decades ago.

"In case you forgot," I said, jabbing at his rock-solid chest, "*I* was doing exactly what *you* told me to. Act normal, like nothing's happened. Don't you think your watchdog Omar might've gotten suspicious if I suddenly decided the sight of you made me want to gag?"

Dimitri's hand clamped around my wrist so hard I winced. Then his warm breath ghosted over my lips as he growled, "You and I both know you don't have a gag reflex, so try again."

"Fine. Then let's say I was doing what I was told. You wanted the show. The farce. So I did just that."

"Bullshit."

"I'm a traitor, a liar, remember? Why else would I have gone to your bed? Why else would I have pretended to like it? Because I wanted you?" I let out a laugh that quickly turned to a gasp when his fingers dug into my skin. "That might be true if I didn't loathe you as much as I do."

"Something I might've believed five minutes ago until you just reminded me." Dimitri jerked me forward. "You're a beautiful fucking liar."

He slammed his mouth onto mine, stealing my retort with a quick stab of his furious tongue. I grabbed at his arm, about to shove him back from me and then punctuate my indignation with a well-placed slap. But just as I was about to follow through, the hand around my wrist loosened, and he reached for the back of my neck.

The red haze of anger that had been driving my words swirled to instant desire as those strong fingers began to knead the nape of my neck and hold me in place. The tongue in my mouth had turned teasing, now urging me to reciprocate, and when I slid my hand across Dimitri's chest and laid it over his heart, the rapid beat made my own pulse throb.

Putain.

This was the last thing we should be doing. And the last *place* we should be doing it. But as Dimitri scraped his teeth over my lower lip and bit down, any thought of secrets, lies, guns, and bullets went flying out of my head.

It didn't help that I couldn't look him in the eyes—maybe that would've jolted me out of my lust, but the darkness only heightened it. I could pretend this was a hot moment with a stranger and not a dangerous man who wanted to punish me for my transgressions.

But two could play that game.

I ripped my mouth away and shoved him back, and he hit the wall behind him hard. He snarled, grabbing hold of my shirt and jerking me back toward him.

"You think that was smart? You think I couldn't do anything I want to you? No one could stop me..."

The words he uttered were meant to scare me, but they had the opposite effect. My cock throbbed with a fierceness, days of being denied coming to a head.

"Do it," I said, moving my hands to his chest and digging my fingers into the hard muscle there. "I dare you—"

No sooner were the words out of my mouth than he had us turned around, and now it was my back up against the wall.

There went my advantage.

"You should know better than to think I won't do it. That I won't fuck you raw." Rough fingers rubbed over my dick through my pants, Dimitri's touch not at all gentle. So why did my hips automatically arch into him—why did I *welcome* the bite of pain?

Because I was a goddamn masochist for this man. That was the only explanation.

His mouth crashed down on mine again, and then his hand was on my neck, holding me in place against the wall. I struggled against him, not giving up so easily, even though my body begged for release. If anything was a traitor in this room, it was my erection, stroked to life by Dimitri's aggressive fingers.

Merde, why did it have to feel so *good?* I wanted to put up a fight, defy any kind of attraction to him now that his disdain for me had become clear.

Maybe this didn't count. We were both dealing with a high-stress situation, and anyone would want to take the edge off in this position.

With my irrational thoughts taking over, I dropped my hands, sliding them down to the waist of his pants and tearing them open.

He jerked his mouth away from mine, his breath hot against my lips, but it was nothing compared to the heat in this room. It was scorching, sweat sliding down my temples and the nape of my neck, our kisses getting progressively messier.

Clothes were too much, and I shoved Dimitri's pants and briefs down before doing the same to my own. I didn't bother kicking them off, since there was no telling if I'd find them again, and pulled my shirt up over my head. Dimitri's fingers disappeared and the rustle of noise told me he was doing the same.

This was a *terrible* idea.

But did that stop me? Hell no. In fact, I grabbed his naked ass and hauled his sweat-slicked body up against mine. He licked a wet path up my neck to my jaw, and I dropped my head back against the wall, wanting more of the hungry kisses he planted along my throat and down to my chest.

"This doesn't mean anything," he growled, mirroring my

thoughts as he flicked his tongue over my nipple then sank his teeth in.

I gasped but didn't back down. Instead, I retaliated by threading my fingers through his thick hair and twisting it as hard as I could.

Dimitri grunted and released me, bringing his mouth back up to mine as he slipped his hand down between us and took my cock in his palm. Strong fingers wrapped around my throbbing shaft, and I thrust my hips into his hand and shoved my tongue deep inside his mouth.

Mon Dieu. This was insane. *I* was insane. Dimitri clearly hated me, but damn if his body didn't still have a hard-on for me—one he was rubbing all over my thigh. One I wanted in my mouth.

The question was, did he trust me to put it there?

I smiled at the idea he might think I'd take a bite, and honestly, it would serve him right, but I'd never harm something that had brought me so much pleasure.

Even if it was to teach the stubborn bastard a lesson.

"Something amusing?" Dimitri growled, clearly feeling my mirth under his lips.

"*Non.* I was just thinking about how much I'd like this"—I rubbed my thigh against his dick—"in my mouth."

"And that's funny to you."

"It's a conundrum," I said, panting a little harder as his stroking increased. "You see, I don't think you're brave enough to put it there."

"Why? 'Cause you might take a bite? Who's to say I wouldn't choke you first?"

I moaned as his hand tightened around my cock. "So we're back to playing games then, *mon monstre?*"

"If you want my dick in your mouth, then yes. A game of chicken."

I shoved him back and sank to my knees. The ground was hard, but that wasn't going to slow me down. I reached out to where I thought he was and smoothed my hands up to his naked thighs.

His cock hit my hand almost like it *wanted* me to take hold of it, and who was I to deny it?

I took hold of Dimitri and guided him to my lips, and because I didn't want any bad juju between me and the one part of him that still liked me, I gave it a kiss.

A muffled sound of what I was choosing to believe was approval met my ears, right before Dimitri grabbed the back of my head and guided me forward. He clearly wasn't in the mood for a slow tease here, and neither was I.

I flicked out my tongue and caught the taste of his pre-cum, and the second it exploded on my tastebuds, I was swallowing him down. Somewhere in the back of my mind was his threat of his choking me, but if that were the case, I could think of worse ways to go.

Choosing to focus on more pleasant things, I closed my eyes and hollowed out my cheeks, sucking him as deep as I could get him.

"Fuck," Dimitri said, increasing the pressure at the back of my head. "Why do you have to be so *good* at that?"

Just lucky, I guess, I thought as I swallowed around him, causing him to shout again. Then I dragged my lips up his length and tongued under his shaft.

"Quit fucking teasing, Benoit."

My erection kicked at the sound of my name coming from his mouth, and if he needed any more proof that I'd told the truth about wanting him, all he had to do was suck the cum dripping from the tip of my cock.

But Dimitri was too mad at me to get on his knees for me

right now. Lucky for him, I was satisfied by making *him* explode.

I cupped his balls, kneading them and not being gentle about it. They were full and heavy in my hand, and I opened wide and sucked one into my mouth.

"Fuck." Dimitri tightened his fingers in my hair, shoving his hips forward and forcing me to keep him inside. I sucked harder, until a hiss escaped his lips and I moved on to the other.

As I pumped his cock through my fist, I swallowed around his sac and moaned, both from the taste of him and to drive him wild. That vibration would be shooting through every sensitive part of his body, and if I could see his face, I knew exactly what I'd see: a look of sheer ecstasy that I'd memorized every time we'd been together. Other than the obvious orgasms, it was my favorite part—watching the pleasure of my partner, knowing that it was because of me.

And Dimitri was so sexy that it amped things up beyond my norm. I didn't want to admit how much I'd been hating the fact that he'd caught me, not only for the obvious reasons but also because it had cut our time together short. I shouldn't have been enjoying myself as much as I was, shouldn't be craving his body in a way that had me on my knees for him, but here I was, nipping at the sensitive skin of his balls and then drawing his perfect cock into my mouth again.

I closed my eyes even though I didn't need to, all my attention focused on blowing Dimitri's mind. It kept my thoughts off everything else—the sweat dripping down my body, the potential for our hideaway to be found and shot up. Maybe he needed this distraction just as much as I did. Or maybe he needed to put his hands on me even though his head told him not to.

"You can take me deeper than that," he said, breathless as

he rammed forward, his dick hitting the back of my throat and causing me to choke around it. I pulled back, coughing as tears stung my eyes, but didn't let that stop me.

Wrapping my hands around his erection, I brought it back to my mouth and grazed my teeth across the head. It was a warning—and a promise.

I felt his body jerk, and then the pressure from his grip on the back of my neck increased. "Don't you fucking dare."

Oh, I dared. If he wanted to play, I could do just that.

Replacing my teeth with my tongue, I gave him long licks around the head and across his weeping slit.

And then I went for it.

I sucked him deep and hard, moving my hands to his ass to hold him tight to me. There'd be no getting away if it was too much. Every single drop of his cum would be mine, in whatever way I wanted it.

He cursed, one hand still gripping my neck while the other slapped against the wall. His whole body shuddered, holding himself back, but it was in vain, because I didn't slow.

"God...damn you, Benoit," he said on a gasp before his dick erupted on my tongue. I swallowed down the rush, relishing the taste of him and unable to keep my own climax from barreling through my body. I tensed, curling my fingers into his ass muscles so hard that I knew I'd leave marks from my nails for him to remember me by.

Then I came, a hot surge of my climax pouring out of me and going God knew where. I couldn't see, and truthfully, I didn't give a fuck, not with the intensity of my release and Dimitri's cock softening between my lips.

Why did it have to be so good?

And why did it have to be with *him*?

28
BENOIT

Location: On a Plane, Somewhere Over an Ocean

T HERE WAS NO reprieve after we were able to leave the tunnel. Dimitri had been right about a sandstorm blowing in, forcing us to take refuge in the main house on the property.

At least there were showers. And air conditioning.

But there was also electricity, which meant light, which meant looking Dimitri in the face and trying not to think about how hot it'd been underground—and I didn't mean literally.

Why, why, *why* did I have to be attracted to the man? It would make this whole situation so much easier if I could just ignore him for the rest of our month together. I wouldn't care about the powerful way he dominated my body and my mind, and I could just go on my merry way.

But no, every time I looked at him, smelled him, spoke to

him, my traitorous body gave me away. My pulse spiked, my blood heated, and my dick had a mind all of its own. One that needed to get with the program ASAP.

We'd been under attack, for God's sake, and all I'd wanted was to rip the man's clothes off. So what if the "attack" turned out to be some yahoo tourists who thought it might be fun to take a few off-roaders and shoot bullets in the desert? We hadn't known that, and neither had they. Poor saps didn't realize how close they'd come to being face to face with a man who traded in guns and could unload a round with more accuracy than trained military personnel.

And the fact I thought *that* was hot meant I needed some serious therapy. Something I might actually consider once this month was through.

I stared out the window of Dimitri's private plane, no clue where we were heading, only that we were flying over a body of water.

"Are you alive over there?" Dimitri's gruff voice broke through my thoughts just in time. The last thing I needed to think about was how I'd need to pay someone to get him out of my head when I got back home.

The man wasn't only going to cause emotional damage but also monetary.

"I'm fine."

"You've been quiet for nearly six hours."

"Isn't that what you wanted?"

"If I'd wanted you to be quiet, I would've gagged you."

I arched a brow, and his eyes narrowed.

"Wow. Still nothing. You're definitely not fine."

"Oh, I'm sorry. Did you think everything would magically be okay because you let me suck your dick? Weren't *you* the one who told me it wouldn't change anything?"

He shrugged. "It didn't."

And there it was, that dismissive attitude that really got under my skin. Why couldn't I be like that? Fuck and run. Oh wait, I used to be—until him. But only because I wasn't *allowed* to run.

At least, that was what I told myself.

"Then why do you care?"

"Because we're about to land, and you need to pull out whatever stick got stuck up your ass between Dubai and now, and smile for the crew."

I turned it on then, flashing him my most charming, fabulous smile that won even him over the first time, and he rolled his eyes.

"Don't fucking push it."

"Hard not to when that's what I get off on. Pushing every single one of your buttons."

Our plane landed in Athens, but then the two of us immediately hopped on a helicopter that headed out toward the islands. Wherever we were going now was definitely more my speed, but who the hell was Dimitri meeting with out here that would need what he had to offer? That seemed strange, especially to meet them alone, but I wouldn't question it. I'd done my job. I was no longer officially spying, had no need to report back every little thing Dimitri did.

Though it wasn't like I could help but notice my surroundings, file information in the back of my mind. Those things came as natural to me as breathing, so if there was anything Dimitri didn't want me to know, he wouldn't have kept me around.

Telltale blue domes set against a pure white cliffside village came into view, and as the helicopter dropped lower, I realized where we were.

Santorini, Greece.

Dimitri's hometown.

When the helicopter landed on a private helipad atop a hill, I turned to look at the silent man beside me.

Non. *There's no way he's taking me—*

"We've arrived, Mr. Stavros," the pilot said in Greek. "Prepare for landing."

I looked out the window and watched as the skids touched ground, and when the rotors stopped spinning, Dimitri pushed open the door and climbed out. He started toward the house, but when he realized I hadn't followed, he stopped and turned to see me still sitting in the chopper, staring at him.

"Do you plan to get out sometime soon?" he asked, marching back to the open door. "I only paid to have us delivered, not for you to sit there for the next two weeks."

"The next two— *This* is where we're staying?" My eyes shifted past his shoulder to the gorgeous home perched on the cliff overlooking the Aegean Sea. "The house is stunning but doesn't look like it has fourteen bedrooms."

"That's because it doesn't."

"Then how can we stay here for two weeks? What happened to your 'I only sleep in the same bed once' rule."

"This house is different."

"Pourquoi? Why?"

He leaned into the helicopter and punched the release on my belt. "Because this is mine, and it's well guarded."

Mon Dieu. I was right.

Dimitri had brought me home.

"Now get out of the helicopter, Benoit."

He started off toward the stone-fronted house, and this time I followed. He wove us up through the landscaped property full of cacti, olive trees, and bougainvillea that added pops of color against the rocky volcanic terrain. It was beautiful, immaculately kept, and gave a rugged, naturalistic aesthetic to the property that somehow fit Dimitri to a tee.

"You brought me *home*?" I finally managed as we reached the top of the stone steps. The idea was still completely unreal to me, considering the utter disdain he'd shown me of late.

"I brought you to where *I* was going," Dimitri said without a backward glance. "Which just so happens to be my home. Yes."

That was a lie if ever I'd ever heard one. Someone of Dimitri's power would most certainly have backup homes or accommodations should he wish to go there. Even if it was on his home island of Santorini.

I didn't quite know what to make of the fact he'd brought me back here, to his actual house. Because despite what he was saying, it was a big deal to bring someone into your inner sanctum. And what about the rest of his crew? Would they be joining us later?

"So let me get this straight," I said as we crossed a terrace and rounded a large infinity pool. But when my eyes landed on the view staring back at me, all other thoughts left my head. "Wow..."

Sweeping views of Santorini and the Aegean encompassed all you could see, and the sight was utterly breathtaking.

Dimitri moved up beside me but didn't say anything as I started at one of the most spectacular sights I'd ever seen.

"Why would you ever leave?" The question was more for myself than him, but I got a response anyway.

"I have a business to run."

His answer was so to the point, so him. But I had a feeling there was more to it than that. This place was beautiful, but the strained expression on his face told me there was pain there too, hidden beneath the beauty.

I was about ask, or at least *try* to engage him in some form of conversation that didn't involve his snapping at me, when he turned and headed toward the double doors.

"So," I said, crossing under the shaded area of the terrace to the doors, "you brought me to your house, are dressing me in your clothes... If I didn't know any better, I would think you might want to keep me forever and ever."

"Two weeks, Benoit. Then I'll give you back."

I ignored the sting of disappointment, because why would I *want* to stay? I had a life in Manhattan to get back to, fabulous parties, friends, and couture. Not to mention my own things. Being without even a phone made me feel too naked and exposed. I didn't like it.

"Well," I said, lifting my chin, "you don't have to sound so excited about it. You're the one who wanted me here."

"Maybe I wanted to keep an eye on you. Make sure you didn't fuck up my meetings."

"Oh, I think you wanted to keep an eye on me, all right. But you really could've chosen clothes that would give you a better view." I pulled at the hem of the plain, boring t-shirt and made a face.

"There's no one for you to impress here. Those will do."

That was what *he* thought.

Venturing over to the set of plush outdoor chaise longues that looked comfortable enough to sleep on, I pulled my shirt over my head, tossed it in Dimitri's direction, and spread out on top of a lounger. The shirt hit his chest, and he caught it as I turned my face toward the sun.

"Ah. Much better."

Dimitri didn't say anything, but he didn't have to. I knew his eyes were on me even though mine were closed. He had such a penetrating stare that I could feel it anywhere, and it made me shiver with unrequited anticipation. Our quick encounter in the desert had been a fluke, not something he seemed eager to repeat.

So why had he brought me here?

I opened my eyes, and just like I thought, Dimitri was watching me, my shirt crumpled in his hands. I couldn't read his expression, and that bothered me more than I expected.

"What are you thinking?" I asked.

He only stared at me, those dark eyes unreadable, but there was a faint line etched between his brows.

I stood up, not sure why I felt the need to go to him. Maybe it was just being sensorily overwhelmed, his striking face and powerful body against such a gorgeous backdrop. Or maybe I sensed that he wanted to tell me what was on his mind.

And that was when I realized I really *wanted* him to. I wanted to know more about this complicated man. Why he'd chosen this life for himself, what he'd lost along the way that had closed him off so much. The things he liked and loved, his family, the people he kept close and trusted.

Why he was really keeping me around...

I took another step toward him. "Who are you, *mon monstre*? Will you show me?"

Dimitri took in a deep breath through his nose, like he was preparing to open up, but the second he let it out, a wary look entered his eyes and he stepped back.

"The house has five bedrooms," he said, thrusting my shirt back into my hands and then heading back inside the house. "There's no chef, so if there's something you want, get it yourself."

I bit back a sigh and followed him inside, forgoing putting the shirt back on. I was so close. I could feel it. He'd almost opened up, just a little. But Dimitri was a stubborn, stubborn man, something I was all too familiar with, and he'd snapped shut and locked himself away like a private diary.

I'd get my hands on that key, though. Being here, in his private sanctuary, was a step in the right direction, and it only proved he didn't think I was as much of a threat as he'd proclaimed. I'd never let an enemy into *my* home, so whether he wanted to admit it yet or not, he didn't see me as his enemy.

What exactly he saw me as remained to be seen.

29
DIMITRI

THERE WAS A very real possibility I'd lost my mind.

Bringing Benoit to my home—my real home. Giving my guards and my staff their leave.

It was an unconventional decision, one Omar had tried to talk me out of until I'd sent him packing. Not for good, but until I needed him again. We were in the thick of the holiday season, and I wasn't such an asshole that I'd keep them away from their families this week.

Benoit, on the other hand, I didn't give a fuck about keeping for myself. I didn't fully understand why, not when he'd proven himself to be a liar. I didn't tolerate liars. Didn't welcome them into my house.

So what the fuck had I been thinking bringing him to Santorini? This island held the memories of my life, both good and bad, and it drew me back time and time again. It was my private sanctuary, the one place I felt the most at ease, though I didn't think I could fully relax anywhere. It just wasn't in my nature.

The morning after we'd arrived, I'd been working in the

living room, in an oversized leather chair that I'd worn in over the years until it was smooth and faded, when Benoit slipped inside. The man didn't know the meaning of rolling out of bed —his skin was always flawless, hair perfectly done to his liking. Even in a pair of linen pajamas he probably never would've worn of his own volition, Benoit was...

Well, he was stunning. And that was the problem.

"I made myself at home in your kitchen and brewed a cappuccino," he said, holding a steaming mug as he came to stand in front of me. "You don't mind, do you?"

With the sarcasm that laced his voice, I knew he wasn't actually asking for my permission. I doubted he'd ever had to do that in his life, not with the way he waltzed through it so easily. He charmed men to get what he needed. Hell, maybe even women. Considering I didn't know if anything he'd ever told me was the truth, I didn't really know all that much about him.

Other than the fact he wanted to push my buttons now.

"I'm surprised you know how," I said, returning my attention to the file in my lap. "Don't you thrive on having some rich schmuck at your beck and call?"

"Nah, just one of their many staff—oh, wait. You don't seem to have any of those here. How peculiar. Did they all turn out to have hidden agendas too, or did you get bored one day and use them for shooting practice?"

"I'm not as high maintenance as you seem to be."

"No? You travel with a team twenty deep."

"And how many secret agents are in King's corner?"

"Touché." He took a long sip of his coffee and turned away, leaving that unanswered, which told me what I needed to know. That there were more members than the ones I'd met, and he wouldn't be divulging their names. Were some of them on the flash drive? Or were those strictly clients? I hadn't questioned Benoit when I thought he was just a dancer, but now I found myself wanting to know more.

How the tides had turned.

Fuck.

"How did you get recruited? Dancer turned spy? Your parents were spies?"

Benoit slowly turned around, arched a brow, and smirked. "Oh, I'm sorry, are we asking personal questions now?"

I rolled my eyes, wishing I hadn't said a damn thing and got to my feet. "Never mind. I don't know why I bothered."

It was going to be a *long* two weeks.

THE NEXT TWO days were much the same, a precarious back-and-forth dance that had us moving in and out of each other's space with caution. I didn't trust him and he sure as shit didn't trust me—not that I'd given him any reason to.

I'd pointed a gun at his head. Threatened his life. Then bartered with his leader to put that very same life in my hands for the last two weeks of our agreement.

I didn't feel guilty, though. Benoit deserved every bit of my disdain. His lies had left an acrid taste in my mouth, one that was difficult to be rid of.

He was the perfect illusion. Beautiful. Fun. Flirty. I should've known it was too good to be true. There was no way someone like him would ever be interested in—

"Are you going to join me for a swim today, *mon monstre*? Or are you still afraid I might try to drown you?"

—a monster.

I glanced out the sliding doors to the glistening pool that beckoned. Benoit had invited me to join him on several different occasions since our arrival, and each time I'd refused. I knew myself well enough to know that being around him wet and nearly naked would only end one way, and it wasn't with either of us drowning.

"I'm working." That seemed the easiest way to be rid of him. Ever since King had shown his hand, Benoit had been about as interested in my business as I imagined he would be in a seminar on accounting.

I could just imagine his opinion on that—*I don't care how I make the money, darling. Just how much of it I can spend.*

"You're always working." The pout was evident in his voice even without my seeing him. But the next thing I knew, Benoit came around the side of my lounger and took the laptop from me. "I think it's time you loosen up."

"And *I* think you're going to want to give that back."

Benoit looked at the weapons catalogue I had open, frowned, then shut the computer. "Nope."

I got to my feet and went to reach for my laptop, but he quickly sidestepped me.

"It's a beautiful day, your pool is heated, and you and I are going to go and get wet."

"No, *we* are not. Give it back."

Benoit's lips curved into a smirk full of wicked promise. Once upon a time I would've taken that as a come-on, but I was now well aware that that promise was full of devious intentions, and there was no way I would fall for it again.

"If you don't give that back, I'm going to—"

"What? Kidnap me? Done that. Handcuff me? That was fun. Threaten my life? Guess what? You've done that too. I mean, really, *mon monstre*, you're going to have to come up with something far more creative than threats if you want this back."

He dangled my computer in front of himself, and as I snatched for it, he laughed and turned, running off through the house.

Fucking Benoit. He was insane. No one talked to me the way he did. I'd thought that the first time we met, and I was thinking it now as I went after him. He headed straight toward the sliding doors that led out to the terrace, and my heart skipped a couple of beats. Who knew what he'd do next? I wouldn't put it past him to throw it in the damn pool.

"Benoit, give me back my fucking computer."

He came to a stop at the edge and, sure enough, held it over the water. "Say please."

"Give it to me, now."

Benoit pursed his lips then looked at the water. "I don't know, that didn't sound like—"

"*Please.*"

He slowly turned his head in my direction, and his expression was full of mischief. "Ooh, now *that* I like the sound of. Say it again."

"I said it once." I took a step toward him. "That's what you asked for. Now give it to me."

Benoit walked over to me, still too close to the water for my liking, but then pushed the computer up against my chest. Then he angled his face up toward mine, and the afternoon sun made his eyes sparkle.

God he was beautiful.

"I'll give you anything you want, *mon monstre.* All you have to do is ask."

Fuck I was tempted. So damn tempted. Who wouldn't be? With his flawless skin, inviting eyes, and sensual mouth, I was trying to remind myself of all the reasons that would be a bad idea.

"You want to," Benoit whispered. "I can see it on your face. I feel it in your stare. And I'm sure if I look"—his gaze traveled down my form—"I can see it in your body. Why are you fighting it so hard?"

"Because it isn't real."

Benoit cocked his head. "What isn't? My attraction to you? Or yours to me?"

My dick jerked as he slid he tongue over his lower lip. I wanted to give in, wanted to take his lying lips with mine. But I couldn't seem to get past the idea that he'd only been in my bed for King.

"I'm going back to work."

I turned on my heel and headed back toward the door, and just as I was about to walk inside, I heard, "I see right through you, Dimitri Stavros. This isn't just another compound. This is your home, the place you keep the things you're afraid to lose, and guess what? I'm one of them."

My feet faltered, but I didn't turn back, didn't respond, because if I did I might have to acknowledge the fact that maybe...he was right.

WE CONTINUED TO circle each other like wildcats as the days passed, and I had to face the truth that, for some reason, I didn't want to let Benoit go. It was irrational. Stupid. I should've tossed him off a cliff the second I learned the truth about him, but there he was, in my private study, nosing around. I happened to see him through the half-opened door as I was passing by and stopped to watch him.

He scanned the books lining the shelves, picking one out and flipping through it before putting it back. Was it fucked up that my first thought was that he was thinking of the best way to hide a camera? It was, but no one could blame me.

Considering I hadn't let him out of my sight or my residence since we'd arrived, I knew he was clean. There was no way he'd be able to get his hands on anything to plant in the first place, and there were no meetings to spy on here.

No, it seemed like he was just browsing, stopping here and there to inspect replicas of old pistols from past wars. His fingers brushed over the worn keys of the piano that sat unused as he passed, pressing them too lightly to make a noise. Then he stopped suddenly, his gaze falling to the lone framed photo sitting on top of the closed piano lid.

A furrow marred his brow as he reached for the frame, but when he brought it closer, he began to smile.

I swallowed and continued to watch silently, my heart starting to beat a little faster.

"This is your father?" he said, and then looked straight at me.

I flinched at the realization he'd known I was watching him. He was more aware than he'd originally let on, something I needed to remember.

Nodding, I shoved my hands in my pockets and entered the room. "Yes."

"He's handsome. He still around?"

"Not for you he's not."

Benoit chuckled but didn't put down the frame. "For you, then?"

I hesitated, then shook my head.

"I see." He looked back at the picture before carefully setting it on the piano. "I'm sorry for your loss."

"It was a long time ago."

"How old were you?"

"Seven."

"Just a child," he murmured to himself. "He was in this world?"

I knew what he was getting at: did my father get killed doing the same thing I was doing now? But the reality was far from his insinuation.

"My father was too smart to get involved with this business. He steered clear of men like me." I sighed and looked up at the ceiling. "He'd fucking hate the person I am now."

As silence fell between us, I tried to picture Dad's face in my mind, but with each passing year it had faded and now I couldn't tell if what I remembered was real or something my imagination made up.

"Where was this taken?" Benoit asked.

"Here on the island, during the Ifestia Festival." When the name didn't seem to ring a bell, I continued, "Some people call it the Volcano Festival, since it celebrates the origins of how Santorini came to be. How even in destruction, something beautiful can be formed." I nodded at the photo, at the fireworks in the background as my father covered my ears from the noise, our faces lit up with huge smiles. I was six, and it was the first time I'd been allowed to go.

It had also been the last.

"It's a beautiful shot." Benoit's lips quirked. "You're smiling in it."

"I was six."

"I know," he said, and moved a little closer to me. "But it's nice to know that somewhere inside you is a little boy who used to smile freely."

"Deep, *deep* inside."

"Are you always so cynical?"

"What do you think?"

Benoit put a hand on my arm, and for the first time since I'd discovered who he really was, I let him.

"I think that little boy is still in there. He's just afraid to come out now."

I shook my head. "Afraid? Hardly."

"You're so used to having to put up a front, show strength, not weakness, that you've buried him. But he started to come out with me."

I swallowed back my denial as Benoit ran his hand up my arm and placed it on my chest. I knew I should shove it aside and walk away, but as he stared up at me with eyes full of understanding, I couldn't seem to bring myself to move, let alone push him away.

"You can let your walls down," he said so softly that I almost missed it. "It's just you and me now."

"Is it?" My heart thundered under his palm as visions of him on the balcony that first night in Prague, sitting in my lap, flashed inside my head.

Benoit was right—with him I'd shown a side of myself I'd rarely let anyone see, a vulnerable side. It had started out as a lustful craving for him that I couldn't quit. But the more time I'd spent with him—been inside of him—the more I'd given of myself, until I'd been planning dates in the hopes of impressing him.

That hopeful boy, the one who might've grown into a young man my father would've been proud of had he lived, had started to re-emerge, and all because this beautiful man had smiled at me.

"When it was you and me, like this," Benoit said, moving in until our toes touched, "it was only ever us."

I wanted to believe him. But I wasn't there yet. So I did the one thing I knew would stop him talking, stop him from pushing me to admit the one thing I wasn't ready to yet—I kissed him.

I swept my lips over his in a gentle brush, a test. If he wanted to shove me away, he could. But the second my mouth met his, the fingers on my chest clenched around the material of my shirt and he opened to me.

I immediately accepted.

I slipped my tongue inside and tangled it with his, and the moan that left him had me reaching for his arms and drawing him even closer. I wanted to touch him and feel him touching me. I reached for the back of his neck, and Benoit angled his head and let me in even deeper.

"Dimitri," he whispered as I kissed my way up his jaw to his ear. "I missed you...missed this."

God, so had I. It felt like forever since I'd tasted him, and even longer since I'd held him, when in reality it'd only been days.

I turned him until his back was to the piano and caged him in, pushing a leg between his as I brought my mouth back to his, not trusting myself to talk. The last thing I needed to do was open my mouth and admit that I cared.

And fuck, that was the real problem here, wasn't it?

I'd finally found someone I could see myself opening up to, sharing myself with, only to find out he wasn't who he'd said he was.

As that cold, stark reality slammed into me, I ripped my mouth off Benoit's.

I stared down into his gorgeous face, memorizing his flushed cheeks, swollen lips, and dilated eyes, and wanted nothing more than to lift him onto the piano and take him.

But just like I wanted to believe him—I wasn't there yet.

I didn't trust him. I didn't know that I trusted *this*.

And until I did, Benoit was the most dangerous person in the world to me.

30
BENOIT

I'D LOST TRACK of the days, and apparently so had Dimitri, because Christmas had come and gone yesterday without either of us realizing.

I chose to blame him, since I didn't even have access to a phone. It was strange to feel so untethered to the rest of the world, to be hiding away up here on his cliffside. The first couple of days it made me anxious, wondering what my brothers were doing, feeling like I was missing out.

But then I noticed the way Dimitri watched me when he thought I wasn't paying attention. Sometimes it was with a wariness that told me my actions were still at the forefront of his mind, but mostly it was with what I thought was interest. He wasn't an easy man to read, but all the time we'd spent together had me almost as familiar with his body as my own, and that look in his eyes? Interest. Curiosity. Conflict.

If I was reading him right, Dimitri found himself wanting to get closer to me even as his mind warned him I couldn't be trusted. And under my usual circumstances, he would be right. I *couldn't* be trusted.

But...

What if I wanted to be?

I tried to shake off that utterly impossible thought. I didn't get attached. It went against every fiber in my body. I'd put up that boundary two decades ago and it had served me well ever since, which was why spending so much time with Dimitri was wrecking my state of mind.

Because the thought that I could possibly care about him? Want to spend these quiet days getting even closer?

Ridiculous.

"What do you think you're doing?" No matter what he said, Dimitri's tone always had a brusqueness to it, a sharp edge that sounded accusatory. Though in this case, it might be.

I didn't bother turning around as I fluffed the potted olive tree I'd dragged in from the terrace. "I didn't know what you usually did for a Christmas tree, but since I couldn't find a nice fir on the island, I had to make do."

He stopped beside me, arms crossed. "I don't."

"You don't what?"

"Bother with a Christmas tree."

"Like...ever?"

He shook his head, and my jaw dropped.

"You've *never* had a Christmas tree?" When he continued to shake his head, I said, "Never celebrated at all? What about presents?"

Dimitri continued to look at me like I'd lost my mind, and that just wouldn't do. From the base of the tree I grabbed the gift I'd wrapped with paper and tape I'd stolen from his office and got to my feet.

"All that changes now," I said, holding out the present. It wasn't my finest wrapping, but I'd had to use what was available. All that mattered was it was something to open, and since he'd apparently never even experienced that before, he had nothing to compare it to.

"What is that?" He eyed it suspiciously. "Did you figure out how to make a bomb with household ingredients?"

"That's child's play. Don't insult me, *mon monstre*. Not when I have a gift for you." I grinned and motioned for him to take it. "Gifts are good things, never bad."

"A bomb would be good for you," he muttered, but then sighed and carefully took the package off my hands.

"And leave me no one to spar with? Never." *And no one to kiss,* I also thought but didn't say out loud. He'd initiated the kiss last night but didn't let it go further, and today he was back to putting space between us. Part of me wondered why he'd bothered keeping me for the remainder of our time together, but I could sense the struggle. The want. The desire. It was all there for me too, and I had to focus on keeping my eyes off his mouth and the way I wanted to devour it. I couldn't just jump the man on our faux-Christmas morning, after all.

As he inspected the package, turning it over in his hands, I tapped my foot impatiently.

"You have to actually open it. The wrapping's not the gift."

He arched a brow. "I should hope not. This looks like... What did you say? Child's play?"

"If you actually owned gift wrap, it would've made my life a lot easier, so stop being rude and open your damn present."

There was a hint of a smirk, all the amusement he was going to show, and then he tucked his finger under the taped flap and opened it.

As he pulled the paper away, I fidgeted with the hem of one of the plain tees he'd given me to wear. I'd taken a huge chance with this, I knew that, but I wasn't about to skip Christmas— and since I didn't have access to anywhere other than here, I'd had to think on my feet.

He'd either be happy or pissed at what I'd done. I was hoping happy but with Dimitri you never knew. After all, I'd basically taken something of his and—

"You fixed it..." Dimitri looked up from the old cuckoo clock he held, a surprised expression etched into his rough features.

"I did," I said as he looked back to the little house carved out of wood. "I saw it on the wall but noticed the hands weren't working. At first I thought it might need a battery, but when I took it down I realized this is the real deal."

Dimitri nodded, running his fingers lovingly over the shingled roof, the balcony where dancers twirled in a circle, down to the little door that held the cuckoo. "It's from Germany. The Black Forest. My father brought it back for me after a business trip. It broke years ago but I didn't have the heart to throw it out." He shook his head. "How did you... I didn't know you were..."

"Good with my hands?" I finished for him, then grinned and waggled my fingers. "Surprise."

He blinked a couple of times before looking back to the clock, his harsh features softening as the hands hit the hour and out popped the little wooden bird.

Cuckoo. Cuckoo. Cuckoo.

Dimitri let out a rumbling laugh, and it was such a boyish, joyous sound that all I could do was stand there and stare. In all the time I'd known him, I had never heard such a relaxed sound come from him, such a happy sound.

It was...*incredible.*

"So you like it?" I said, moving closer.

He looked up, his eyes shining. "I love it."

My heart just about stopped at the emotions swirling in those dark eyes. There was a battle going on there, the same one going on inside me. One minute I wanted to walk away from him and never look back, and in others, like this one, I wanted to walk into his arms and never leave.

But it wasn't only my mind that was conflicted. It wasn't only my body. I knew that now, as Dimitri's happiness slipped through the cracks of my own armor. My *heart* was conflicted.

I shouldn't want his trust. Shouldn't need his approval in any way. But as I stood there with my hand in his, and his eyes searching my face for the same answers I was looking for, I almost forgot that I was his prisoner.

And wasn't that terrifying?

"I'm glad," I finally managed. "I wasn't sure if you'd think I was crossing a line by working on it in secret."

"Why? It's no worse than any of the other things you've done behind my back."

The caustic comment was no more cutting than half of the things he'd said to me since finding out about my true identity and mission. But in that moment, it hit harder than any slap could. I tensed and pulled my hand back from his.

"You just can't help yourself, can you?" My words were quiet but I knew he heard them, because he immediately looked away from me.

"I'm not going to apologize."

"No, of course not. Why would you?"

Dimitri took in a deep breath and then let it out as he placed the clock on the table. "Look, you did something nice for me, and I appreciate that—"

"*Do* you?" I shouted much louder than I meant to. "Because to me it sounds like you're an ungrateful bastard who's still holding a grudge."

"A *grudge*? Do you know what I'd usually do with someone who did what you did?"

"It's not hard to guess, since you aimed a gun at my head. But I thought we were past all that."

Dimitri moved in close to me, his eyes blazing. "*Past it?*"

"*Oui.* Isn't that why you brought me here? Why you demanded to keep me like some kind of prisoner until our time was over?"

"You think I'm keeping you like a prisoner?" Dimitri grabbed my wrists and hauled me up against his chest. "If I was holding you prisoner, you'd be tied in some basement with a lock on it. Not standing in my home driving me fucking crazy."

"Then why am I here? It's obvious you don't want me anymore—"

"Then you aren't looking close enough. All I *do* is want you. When I wake up, when I eat, when I fucking sleep. I never *stopped* wanting you." He shook his head. "And another thing I can't seem to stop is wondering whether or not I'm just a job to you."

My pulse thumped hard and fast under his fingers. "You already know the answer to that. You're just too stubborn to admit it."

He swallowed, and it took everything I had not to lean in and lick a path over that strong throat.

"There's no way this can work. No way you and I will ever work."

"Not even for a moment?" I said, and licked my lips. "Not even for right now?"

Dimitri's chest heaved against mine, and just when I thought he'd push me away and leave me wanting, he grabbed the back of my neck and stole the moment for the both of us.

31

DIMITRI

FUCK, IT WASN'T just that I wanted Benoit—I needed him. I couldn't even deny it to myself anymore, and the second I touched him, he knew it too.

I'd meant what I said. I didn't see a way the two of us could be together, but every one of those thoughts flew out of my head the moment my mouth was on his.

He reached for me, threading his fingers through my hair, his tongue eager to tangle with mine. I hauled him into my arms, never breaking our connection, and he wrapped his legs tight around my waist. With every step I took, his growing erection rubbed up against mine, and fuck, I needed to get us somewhere, and fast.

When my foot smacked against the edge of the couch, sending us stumbling into it, that was enough of a sign for me. My knee hit the cushion and I lowered Benoit down onto it.

Then the frenzy began.

His mouth left mine briefly as we tore off our shirts and shoved our pants down, impatient to finally take what we'd both been missing. I couldn't get mine off fast enough, so I stood up and kicked them off, and saw Benoit's pants still wrapped around his ankles. I reached for them, and with one yank they were gone, tossed into the pile along with mine.

"You are..." Benoit licked his lips, already breathless as his gaze ran down my body before returning to my face. "...the sexiest man I've ever seen. *Mon monstre.*"

He punctuated that by reaching down to stroke himself, and he was already so hard and flushed that I knew it couldn't be a lie. He really was as turned on by me as I was by him.

I grabbed a bottle of lube from a drawer nearby and drenched my dick with it. I'd usually want to edge him for a while, make him so crazy for me that he'd be begging for me to fill his ass, but foreplay wasn't in the cards right now. I needed inside him more than I'd needed anything.

"On your back," I said roughly.

He didn't hesitate to follow my order, nor did he take his eyes off my fist around my cock.

As I moved back onto the couch and spread his thighs wide open for me, I said, "You obey so well in bed..."

I didn't have to finish my sentence, not when he knew exactly what I was implying. Benoit didn't mind submitting during sex, but that rebellious, headstrong nature wouldn't allow him to do it outside the bedroom.

"Pull your legs up. I want to see what trouble I'm about to get into."

Benoit bent his legs, grabbed hold of his knees, and pulled them up to his chest, his eager hole on proud display.

"This what you want?" he asked when I didn't move, didn't speak. I was too enthralled by the sight of him so open, so willing after all that I'd done to him, that it took me a moment to remember that he was offering himself to me. I wasn't taking anything he didn't want to give.

I scooted forward between his spread thighs and put a hand on one of his shins as I lined the head of my cock up with his tightly wound body.

"It's exactly what I want. And *this*," I grunted, shoving inside him in one hard thrust, "is exactly what I need."

Benoit moaned and arched his head back on the cushion, exposing the long line of his throat to me, and I leaned over him and licked a path from the hollow of his neck to his ear.

"I hate that I love this."

Benoit turned his head and nipped at my lip. "But you do, don't you? You love being inside me."

Yes, I fucking did. It was like heaven and hell rolled into one, the possibility of everything I could ever want clouded by dark deception.

"I don't want to," I confessed as he slid a gentle hand in my hair, pushing it back from my face.

"Sometimes we don't have a choice, *mon monstre*. It's fate..."

I shook my head, refusing to believe that the one man I felt this deeply for, connected with this explosively, was the one who'd lied his way into my bed.

"Then we're well and truly fucked, aren't we?" I reached over his head to brace a hand on the arm of the couch. "Fated couples never end well."

I punched my hips forward, and Benoit gasped, shifting under me with the force of my penetration, his cock never softening even with my rough handling of him.

But that was what made us such a perfect pair. We both knew what the other needed, what the other could take when we came together in moments like this. And right here and now we were tearing open old wounds, exposing our crimes, and laying bare the ugliness that had brought us to this point.

He'd lied his way into my life and I'd paid to have him

there. Who was more at fault? Or was he right? Were we fated to end up this way?

A fight to the bitter end. A game of push and pull. Control and submission.

My balls tightened at the idea, the delight I took in having Benoit so vulnerable, so open, as arousing as it was satisfying. But instead of punishing him in this moment, I wanted to devour him—just in case I never got the chance again.

With my climax only a hair-trigger from explosion, I tunneled in and out of the tightest, sweetest body I'd ever been buried inside of. But I needed more, needed forever to get what I wanted from him, and knowing I wasn't going to have that made me let go of his leg and brace my other hand over his head.

Benoit wound his legs around me, understanding shit was about to get wild. As I intensified my pace, his thighs clenched around me at the same time his ass did.

"Fuck," I growled, lowering my head into the crook of his neck, the sensations coursing through me overwhelming, the emotions ones I'd never experienced. "Why you?" I panted. "Why did it have to be you?"

He didn't answer, just arched his head back against the pillow as I thrust into him so hard he gasped. My mouth grazed over the jackhammering of his pulse before moving down lower and sucking at the tender skin.

With a moan, he grabbed the back of my neck, holding me there as I pounded into him. With every drive, I could feel his cock pressed between our bodies, his arousal smearing our abs, and damn if that wasn't a turn on.

It felt so right being inside him again, like I never should've left. When I heard him whisper, "Dimitri," his hazel eyes locked on mine, and the look he gave me made my chest clench and my body falter for a split second. It was intense, this connection, no matter how much I tried to fight it. No matter how wrong it was. No matter that I couldn't keep him.

Benoit lifted himself up, just enough to capture my lips and stop the barrage of thoughts trying to slam sense into me. He wound his arms around my neck and tightened the hold his legs had around my waist, keeping us joined completely, not letting me escape.

"Fuck me," he whispered against my lips. "Make up for all these nights we didn't get."

There was no time for regret, not with my cock lodged so deep inside him. And then Benoit, the minx, clenched his ass tight around me, and that was all it took—I went full throttle.

I braced myself on the arm of the couch, pulled out of his warm body, and then drove back in, just enough that I nailed his prostate on the first go.

The sound he made, a mix of a moan and a desperate cry, was music to my ears. I repeated the move, over and over, until Benoit shook so hard he could barely keep his legs wrapped around me.

"Give it to me," I said. "Every last bit of your cum. It's mine. *You're* mine."

Benoit trembled, his breath catching, and then the warmth of his release erupted between us. He dug his nails into my back and held on for dear life, and I didn't give him an ounce of reprieve as I continued to rail him.

The edges of my vision started to cloud at the force of my impending climax, but I didn't slow, didn't stop barreling toward it.

"Yours, *mon monstre*," he said, "for however long you want me."

I wasn't going to acknowledge the way my mind refused a time limit, focusing instead on his admission. *Yours.*

Mine.

My body tensed and then I came, holding on to him and that promise like it was a lifeline—one I wasn't sure what I would do without when I eventually had to let it go.

32
BENOIT

"WAS *ANYTHING* YOU said true?"

Dimitri's words came from out of nowhere as we lay in front of the crackling fire the next day, curled up together on a soft pile of blankets after a night spent making up for lost time. With the rain coming down in sheets against the wall of windows, it was hard to know what time it was, but it didn't matter. I wasn't planning on leaving this spot anytime soon.

I ran my fingers down his arm and watched the flames dance a few feet away, my back warm against Dimitri's chest and our legs tangled together. *Was* anything I'd said true? I was wondering when he'd finally ask.

I nodded. "Yes."

"How much?"

"Everything but the reason I was there."

His hum vibrated against the back of my head, and I could sense there was more he wanted to ask. There were so many questions I had, too, and if this was the time he wanted to lay it all out there, I was ready to do that.

I turned in his arms to face him and was taken again with just how striking he was. That was the best word for him, because even though, yes, he was beautiful, it was too soft a word to encompass all that Dimitri was. He was a man who was hard and unyielding, but protective and far too captivating to look away from.

"Ask me," I said. "Whatever it is you want to know."

His dark eyes narrowed slightly. "Will it be the truth?"

"Guess you'll just have to trust me. We don't have the best track record with that, but we've got to start somewhere, *non?*" When he hesitated before nodding, I said, "This goes both ways. Why don't you tell me something true about you, and then I'll reciprocate? Come on, *mon monstre.* Indulge me."

Dimitri let out a sigh. "I never wanted to be a...*monstre.*"

My nickname for him fell softly from his lips as he stared down into my face, his expression inscrutable. From the little he'd told me about his father and his childhood, I knew what he said was true. It was unlikely that child had dreamed of growing up to be one of the most feared men in the world.

So what had set him on that course? The loss of his father? The manipulations of a bigger, badder monster? I wanted to ask, was dying to peel back every damaged layer of this man who hid away in isolation, but I didn't want to push. I wanted Dimitri to tell me, to *trust* me.

After all, that was what this was about—we trusted each other enough not to physically harm one another. But emotionally? That was a whole other story.

"I believe you."

His lips quirked at the edges. "Why? It's not like I've ever given you a reason to believe otherwise."

"That's not true. I've glimpsed behind that scary façade of yours. I've seen moments of kindness." I turned and settled back into his arms, hoping he'd open up more if my attention was elsewhere. "You played chess with me by the fire one night, took me to the Christmas markets, planned a night out dancing..."

Dimitri wrapped his arms around me and rested his chin atop my head. "I did do that, didn't I?"

"You did." I lowered my head to kiss his arm. "Why?"

"Honestly?"

"*Oui.* That *is* the theme of the moment."

He chuckled, and it was such a relaxing sound from him it warmed me more than the flames in the fireplace.

"I wanted to impress you. Stupid, really. When you were only there because I paid you to be."

"Maybe at first," I said without thinking. "But King and the money?" I reached for his hand and interlaced our fingers. "They were a distant thought in my mind whenever you were in a room with me. You took up all the space. All my thoughts. Until I started to forget why I was there in the first place."

"That's a dangerous admission. Especially to a *monstre.*"

"Not to *mon monstre.* You won't hurt me."

"You trust too easily."

"And you don't trust enough."

"That's what happens when your father is taken from you in the middle of the street on a sun-drenched afternoon." The confession was soft, but the impact was harder than any strike could've been. "You stop trusting perfect situations."

I wanted to know more, was about to push for more, when he cleared his throat.

"You mentioned a betrayal," he said, turning the focus back on me. "Was that true?"

"You remember that, huh?" *Mon Dieu.* That time in my life was the last thing I wanted to talk about. But if we were baring our souls, learning to trust, then I supposed I couldn't deny him the full story.

"I remember everything."

"Maybe you should be the one spying," I teased, but when he didn't respond, clearly waiting for more, I swallowed a sigh and took myself back to a place I never allowed myself to go.

"I wasn't always such a...well, man-eater, as my brothers would say." I glanced at Dimitri who arched a brow at the mention of family, and I waved a hand. "Not blood family but chosen family. You've met three of them already."

"I see. And your blood relations?"

"Nonexistent. No siblings and I haven't spoken to my parents in"—I thought back, counting the years—"has to be at least a couple of decades." More like they hadn't spoken to me, but that was just semantics. There had been no communication between the three of us, and at this point, that was fine by me. "My mother is French, my father is from the U.K., so I grew up splitting time between France, London, and New York."

"That accounts for two languages," Dimitri said, and I cracked a smile.

"Keeping track, are you? How many am I up to?"

"At least six."

"Remind me to whisper sweet nothings in a seventh later."

Dimitri nodded against my neck, tightening his arms around me, and I swallowed a sigh.

"I guess by now you've figured out I come from money, but what you don't know is that the generational wealth and status goes back centuries. Both sides of my family are part of the aristocracy and are worth... Well, add a few more zeroes to the check King gave you and you'll understand."

"So you planned to spend the couple million I gave you on what, lunch?"

"Couple million?" I said. "I do believe the agreed-upon price was four."

"Lunch and dinner, then."

"Exactly. Maybe even a couple bottles of the best brandy." My lips quirked as I faced the flames again, but my smile soon fell. "What I didn't realize as a young man going out into the world was that there are people who would take advantage of my family's money and connections. I was... What did you say? Too trusting?" I shook my head. "Not so much anymore, but I was then. I went off to university in Manhattan and got swept up in a romance with a much older man, someone I had no business being with."

"Sounds familiar."

"Ah, but you're not the love-bombing type, *mon monstre*. You're also not a diplomat. Or my father's closest friend."

When Dimitri made a noise in his throat, I nodded.

"Scandalous, isn't it? I wasn't the one who made the first move, but you can imagine when a brilliant, worldly man makes you the center of his world that it's hard to resist. Ulterior motives never entered my mind because of his supposed relationship to my father, but it turned out he'd embellished that bit. They'd been friendly at one point, but playing up their closeness made me all too comfortable opening up about things I never should've. Private family affairs, business dealings...things this man could leverage for his own personal gain."

"So he used you?"

"Pretty spectacularly, *oui*. It was humiliating. While I'd been falling for him, he'd been looking to make my father's empire fall. Turned out I unknowingly gave him a key piece of information—the name of the man my father was thrilled to be signing a multimillion-dollar global contract with." I shook my head, remembering the disgust and disappoint my father aimed my way when he'd found out. "Let's just say the fallout from that mistake was more than my broken heart and his broken contract. My father pushed me out of the family after that. Said that if I couldn't be trusted, I shouldn't be there."

"But I thought your father was generationally wealthy. A few million shouldn't have hurt his bank account."

"He was, and still is. It wasn't that it hurt him financially, it was that in his eyes I had betrayed the family, betrayed him. He never once stopped to ask me how I felt. I thought I'd been sharing an exciting family moment with my 'boyfriend,' but let's just say that experience woke me up real fast." I turned around and pressed my finger against Dimitri's parted lips. "And before you say 'once a betrayer, always a betrayer,' I learned from that mistake to always keep my mouth shut."

But there was no accusation in Dimitri's eyes, only a flicker of empathy that I hadn't seen there before.

I forced a tight smile and lowered my hand. "Oh, don't go feeling sorry for me now. I'm fine. Better than fine. *"Je vais très bien."*

"Not sorry. It does give me an insight into you, though. Why you use charm as a weapon and view vulnerability as a weakness." He tilted my chin up and traced my lower lip with his thumb. "You fell for someone who used you, so you decided to become untouchable. To never let anyone get too close or see the real you."

Putain. How did he do that?

"Sounds like you might know something about that," I said.

"I do."

I reached up to circle my fingers around his wrist to keep him touching me. "Tell me. My truth for yours."

He shifted, moving his leg between mine and pushing me

onto my back. As he lowered his head, he whispered across my lips, "One traumatic tale is enough for today."

His mouth moved to my jaw, and I arched into his kiss. "That's cheating. You promised."

"I'll keep it. Just not today."

I started to protest, but Dimitri stole my lips, cutting me off and doing a damn good job of distracting me.

But I'd let him keep his secrets for another day.

33
DIMITRI

"OKAY, I KNOW we've been working on rebuilding our trust, *mon monstre*. But this is asking a lot."

Benoit eyed the scrap of material hanging over my finger with a healthy amount of caution. I couldn't blame him, not really. With the way I'd treated him—up until a few days ago—he was smart to question my intentions. Even if he had no reason to.

"And here I thought we'd moved past all of that."

"We have," he was quick to assure me. "But a blindfold?"

Just because we'd moved beyond the name calling didn't mean I was going to let him think I was a total pushover. But, truth be told, I was starting to think I'd let him get away with just about anything.

"Then you should trust me enough to put this on." I moved closer, dangling the piece of black fabric at him like one might a cape at a bull. I was daring him, and if there was one thing I'd come to know about Benoit, it was that he couldn't resist a challenge.

"Fine." He snatched the narrow strip from my finger and

wrapped it around his eyes. "But please tell me I'll eventually see the light of day again. I would hate to think I let you talk me into walking off the edge of your cliffside retreat."

He turned his back, and I tied the blindfold in place. "Maybe I should look into a gag for you as well."

Benoit turned his head and, when our noses bumped, moved back a fraction. "Your choice, really. But I have to tell you, I'm way more fun when my mouth is unoccupied."

I grinned despite myself—and because he couldn't see— then leaned in to brush a kiss across his lips. "I might have to disagree with you on that one."

Benoit sighed as I reached for his hand and laced our fingers.

"Now come, follow me."

It'd been several days since our faux-Christmas, and with only several more remaining until he was due to leave, I'd found myself developing quite the obsession with time.

It was going by too fast. Not that I'd ever admit that to him.

But somewhere between my demanding he stay with me the remainder of my trip, and our actually spending those days together, I'd grown accustomed to having Benoit around.

Whether it be in the kitchen or living room, sharing a meal or a swim in the pool, I'd gotten used to hearing his bare feet on the slate floors, his humming whenever he made our morning cappuccinos, and the soft sounds of a man in a deep, peaceful sleep.

I never thought I'd have that. Someone to share the quiet moments with, to share *this* side of myself with—but I really didn't.

This was a false sense of reality, a moment I'd stolen for myself by threatening Benoit's boss. But I wasn't going to think about that, not yet. Not until I had to give him back. And that wasn't today.

I led Benoit around the pool and down the paved path we'd walked up when we first arrived. There were only two ways off this island my house was built on—one was by air and the other, of course, by sea.

"Stop," I said, drawing Benoit to a halt. "There are steps you have to walk down now. There's a rail to your left, and you can use me—"

"*Ooh*, can I?"

"—to lean on, here on your right."

Benoit's fingers gripped mine a little tighter as he followed my instructions, and soon we were at the bottom of the stairs, standing on my private pier.

"I'm going to take off your blindfold now, okay? Don't move, or you might not like where you end up."

"Um," Benoit said as I let go of his hand and moved behind him, "if that's supposed to be reassuring, it's not."

I chuckled as I reached for the knot at the back of his head, and when the material fell away, Benoit gasped.

"*Mon Dieu,*" he said as he stared out at the catamaran docked in front of him. "Is she yours?"

"She is. And tonight, she's ours."

Benoit walked up the pier, looking over the sixty-seven-foot sailing boat I'd had delivered this morning.

"Tonight?"

I slipped my hands into my pockets and wandered up the pier. "I'm not sure if you realized, but it's New Year's Eve."

Benoit spun back to face me. "New Year's?"

"Yes."

I could tell by his shocked expression that he'd totally lost track of the days, and had I not been hyperaware of when he was due to leave, I likely would've done the same.

"You don't strike me as the type to stay home on such an occasion. So I thought I would take you out. The safest way I could, that is."

"I can't believe it's New Year's Eve already." He walked back to me, shaking his head. "The week flew by."

"It did," I said as the wind whipped up and blew some of his hair across his forehead, and I reached out and brushed it back from his handsome face. "So, what do you say? Want to ring in the New Year with me?"

I wasn't really giving him a choice, but when Benoit looked up at the magnificent boat, then back to me, his bright smile told me he would've said yes even if he did have one.

"Do I get to kiss you at midnight?" he asked.

"What do you think?"

"Well, in that case, I'd love to."

I gestured to the stairs that led to the main cabin. "After you."

FOR A FEW hours the catamaran sailed along the coastline, giving us magnificent views of the island that Benoit hadn't seen from this angle before. It was one thing to view Santorini from high above, but out here on the water he could see it all: the villages, the iconic caldera. No matter where I went, nothing ever compared to this place. But now that I was seeing it through Benoit's eyes, I could appreciate just how beautiful it really was. Wild I'd never paid attention before.

"Looks like we weren't the only ones with this idea," he said, pouring himself another glass of his favorite brandy that I'd tracked down. He took a long, appreciative sip, poured a little more, and then nodded at the other boats all around us.

"Want me to get rid of them?"

His brow shot up. "I'd love to know how you'd do that."

"A couple of shots fired usually does the trick."

"*Usually*? So you do this often?"

"Do I value my privacy and hate anyone coming too close? You know the answer to that."

Benoit let out a laugh and shook his head before reaching for my hand, pulling me out onto the beach platform of the boat with him. Usually this was the spot for tanning or lounging after a swim, but tonight it was set up with a plush assortment of blankets and pillows, perfect for watching the night sky.

Who the fuck *was* I?

A sudden explosion to my right had me moving fast, shoving Benoit down on the ground and reaching for my weapons stored in the lockbox. No hesitation, just action. Whoever was popping off would regret it, and the second I had the gun in my hand, I got to my knees and—

"It's okay," Benoit said, placing a palm on my ankle. "They're just testing the fireworks."

What?

Another bang sounded, coming from the same direction as the first, and when I lifted my gaze to the sky, I saw the green and gold flashes lighting it up.

Fuck. My shoulders dropped as the rush of adrenaline eased off, and Benoit gave my leg a squeeze.

"Sorry," I said as I put the gun away and turned back to face him. Miraculously, he still held his full glass, not a drop spilled even when he'd hit the floor.

"It's okay. We're safe."

But paranoia still had me looking around, memorizing each of the faces on the nearby yachts and party boats, searching out anyone with an ill intent. Shit, maybe this had been a bad idea. Too many people and no way to protect the two of us if—

Benoit's lips crashing down on mine had those thoughts instantly ceasing, jolting me back to reality. That delicious tongue, sweetened with brandy, stroked mine, unhurried.

I fell into his kiss easily, giving him the focus he deserved, and then he pulled back and rested his forehead against mine.

"Better?"

I nodded and ran my hand down his back. "Much."

"Good." He handed me his glass and then rose to his feet, heading back to the bar cart inside to pour another drink. When he came back, he also had a box of cigars and a devilish smile. "You know, I have to say, seeing you jump into hot protector mode is sexy. A little alarming, but it's nice to know you weren't going to let me get riddled with holes. Doesn't really work with my outfit."

As he settled in beside me on the blankets, I took a long swallow of brandy, my heart rate finally coming back down.

Everything was fine. It was just an overreaction, but it'd triggered me, sending up a rush of memories I tried to keep locked away.

"I think we deserve these after that," he said, choosing a cigar from the box and cutting off the tip. He toasted the foot before bringing it to his lips and gently puffing, then handed it to me.

"No, it's yours."

"*Non, mon monstre.* To my hero." He winked and placed the stogie between my lips.

"Hardly," I said, but I couldn't complain once I drew the smoke into my mouth and savored the smooth, rich flavor. It instantly brought a calm to my body that only Benoit had been able to match, and when I blew out the smoke and opened my eyes, the affectionate way he was looking at me made my heart stutter.

"My father died in an explosion," I said abruptly. "Things

were more tense here back then. There were some gang-related issues that spilled over onto the streets, and my father got caught in the crossfire."

Benoit moved to face me, listening with his brandy in one hand and his own lit cigar in the other.

"The man who broke it up was terrifying. My friends and I had called him the scariest man on the island, because he always traveled with a pack of men and all of them carried more weapons than an army." I paused to take a drink, my throat feeling dry. "But that day he wasn't any of those things. He was kind and compassionate to a kid who'd just lost his father."

"Giorgos?" Benoit said, and I nodded.

"I didn't have any family, and he took me in. Raised me. Taught me ruthless survival over the kindness he'd first shown me." I let out a humorless laugh. "Taught me how to shoot before I learned how to shave. He burned all the soft parts of me and honed me into the perfect weapon. So perfect he never saw me coming."

Silence fell between us as my confession lingered in the air with the smoke of our cigars. Benoit hadn't asked, but I knew what was on his mind. Were the rumors true? Had I taken out my former boss? The man who took me in and raised me?

The answer to all of those questions was as simple as it was complicated: yes.

"Ask me." My words were soft, but I knew Benoit had heard them. It was the expression on his face, the struggle between wanting the truth and wanting to stay blissfully unaware.

"So you did kill him? Giorgos?"

I could've lied. Could've reshaped the truth. But for the first time in my life, I wanted someone to know me. *All* of me. Even the ugly parts.

"Yes," I said, that one word heavier than any I'd ever

spoken. "His was the first life I took. He raised me, but he didn't protect me. No one did. He fed me, trained me, and when I became too popular within his organization, became the *leader* he was molding me into, he became threatened and plotted to take me out."

Benoit's eyes widened, but he didn't say anything, and I continued.

"Omar had heard that the meeting Giorgos had sent me to attend was a trap. He was planning to confront me, find out my true motives with his crew, demand to know why I was trying to overthrow him—"

"But you weren't?"

"No, I wasn't." I shook my head and put my drink aside. "I never wanted this life. Never wanted to be a monster. He was becoming more and more brutal in his dealings, and those he was partnering with weren't the kinds of people I wanted to associate with. I'd trained to kill, but I'd avoided it until that night."

Benoit put his glass and cigar down, then moved to his knees in front of me.

"What happened?" he asked, laying a hand over mine.

"I arrived at the meeting spot early. An old, run-down warehouse on the coast. Used to be a fish-packing plant. And I waited. I waited for what felt like hours. I almost talked myself out of it. I tried. But there was no other way. It was him or me. If I was going to survive the night and the days that followed, I knew what I had to do. What his crew would expect of a coup. And like I said, no one was going to protect me, so that night I protected myself. I became the monster no one could touch. The one *he* had created."

Benoit swallowed, and while I would spare him the most heinous details, he needed to know something.

"I don't regret it."

"I didn't ask."

"But you're wondering." I turned my hand over and laced my fingers with his. "If I hadn't taken him out, he only would've gotten worse. His desire for power knew no bounds, no restrictions. He was going to kill me, and he almost did—"

Benoit brought his other hand up and gently touched the scar by my cheek. I closed my eyes, remembering the moment Giorgos's knife had cut through my skin. The burn, the pain— it had been the final push I needed to end it all.

"But I was the bigger monster that night."

The weight of my truth fell from my shoulders like a sack of bricks. I'd cut open my most vicious wound, and it was as freeing as it was terrifying to know I'd just laid my soul bare.

"You're not a monster." Benoit's voice was soft, gentle, as he stroked his thumb over the jagged mark of my predecessor. "You're a survivor. You witnessed and lived through something no child should ever live through, and somehow came out the other side stronger for it. You took his empire and made it your own. You took it out of the hands of the truly depraved and only agreed to work with those of your choosing. You're brave, strong, and at times truly terrifying."

I opened my eyes and stared into earnest hazel ones full of pity, compassion, and awe.

"But I see you, Dimitri Stavros. I see the man under all of those things, and I—" Benoit swallowed again and squeezed my hand. "I'm not sure how I'm going to say goodbye to him."

I took his hand and tugged him into my arms, capturing his mouth in a kiss that was as painful as it was tender. The kiss of an inevitable ending. One I wasn't sure I knew how I would survive.

The loud *bang* of fireworks rent the air, surprising the both of us, and Benoit pulled back to look up at the sky. His eyes shimmered from the sparkles and emotions filling the both of us, and I pulled him back into my arms where he belonged.

"Thank you," he said as he settled in, his back to my chest.

"For?"

"Finally trusting me with your truth."

I wrapped my arms around him and squeezed him even tighter, knowing there was one more truth I needed to give.

"I lied that day I told King I'd found something I want more than you," I whispered as I kissed his temple. "The truth is, I don't think I'll ever want anything more than you. But I also know I can't keep you."

Neither of us said anything after that as we stared up at the colorful display above, knowing that *that* truth was now only days away from becoming our reality.

34
BENOIT

I CLAMPED MY hand down on Dimitri's wrist as he tried to take the wallet in my jacket pocket. "That was so slow I think the cop down the street saw you reach for it."

"Bullshit. You just knew I was going for it."

"You have to make me forget." I smirked as I removed his hold on the wallet, tucked it back into place, and then stepped in closer. "Remember, it's all about misdirection. You don't need to be faster than the eye necessarily; you just need to make the eye look somewhere else." I ran my hand along his waist and lifted my chin to graze my lips over his. He still tasted like the coffee we'd brewed earlier, and it took all my willpower not to fall into the kiss.

When I pulled away suddenly, Dimitri started to protest, and it wasn't until I held up his watch that he realized what I'd done and cursed.

"How the fuck did you do that?" He examined his now-empty wrist and shook his head. "I didn't even feel you take it off."

"Told you I'm good with my fingers," I said with a wink.

"I already knew that much."

"Aww, don't pout, *mon monstre*. With my help, you'll be a pro in no time." I fastened his watch on my wrist and then moved the wallet from the outer pocket to the inside one as Dimitri watched with an expression full of doubt. I crooked a finger. "Come here."

When we were toe to toe, I reached for his hand and brought it up to cup my face. "The hand they're watching isn't the one doing the stealing. So if you have me focused here, on your touch"—I leaned into his caress as his fingers brushed my cheek—"then you have the perfect opportunity to keep me distracted so I won't notice what you've taken."

With my other hand, I guided his to the hidden wallet, our eyes locked on each other. He easily grabbed it this time, and I barely felt it slide out of my pocket.

"See?" I said. "We're naturally distracted when we're being touched, so use that to your advantage."

"I can do that."

"I know you can. You've been distracting me for weeks." I grinned and pressed a kiss to his lips.

"The problem is, how the hell do I distract someone when it's not you?"

"Meaning?"

Dimitri narrowed his eyes. "I know you don't have a problem seducing someone to get your way, but I'm not about to kiss a bunch of assholes to get what I want."

"Touché. I won't take offense to that, since I don't want you kissing a bunch of assholes either, but it doesn't have to be a sexual distraction. For instance..." With my hands on his shoulders, I guided him to where I wanted him and then brushed by him like a stranger on the street. "There are a lot of ways you touch someone every day without even realizing it. Just moving past them like this on a street can make it an easy grab—or easy to place. Or when you're making conversation" —I moved to stand in front of him—"maybe they have something on their shoulder you can help them brush off while your other hand is doing the real work. Maybe you need to place something and you drop your keys—"

"Like you dropped your ring on the train?"

I smiled proudly, glad he was catching on. "Exactly. You were all so focused on looking for my lost ring that you didn't notice me planting something in the curtains."

"The curtains? I wouldn't have guessed that."

"Another good thing. You don't want to be predictable. After all, there are a million ways to use distraction to your advantage, so don't rely on the same trick to get what you want."

Dimitri stared at me for a long moment, and then rubbed at his jaw. "You're impressive, I'll give you that. No one could ever see you coming. Certainly not me."

"I beg to differ. You saw me coming several times."

The awe swirling in those dark depths quickly took on more than a trace of arousal, but I wouldn't let him use that to distract me. When we'd dived in and started asking each other the hard questions, I was surprised to find Dimitri more than curious about my tricks. They were things that could be particularly useful for him in knowing who he could trust. If he ever had doubts about his inner circle or someone he was conflicted about, he could easily plant a device the way I had to get the information he needed. It wouldn't have been anything he needed to learn if I were around, but considering we were down to our last hours together, I figured helping him in whatever way I could to remain a strong leader was the best thing I could do.

For one, it kept my mind off the fact that I was leaving soon, and two, Dimitri had established himself as someone the Kings and I could trust, someone we'd want to be in business with, so really this was the smart thing to do on both accounts.

A twinge in my chest had me swallowing hard, and I shoved all those feelings into a box and struggled to lock it up tight. These past few days with Dimitri had been everything, and I didn't want to think about the fact that I didn't know when I'd see him again. *If* I'd ever see him again.

"Okay, teach me something else," Dimitri said, making me laugh.

"Ah, such an eager student. I like that."

"I'm sure you do."

"Mhmm, let me see." I tapped my finger against my lips. "While tricks and technique are important, when it comes to picking someone's pocket, your attitude is key too."

"My attitude?"

"*Oui*. You need to be confident about what you're doing. You can't fumble. You have to go to your target with a purpose. Know what you're looking for, where it is, and zero in. Hesitation is a confession. But if you strike with confidence, then they will believe exactly the lie you're selling them."

"That makes sense." He nodded. "Like shooting a gun."

"Uh..." My brow furrowed. "I'll take your word for it."

Dimitri chuckled at my obvious displeasure. "So you really *don't* like to use weapons."

"That would be a negative. The idea of holding something that can take another's life? Not for me. I'm more about information gathering—"

"Plus, that body of yours is weapon enough."

My lips curved, and I moved back into Dimitri's arms. "Is it now?"

He wound his arms around my waist and cupped my ass. "Almost had my heart giving out several times over."

"Now that would've been a shame." I gave a flirty wink and smoothed my hands up to cradle the back of his neck. "Especially when I was just about to show you how I was going to steal it."

Dimitri grazed his lips over mine. "Who says you haven't already?"

It was a good thing he had a hold of me then, because while I was being flirtatious and demonstrating my craft, Dimitri was dead serious.

I pulled back a fraction to make sure I wasn't reading more than what he was saying, but when I caught the emotions swirling in his eyes, I knew I was right.

My heart began to thump a little harder as my stomach flipped, and just as I was about to return the sentiment, a phone rang.

The sound was so intrusive, so jarring in this otherwise perfect moment, that I cursed the blasted object and pulled out of Dimitri's arms. He looked down at me as though he didn't understand why I'd stopped. And while I knew my anger was irrational, I'd be damned if I got interrupted confessing my feelings by some gun deal.

"Well, aren't you going to answer it?" I demanded. "I know it's not mine."

Dimitri smiled at my annoyance, and that only made me more irritated.

"What?"

"Nothing," he said, casual as you please, as if he hadn't just told me I'd stolen his damn cold heart. *Bastard.* "I just hadn't realized how adorable you are when you're angry."

I planted my hands on my hips as he strolled over to where

his phone was vibrating on a table. "Well, you've had plenty of opportunities."

"That's true," he said, picking up his cell. "But I was too mad at you then to really appreciate it. I'm seeing it now, though, and...adorable."

I was just about to give him a piece of my mind for laughing at me when he answered the phone.

"Stavros," he barked.

I spun away from him and walked over to the window that looked out over the pool and sea. With only hours until I left, the intrusion was unwelcome, and whoever was on the other end of that call could go straight to—

"It's King."

Oh.

I let out a sigh and turned to see Dimitri crossing the room to me, a smirk on his lips, the phone held out in his hand. I didn't think I'd ever been irritated to hear from King, and I had to mentally slap myself out of my mood before I took the phone. He wouldn't be calling if he didn't have a good reason, and I instantly went on high alert.

"King," I said, "what's wrong?"

"Hello to you too, Benoit. No 'nice to hear from you' today?"

Considering he'd barged in at the worst possible time, I wasn't exactly ready to greet him with my usual flair, but more than that, I was unnerved he'd called at all. I hadn't heard from him this entire trip.

"Has something happened?" I said. "What do you need?"

"More like what *you* need."

I blinked. "Me?"

"According to your location tracker, it appears you're not in an easy place to get to, and I'm assuming Dimitri isn't offering his services to help you leave."

Oh. Right. King wanted to help me get off this island and back home now that my time here was at its promised end. He wasn't calling because anyone was in trouble; he was calling to take me away.

I didn't know which was worse.

"Uh..." I looked up to see Dimitri watching me, his arms crossed tight over his chest. "We haven't discussed those plans just yet."

"No need. Lachlan and I are already in Athens. We'll send a helicopter to you within the hour—"

"No," I said, the word coming out a little too forcefully. "I mean, uh, that time frame isn't going to work for me."

There was a pause on the other end of the line. "Are you in danger? Yes or no."

"*Non*, of course not."

When I didn't elaborate, I could practically see King's frown forming. "Tomorrow morning, then?"

Putain, that was still too soon, but I wasn't about to wear out my welcome here...or be the reason their tentative agreement went to shit. I bit the inside of my lip, hard, and forced the words out.

"That works. Thank you, King."

"Are you..." He stopped. "Need to say goodbye?"

"Something like that."

"All right. Be ready at seven."

My body instantly rebelled at the early hour, but I found myself nodding and agreeing anyway. "Will do."

I ended the call and handed the phone to Dimitri, but before I could turn away, he grabbed my arm.

"Is he on the way?" The harsh set to Dimitri's jaw was as sharp as his words, as his eyes searched my face for the answer he sought. "Why aren't you happier?"

"You know why," I whispered, and gently pried his fingers from my wrist. "And no, he's not on his way...yet."

Dimitri swallowed and looked down at where our hands were connected. "When?"

"Tomorrow. Early."

"But your time is up tonight."

"I know." I brought his fingers up to my lips and pressed a kiss there. "But tonight it's my turn to steal a moment for us."

35
BENOIT

I SHOVED ASIDE the bitterness that had crept in at how the countdown had already started. But it could've been worse.

I could be leaving now.

I slid my hands beneath Dimitri's jacket and shoved it off his shoulders as I walked him backward out of the living room. We'd both put on suits to practice the pickpocketing techniques I was so adept at, but now there were far too many clothes between us.

As I started unfastening the buttons on Dimitri's shirt, he said, "Fuck it" and ripped it off himself. Then he yanked my shirt out of my pants and tore it open, sending buttons flying in every direction down the hallway.

"That's one way to do it," I said with a laugh, taking off the ruined shirt along with the jacket and leaving them on the floor.

"You're not allowed to wear anything for the rest of the night." There was a rough, take-no-shit edge to his voice that shot straight to my cock and made me want to obey instead of rebel. Had it been anyone else, maybe I would've, but with Dimitri I wanted anything and everything he had to give.

I backed him through the door to his room and unbuttoned his pants. "Not allowed? You think you're calling the shots tonight?"

"Always." Dimitri nipped at my lower lip, and I moaned.

Putain, I was going to miss this. The way he never let me get away with anything. The way he could make me melt with one touch. No one else could do that.

His fingers found their way into my hair, his strong hand cupping the back of my neck as he angled his head and swept his tongue inside my mouth. Just like that, every thought, every worry, left my mind. There wasn't the impending arrival of King; there wasn't Dimitri's crew; there wasn't our jobs and responsibilities or betrayal or lies or anything else.

There was just us, holding on to each other and relishing our last hours before we left this room and the real world came back in. It was the soft growl in the back of Dimitri's throat when he wrapped me up tight in his arms and the feel of his stubble grazing my cheek as we inhaled each other. I'd known from the second I saw him that I wouldn't mind spending a few hours in his bed, but what I didn't know was how much I'd come to crave being there. How much I'd crave being with *him*.

Curling my fingers into the waistband of his pants, I shoved them down before getting rid of my own.

There. Naked, just the way he wanted me.

When he leaned in to steal my breath again, I put my hand on his chest, holding him back, and a furrow creased his forehead until he saw why.

I was taking a mental picture, running my eyes over every inch of his incredible body. All of that tanned skin I knew as well as my own now, those broad shoulders made for holding on to. Powerful thighs that could hold the both of us when he fucked me, and, of course, that spectacular cock.

But somehow, even with every perfect inch of him, nothing compared to his face—those dark eyes that hid a deeply soulful man. The jagged scar across his cheek that didn't detract from his looks but somehow added to it.

And those full lips, the ones that fit against mine like they were made to be there and whispered sensual words in my ear in the dark of night.

How was I ever supposed to leave this man?

An unexpected sting behind my eyes had me blinking fast and pushing Dimitri back onto the bed before he could see. That was a little too much vulnerability for me. The last thing I needed was his seeing unwanted tears in my eyes.

As Dimitri's back hit the mattress and he shifted up the bed, he reached for the side table and grabbed a bottle of lube. He tossed it to the foot of the mattress, and I picked it up and eagerly followed him up the bed, crawling between his spread thighs until I straddled his hips. It was as if I couldn't stand for him to be too far from me, knowing that soon he'd be a whole world away.

Dimitri went to grab for me, no doubt to roll me to my back, but I wasn't having any of that tonight. Up until now he'd been in full control—not that I was complaining. But tonight I wanted his trust. I wanted to mark him, brand him as mine. I wanted to imprint myself on him the way he had me— and to do that, *I* needed to be the one in control.

I took hold of his hands and laced my fingers through his, then leaned down until I had his palms trapped on the mattress.

"Uh-uh," I whispered across his lips. "Tonight, *I'm* calling the shots."

Dimitri arched a dark brow, but where I thought I'd get pushback, all I got was a challenge. "Do your worst."

I chuckled and nipped at his lower lip. "Don't you know by now? That's when I'm at my very best."

"I'm counting on it." Dimitri grabbed the back of my neck and held me there for a fierce kiss that had me moaning.

I sat up and stared down at the most magnificent man I'd ever had between my thighs. Talk about a beast. Strong, powerful—and right now, completely at my mercy. I reached for the bottle of lube, poured some into my palm, then wrapped a hand around his thick length. I gave a rough pull that made him groan, but not once did he take his eyes from mine.

"*Mon Dieu,*" I whispered as I rocked in time with my stroking of his cock. "I love seeing you like this. Aroused, unrestrained, free of any worry but your next orgasm."

Dimitri's nostrils flared as the cords of his neck strained and he shoved his head into the pillow, arching up to push his dick through my fist.

It was so sensual, so erotic, the way he was moving under me, that pre-cum leaked from my own cock at the sight.

"*Oui, mon monstre.* Feel it. Let go. Let me take care of you tonight."

Dimitri swallowed, that intense stare of his softening, then slid his hands up under the headboard and nodded.

My heart skipped at his submission, at the trust he was giving to me, as he closed his eyes and surrendered control.

I pressed kisses across his chest, first to one nipple then the other, biting and sucking at the hard nubs until the cock in my hand jerked at the attention. Then I kissed a path up his neck, where I scraped my teeth along his sharp, stubbled jawline.

Dimitri was beautiful in his acquiescence. A man of beauty, strength, and power.

A man that I—somewhere along this wild, crazy ride—had fallen for.

"Benoit..."

The sound of my name in that gravel-rough voice made me tremble as I slid my tongue over his top lip and teased my way inside. Dimitri groaned and my fist tightened, and as he bucked up underneath me I knew it was time.

With a final kiss I moved back to straddle his body, and when he opened his eyes I could see the same emotions that had to be swirling in mine.

Desire, attraction, sadness, and an emotion neither of us was brave enough to voice. So I decided to show him.

I moved up to my knees and positioned him against my body, and with our eyes locked, slowly lowered myself onto his shaft. The delicious burn sent a wave of pleasure through me, and as I braced my hands on his chest to keep myself upright, I could feel the rapid thump of his heart beneath my palms.

"Put your hands on me," I said, needing his touch to ground me, needing it to remind me that this was real. *He* was real.

Dimitri lowered his hands from the headboard and ran them up my thighs, then whispered, "Make me forget."

Tears pricked behind my lids as I blinked them back. He didn't have to elaborate. I knew exactly what he meant.

Make him forget that this was it.

Make him forget that this could never be.

Make him forget that after tonight, we would be no longer.

But how could you forget a person when they were written across your heart?

I swallowed back the emotions bubbling up and instead focused on the feel of having him deep inside me, filling me in ways no man ever had.

I clenched my thighs around his hips as I dug my fingers

into his pecs, then began to rock over the top of him. Slow at first, finding our rhythm. It was exactly what I wanted, but somehow it still wasn't enough. I wanted to be connected to him everywhere, wanted to feel his breath on mine as I sank down onto him again and again.

"Come here," I said, sliding my hand to the back of his neck. "I need you."

His eyes flared, and for a moment, I couldn't believe I'd said that out loud. But then Dimitri sat up, adjusting our bodies so our chests met and I was fully in his lap.

Putain, this position was so much more intimate. It matched everything I was feeling, dialed to ten. He was deeper inside me than he'd ever been.

It was so much, so overwhelming, that I stilled and dropped my head on his shoulder, needing a minute to get a hold of myself and stay in the moment.

"Benoit..." My name on Dimitri's lips sent a shiver through me. Then his hand was in my hair, gently tugging me back to look at him.

Everything swirling in his eyes was exactly why it'd been hard to look at him. I felt like I was going to crack open and spill all the thoughts running through my mind. But one look and I realized—he already knew.

"You're in charge," he said. "Touch me. Fuck me like I'm not a monster."

I shook my head and ran my fingers down his face, over his scar. "You were never the monster. Just a man in a cage of your own making. *Mon monstre*."

He nodded as his lips met mine. "Yours."

My heart squeezed. For the first time in my life, I wished that could be true. I'd never wanted anyone I could keep before. And of all the people I'd met over my forty-two years on Earth, it had to be Dimitri Stavros. Our paths couldn't be more different. I'd been sent to betray him, spy, find out who he really was and then get the hell outta Dodge.

And yet...

Here we were. And I wouldn't regret even a second of the time we'd spent together.

I fell deeper into his kiss and began to slowly rock on top of him again. As I clenched my ass around him, Dimitri brought me in closer, wrapping me in his arms and keeping every inch of us connected. He surrounded and filled me so completely that I didn't think anything could tear us apart.

His moan when I sucked on his tongue and began to move my hips faster spurred me on. I wanted to give him back all the pleasure he'd taken from me the past weeks. Keeping our mouths connected, I lifted up from his lap before slamming back down on his cock. The sounds ripping out of Dimitri with every thrust as he chased my hole were feral, untamed.

I jolted as he reached between us to take hold of my cock and give it a firm stroke.

"*Oui*," I breathed, arching my head back as he worked his fist up and down my length and then dropped his mouth onto my neck. The way he sucked at me would bruise, but I welcomed it, wondering if he just wanted to mark me in a way that would last beyond tonight.

When sweat dripped down my temple as we raced to see who could get the other off first, Dimitri licked the path it left on my skin, and I almost lost it.

My legs began to shake every time I lowered onto him, and then my pace started to become uneven. I needed to come, but I didn't want this to be over yet.

Our bodies had other ideas.

As Dimitri jerked me off, his hand stuttered, and then every muscle in his powerful body tightened.

"Fuck, Benoit—" His words cut off as a hot rush filled my

ass and he gasped. I didn't even need his fingers to make me come. Just watching the ecstasy on his face as he locked eyes with mine had my dick exploding between us.

With my hips rocking us through the never-ending waves of our climaxes, I held on tight to him, breathing in his scent where it was strongest beneath his ear.

This was perfect. Heaven. Why I hadn't realized it before now was one of the great mistakes of my life.

I wish I could—

"Wish you could what?" Dimitri's question had me realizing I'd started to say those private thoughts out loud, and I snapped my mouth shut.

He leaned back, taking my chin in hand and searching my eyes. It didn't matter what I said; it had to be written all over my expression.

There went having the best poker face among my brothers.

"Tell me," he demanded, and I couldn't find it in myself to lie to him anymore.

I brushed his hair back from his face. "I wish I could stay. I wish I could love you."

What I didn't say was *for the rest of our lives*, but that had been enough.

Those dark, piercing eyes softened and he swallowed. "I know," he said quietly, bringing my hand to his lips and pressing a kiss to each one of my fingers. "I wish that too."

And that was almost worse than silence.

36
DIMITRI

H E WAS GONE.

It had happened. The inevitable.

I knew it the second I woke. Not because I opened my eyes but because I could feel his absence as acutely as a lost limb.

The sun was just now trickling through the open windows as I rolled to my back and stared at the empty pillow. I could still see the indentation from Benoit's head and found myself reaching out to touch, just in case it was a dream.

But no, it was real.

He was gone.

I sat up and turned to look out at the beautiful view that greeted me, the sun sparkling off the blue of the Aegean Sea, and not even that could fill the void Benoit's absence had left. Nor did it replace the loneliness that threatened to reclaim me.

Damn it.

It wasn't supposed to be like this. It wasn't supposed to hurt this fucking much. But as I sat there in the place that used to be my sanctuary, my refuge, I felt alone.

I looked over at the empty side of the bed, at the rumpled sheets, and remembered Benoit's smile as he'd drifted off to sleep: peaceful, satisfied, and a little bit sad. I lay there for hours after that, memorizing everything about him—his long lashes, full lips, his delicate jaw and the messy hair I'd run my hands through as I held him close—refusing to acknowledge I'd have to let him go.

But when I finally drifted off, it had been into a sleep so deep, I hadn't even heard him wake. Maybe he'd planned it that way. After all, he was a master thief, a skilled pickpocket. Maybe he'd slipped out in silence on purpose, not wanting to face "the end" head-on either.

I shoved the sheet aside and got to my feet, wondering what time he'd actually made his move. It was just turning seven now, so when had King sent in his men? The ass crack of—

Whop. Whop. Whop.

The familiar thumping sound of rotor blades overhead had me grabbing the robe off the chair in the corner and shrugging it on. I pulled open the sliding door and stepped outside as a sleek black H130 helicopter soared over my house and headed toward the landing zone.

Benoit...

He had left the house, but not my island.

Not yet, anyway.

I quickly belted my robe and crossed the terrace as the helicopter began its descent, and when I reached the edge of my property, I spotted him.

Benoit was standing with his back to the house, the linen pants and shirt he wore plastered to his body. I wanted to call out to him—to say what, I had no fucking clue. But he was too far away and the sound from the blades was too loud. The wind was whipping his hair around his head in a way that wouldn't allow him to hear a thing as he stared up at the black bird that had come to rescue him.

From the mission.

From the island.

From me. The monster.

A growl rumbled up inside of me, every possessive instinct clawing to the surface as the skids touched down and the door to the helicopter was pulled open. Then that motherfucker Lachlan—*of course it's him*—waved Benoit forward.

Fuck. That.

I ran toward the path that led down to the landing zone, and as my bare feet hit the gravel I stepped on several cactus spines that had fallen off. I cursed as the pain sliced through me, and I wasn't sure if he heard me or felt me there, but Benoit stopped as he reached the door of the helicopter.

He looked back over his shoulder to where I stood as though frozen in time, and the second our eyes met, I knew—it was really over.

It didn't matter if I hobbled down to him or crawled—he was going to get in that helicopter and fly back to whatever life he had before me, and I just needed to get on with mine here, without him.

It was easy, right? I'd done it before. Existed without him.

So why did it feel as though he tore my heart out of my chest when he turned back to Lachlan and climbed into the helicopter?

I stood there at the top of the hill and watched as he slammed the door shut on what we had, and as the helicopter began its ascent, I heard the faint ringing of my phone from inside the house.

Like a man in a trance, I turned from the life that might've been and headed inside to the life that was to answer the call.

"Stavros here."

"Boss." Omar's voice was like a hard, cold slap back to reality. "Sorry to bother you so early, but I just got a call you need to take. Are you back at work?"

As the helicopter faded in the distance, I shoved aside any fanciful notions I might've had about falling in love, having a life beyond the violent one designated to me as a child, and instead focused on what was.

It was time to wake the fuck up. Time to remember who I was.

And with that I snapped, "Yes. Put them through."

37

BENOIT

"WHAT EXACTLY AM I looking at here?" Archer, my best friend since college and a member of the Libertines—though he hadn't chosen to be one of the Kings—stared down at the open trunk in my parlor as I sipped on my fourth glass of wine.

"Don't pretend you haven't seen four million dollars before," I said, stretching my long legs out on the leather ottoman in front of me. Thank God the alcohol was finally kicking in, giving my brain a reprieve from the constant over-thinking and pining of the last few days.

More specifically, since I'd seen the look on Dimitri's face as he stood outside his house watching me climb into King's helicopter. I'd never get over it. It was so full of want and need and regret—but also, strangely, hope, like for a moment he thought I'd turn around and come back.

But staying wasn't part of the deal. And neither of us was the type to have a relationship, especially not with our respective jobs.

Still...

I drained the rest of my glass and held it out toward Archer for another.

He arched a brow and came over to take it. "You've polished off a bottle since I arrived. You sure opening another is a good idea?"

"It's a fan-fucking-tastic idea," I said, waving him in the direction of my wine rack nearby. "Make it a good one, please, Archer dear. The older the better."

When he returned, he carried an extra glass with mine and a vintage bottle, maybe the oldest in my collection.

I gave him a lazy grin. "That's perfect. *Merci*, darling."

Archer shook his head as he peeled off the top wrapping and began to unscrew the cork. He started to pour it into the decanter, but I reached for the fancy crystal and set it out of his reach.

"The glass, please."

He made a face as if to say, *Really?* but poured us both a glass anyway and handed me one. "Care to explain why you have four million dollars sitting in front of your fireplace like you're about to toss it in?"

"I'm not so far gone I'd burn money." I brought my glass to my lips and paused. "I don't think."

"This have anything to do with disappearing for a month?"

"Kings business."

"You don't ever come back from Kings business so depressed. Actually"—he took a seat in the leather chair across from me—"I don't think I've *ever* seen you depressed. At least not since..."

I was grateful he didn't continue that thought. Archer had been there for all the family and relationship drama in college, and it wasn't something we ever spoke of out loud. There was no need. I was fine. Absolutely fabulous.

And now I had a nice buzz to go along with all my fabulousness.

"Okaaay," he said when silence filled the air between us. "You called me over, I'm assuming to chat. Vent. Drink all your wine with you."

"Mmm, yes. Drinking sounds good."

"What did you have to do for that money, Benny?"

I swirled my glass and stared into its rich red depths. "Nothing I didn't want to."

Archer took a sip of his drink, his stare louder than any words as he watched me over the rim of his glass.

"Or should I say no *one.*"

"Ah." The smug bastard grinned. "Now we're getting somewhere."

"No, we're not." I pouted. "Because I'm not talking about it. Not now, not ever."

"Because you can't?"

"Because I don't want to."

"That's obvious, since you literally asked me to come over here for a chat."

"*Oui*, but I didn't say about what." I rolled my eyes. "Maybe I wanted to see how life is going with your pretty young thing."

"He said with such obvious interest."

"You know, you're not usually this obnoxious. Maybe I called the wrong friend."

Archer chuckled and reached over to pluck the wine glass from my fingers. "I don't think that's it at all. You look miserable. And there's only two reasons I've ever seen you look that way—the first when you had to miss Fleet Week, and the second when he-who-won't-be-named broke your heart."

This was the problem in inviting over the one person who knew you almost as well as you knew yourself to commiserate with.

"And since Fleet Week isn't for another five months, I'm thinking—"

"Well, stop that."

"—you've had your heart broken. The real question is: by whom?"

I waved him off and turned back to face the crackling fire, and an image of me and Dimitri tangled in front of *his* fireplace flashed before my eyes.

Ugh, anytime these memories wanted to exit my brain would be great.

"Benny?"

"Huh?"

"Who is he? Or can you not say?"

I gave him a droll look. Archer knew better than that. He was my vault and I was his. That was why he'd trusted me with his little—okay, enormous—scandal when he fell for his daughter's boyfriend.

So the least I could do was return the favor and let him know I'd fallen for one of the most dangerous men in the world. It was kind of the same, right? Both relationships had the potential to blow up in our faces—mine just might include real explosives.

"His name is...Dimitri."

Archer grinned. "Greek?"

"*Oui.*" I let out a sigh and closed my eyes, picturing Dimitri's dark hair, intense eyes, and sculpted jawline. "A Greek god."

A low chuckle had me opening my eyes and turning to my so-called friend. I was seriously thinking about revoking that title.

"You've got it bad."

"I've got nothing."

"Not true." Archer gestured to the trunk my feet were still

propped up on. "You've got four million dollars. So, um, want to tell me why a man you're pickling your liver over while crying sent you said dollars?"

"I'm not crying." Although I might've been last night. Those eye patches I spend way too much money on clearly don't do shit for puffiness.

"What happened? And don't say nothing. Not when you're usually telling me you have a man in every port."

"I usually *do* have a man in every port. It just so happens that this time it was the same man in every port."

"This Dimitri guy."

"Right."

"And where is he now?"

"Not here." I held my hand up with a flourish. "He'll never be here..."

I thought of the steely resolve that had crossed his features as the helicopter finally flew away. If there'd been any chance of seeing him again, an iota of hope that maybe one day our paths would cross again, I had destroyed it in that moment.

"But you want him to be?"

I couldn't blame Archer for the question. This kind of behavior wasn't normal for me. I didn't lose my mind over men, and I certainly never cried into thousand-dollar bottles of wine over them.

Not until Dimitri.

"I don't know what I want."

"Oh, I don't know." Archer handed me back my glass. "I think you know exactly what you want. In fact, I'm going to go out on a limb and say that you, my friend, are in love."

I started to laugh...hysterically. Because of course I was in love. I'd gone and fallen for the one man I couldn't have. A man I'd been sent to spy on. A man who had paid for my body and stolen my heart.

"Is he dead?"

I whipped my head in Archer's direction, and he shrugged. "Well, is he?"

"*Non...*" At least, he wasn't when I last saw him. *Please, God, don't let him be now.*

"Then why can't he be here?"

"Because...he could be anywhere." Even as those words tumbled off my tongue, I knew how ridiculous they sounded. But Archer didn't understand the complexities here. Dimitri and I had completely separate lives, heavy demands placed on the both of us. It would never work.

Or maybe that was just what I told myself to stop the ache in my chest every time I thought about the fact that we *could* but chose not to. We had the means to travel. I could be on his doorstep in a few hours. He could be on mine.

I took a long sip of wine and shook those thoughts out of my head. "It could never work."

"Sounds like the same thing I told you about Preston."

"And look at you now. Living with your pretty young thing in unwedded bliss."

"For now." He shot me a wink, and even in my inebriated state, I read between those lines.

"*Mon Dieu.* Does that mean...? Are you thinking about—"

He smiled broadly. "Soon. You've got great taste, so I'll need your help finding the perfect ring."

My jaw continued to hold court on the floor as I stared at my friend. Even with the weight sitting on my chest, I couldn't help but return his grin. It was contagious.

"I'm so happy for you, my friend. Truly."

"Thank you. It feels right."

"I can't imagine a hot twenty-something who wouldn't." When Archer rolled his eyes, I added, "I'm kidding, of course. I like him. And I like him for you. I also feel responsible for encouraging this pairing, so I'll take all the credit when you get engaged."

"But of course." He smirked and held my gaze, but the longer he watched me, the more serious the set to his lips became. "What can I do to help?"

"You're already here and drinking my best wine."

"You want this guy? Dimitri?"

"I can't have him."

"Has that ever stopped you before?"

I couldn't argue with that. A challenge only made me put in more effort.

So why did this feel different? Was it the fear deep down that maybe after all this, Dimitri would reject me?

"I'll tell you how you can help me," I said, and nodded at the trunk. "Call your boyfriend and tell him you're staying with me tonight to make sure I don't burn four million dollars."

"If you want it out of your sight, I'll gladly take it off your hands. Or you could donate it. It might make you feel better about your...deal."

Those were tempting ideas, but getting rid of the money, no matter how little I needed it, would be like getting rid of the last of Dimitri, and selfishly, I wanted to keep him close just a little longer.

It wasn't the healthiest decision, but neither was refilling my glass for a fifth time. Or sixth. I'd already lost count.

Without any prompting, Archer topped off my wine, and I held my glass out toward his.

"Why don't we toast to something happy? To your impending engagement and my return to bachelorhood."

I forced a smile as Archer's glass clinked against mine, but as I swallowed down the cabernet, all I could think about was where in the world Dimitri was laying his head tonight.

And if he was thinking about me.

38

DIMITRI

WITH OMAR BY my side, I waited inside the lounge of the yacht anchored off a marina in Hamburg, Germany, while my guards stood out front for the men I'd be meeting with.

It'd been two weeks since Benoit left, and I'd thrown myself into work with a vengeance, making deals up and down the Mediterranean Sea and back into Europe. The distraction had been a welcome one, keeping me even busier than I had been, but Benoit still found his way into my thoughts in the quiet moments in between.

Even now, being on the yacht had my mind drifting back to the night we'd spent on the catamaran. It felt like so long ago now, another world.

I let out a sigh and cracked my neck from side to side, trying not to wonder what Benoit was doing right now. Or *who*. Fuck, that thought instantly filled me with rage, and when my hands balled into fists, Omar glanced over at me.

"Everything good, boss?"

"Fine."

The clipped response had him nodding once, and I thought he'd drop it, but then he added, "They seem willing to compromise."

I didn't have to ask who he was talking about. My mind had been on a man I couldn't have, and Omar was focused on this meeting with the Redwater Syndicate. They'd requested to touch base, and the general consensus from our sources was that they were willing to fall in line for a better deal.

Compromise hadn't been in Giorgos's nature, but I was willing to try a different approach and hear them out. Let them plead their case.

At least for now.

But this was the last thing I wanted to be doing. Which frustrated the hell out of me, because I'd signed up for this, basically demanded the right to it after overthrowing our leader. But that was before...

And that was how my life felt right now, split in two. Before Benoit, and after.

Before Benoit I knew exactly where my place in this world was and what I had to do to achieve it. I knew the risks and was willing to take them to get to the top. Hell, I had the scars to prove it.

This past month had been about solidifying relationships that Giorgos had damaged and forging new ones that would establish me as the reigning arms dealer despite my mutiny. I'd been on a mission to demonstrate my ability to provide to products requested and lead my men in a way that made them want to follow, but then something had happened.

Or should I say some*one*.

From the second Benoit had strutted into my life, establishing my position in this world had taken a back seat to getting to know the enigmatic dancer/spy who'd infiltrated it. He'd consumed my time, my mind, and my body until the month I'd meticulously planned to woo our international clientele turned into my wooing the gorgeous, multilingual pickpocket.

Talk about a fucking wild card. Never in a million years could I have imagined Benoit. Not for someone like me. Which, in the end, was why I'd let him go.

Not that I'd had much of a choice. He'd run to the helicopter that day, barely given me a look back before climbing inside and slamming the door shut on...what? A possible life of being put in insanely dangerous situations like this?

I scoffed and thought of his aversion to guns, which just so happened to be my bread and butter.

It was probably for the best he'd left.

Probably.

Then why did I feel like absolute shit?

He was better off wherever he was—at least, that was what I tried to tell myself. I knew he'd been in Manhattan as of a week ago, because that was where the rest of what I owed him was sent. Knowing he enjoyed a dramatic flair, I hadn't sent a check, but a trunk full of cash instead, courtesy of my team.

Had I considered making a personal delivery? Yes. I could've squeezed it in between stops, and maybe I would've if I thought Benoit would want to see me.

Closing my eyes, I took a deep breath in through my nose. *Just forget him. Don't think about the man you fell for—think of the man with bad intentions.*

If only it were that easy.

Omar's radio crackled to life. "They've arrived," one of the guards said.

"Report back when clear," Omar responded, just as my phone rang inside my jacket pocket.

I pulled it out to turn it to silent when I saw the text from an unknown number.

Probably spam, I thought, opening my messages to delete it.

UNKNOWN NUMBER

Had an incredible lunch AND dinner, so thank$ for that. All that was missing was a scowling monstre.

~Your favorite private dancer, B

My body went hot as I read the message again, then a third time. I should've probably been more surprised that he'd gotten my number in the first place, but I'd long since stopped doubting Benoit's abilities.

Instead, I was more curious why he was reaching out in the first place. I'd never expected to hear from him again. He couldn't wait to get away from me.

Was it possible he missed me too?

No, that was wishful thinking. But as I read the message for the fourth time, I felt the smallest spark of hope spring to life.

What if...

The crackle of the radio and the guard's "All clear" had me shoving my phone back inside my jacket pocket and straightening my shoulders.

Omar glanced at me, a dark brow raised like he knew I'd just gotten distracted.

"Do it," I said, my voice coming out in the sharp, authoritative tone that demanded obedience, even though my insides were now a goddamn mess.

Focus, I told myself as Omar brought his radio to his mouth and barked, "Bring them up."

As the door to the lounge slid open, I forced all thoughts of Benoit and his text from my mind, and became the monster I needed to get this deal done.

39
BENOIT

One Month Later

T HE VALENTINE'S DAY soiree was in full swing as Shep and I stepped out of the elevator and onto the eighteenth floor of our private Libertine building. Located off Park Avenue in Manhattan, it was where the most powerful, influential members of international society gathered to network—and where my brothers and I headed up the organization down in our underground headquarters. The influence we had on governments and corporations around the world couldn't be understated, and with the cutting-edge technology Alessio created and procured, along with the latest and greatest weapons from Dimitri, we were a secret, elite group that even our members didn't fully grasp the entirety of. It was a privileged life I led, no doubt about that, and one I'd always enjoyed.

At least until I'd left Santorini weeks ago.

I'd gone back to business as usual and long dinners with Archer and my brothers, but every night when I went back home it was always the same—empty. Quiet. Alone.

It shouldn't have felt so lonely, not when I always kept my one-night-only conquests confined to places outside my bedroom. But the weeks spent with Dimitri had changed all that, and God I hated admitting it.

I was perfectly fine before he and all that dangerous swagger walked into my life, or rather, bought their way into my life—before King had issued a challenge I couldn't stop myself from volunteering for, before I laid eyes on the man I was now unable to stop thinking about.

I hated it. Hated that I thought of him every day and had to hold myself back from reaching out. I'd sent him a text weeks ago to feel things out, even embarrassing myself in front of Alessio to practically beg him to track down Dimitri's number, only to get nothing in return.

Total silence.

Now that I thought about it, it was the first time I'd ever been rejected by a man, and of course it had to be the one I wanted and couldn't have.

Wasn't that always the way? At least from what I heard. I'd never had the unpleasant experience, and it wasn't something I wanted to repeat or dwell on.

"About time you two showed up. I was about to ping your trackers." Alessio smirked as he headed in our direction, tapping the shoulder of a waiter carrying drinks on his way and pointing them in our direction.

I didn't bother asking what the different drinks were, simply took the cutest one—garnished with a swizzle stick of strawberries lying across it—but instant regret hit me when I brought it to my lips and noticed the heart design floating on top.

Ugh. Just drink it down fast and don't think about any of this lovey-dovey Valentine's stuff. It wasn't like this was in the Kings' usual wheelhouse; it was because King was in a happy throuple relationship and wanted to spread the monogamy vibes, or whatever this was.

But as I looked around at all my brothers, I had to laugh. He was barking up the wrong tree if he thought this group would find love. Well, except for Lucien, but he was always more of a lover than the rest of us. And who could blame him for falling for the cutest young thing I'd ever seen?

A far cry from a certain Greek arms dealer, that was for sure.

Shit, and Lachlan was with someone too, but I couldn't be blamed for forgetting that anyone found him loveable. He may have been easy on the eyes, but he was a little too hotheaded and trigger happy for me.

Also like someone else I knew, but *wasn't thinking about*. At all.

I drained the fruity cocktail, set it on the tray, and then went to choose another, but the love theme was killing me. I flicked off the cupid figurine sitting on the lip of another glass before taking it, and Shep grunted beside me.

"Good to see someone else finds this shindig as nauseating as I do."

I side-eyed our second-in-command, who was clutching his glass tumbler so hard that I was surprised it hadn't shattered. It wasn't that unusual for him to sport such a serious expression, but the irritation coming off him was new. Shep was used to smiling under false pretenses, having been raised in the world of politics.

He was also one of the most recognizable people in the world, constantly under surveillance from the press, whether it be for his fashion choices or political affiliations. So you could imagine the kind of shit that would hit the fan if someone were to find out the son of a former U.S. president was the second-in-command at Libertine.

But that wasn't what was bothering him tonight. No, that was the two men hanging off the arms of our boss—Shep's ex.

"It's a little on the nose, I'll give you that."

"A little?" He swallowed his drink and glanced my way. "Is this really the kind of image we're hoping to portray?"

I scanned the bustling floor full of partygoers laughing and zeroed in on King's most interesting choice of partners: James "East" Easton. He was an obnoxious little shit, that was for sure. I'd heard about him first through Archer and his man Preston, the latter of whom had gone to Astor—our alma mater. But never had I expected to have to deal with him in person.

Good thing King knew how to rein him in. And maybe that was half the appeal for him. East and Zac—King's former teaching assistant—allowed King to be his natural, dominant self. Whereas Shep had always bucked against it.

Two alphas could never work. Hell, I'd learned that first-hand. One had to be willing to bend. The problem with Shep and King was that neither had been willing to.

"I mean, everyone *seems* to be having fun," I said.

"Everyone is drunk. Of course they're having fun."

I turned to my forlorn friend, understanding his frustration. There was nothing worse than being the only one without a date. But again, this was new territory for me.

"Then maybe *you* should drink a couple more of those and try having some fun yourself. Forget about them."

"Forget about who?" Theo stepped up beside Shep, his usual kretek between his fingers, the sweet smoke billowing as he looked across the room. "Oh, no need to answer. I see them."

"Kind of hard not to," Shep muttered, and signaled for the waiter passing by with a tray of fresh drinks. "They're like a fucking boy band."

Theo looked past Shep's shoulder, his eyes wide as he caught mine.

Oui, it was very out of character for Shep to be so open in his contempt and feelings in general. But if I thought *I* was wallowing, I had nothing on this guy.

That would probably change, though, if I had to stand across a room and watch two younger men fawn all over Dimitri.

That would make me feel fucking murderous.

Theo took a drag of the kretek and blew it out. "So. Everything set?"

"*Oui*. The second shipment is all safely tucked away." I knew Shep was probably grateful for the subject change, but all it did was remind me of the man I was trying to forget. After Dimitri's first shipment was successful, King had immediately placed another order, and tonight Shep and I had overseen their delivery.

Had I volunteered in the hopes that *maybe* a certain arms dealer would deliver them personally? Perhaps, but over my dead body would I ever admit it.

"Glad to hear it," King said, walking up behind me and leaving his two twenty-somethings behind. "Looks like Stavros is proving a reliable asset."

Asset. The word chafed. Dimitri was so much more than that. He wasn't just someone who dealt in weapons. He was a complicated, layered, incredibly sexy—

"Benny?" Theo was looking at me expectantly, but I hadn't the faintest idea what he'd said.

And that was the problem. The reason I had to get my mind

off Dimitri. He wasn't even around and he still had my attention as if he were standing beside me.

"*Pardon?*" I said, but Theo was no longer looking at me.

Actually, none of my brothers were. They were all staring over my shoulder, a mixture of expressions on their faces that ranged from surprise to confusion to wariness. Except for King, who put his hand on my shoulder, gave it a squeeze, and then turned me around in the direction of—

Mon Dieu. My breath caught in my throat as the music stopped and every head in the room swiveled to look at the unexpected guest who'd just walked in.

But...it couldn't be. Whatever was in that fruity cocktail had hallucinogenic properties and I was conjuring up a vision of Dimitri, because there was no way he'd be here, certainly not within the privacy of Libertine headquarters, and certainly not without his ever-present guards.

I blinked, expecting him to vanish, and when he didn't, my hands started to shake.

King gently took my drink off my hands and nudged me forward. "He came here for you. Better not keep him waiting."

I nodded faintly, willing my legs to start moving, but they refused, and all I could do was stare at Dimitri in his all-black tux looking like a vision from my dreams.

A lethal, stunning, completely unreal vision.

Those dark, piercing eyes met mine, making my heart stutter, and then he was walking toward me. The crowd parted for him, no doubt feeling the dominance that radiated off him, the whole room silent as he made his way across the floor.

I drank it all in, from the slicked-back hair to the thicker stubble that lined his jaw. How was it that he looked even better than I remembered him?

But more to the point, how was he here?

And...for me?

Dimitri stalked me from across the room, laser focused like a predator on the hunt, and damn if my heart didn't skip several beats at the idea of being his prey.

I'd dreamed about this moment, fantasized he'd come to get me, and when he stopped in front of me, so close we could touch, I breathed in his familiar scent and all but swooned.

He was here. For me. I wasn't going to question it anymore.

And just when I thought all of my romantic fantasies had come true, Dimitri's eyes shifted over my shoulder to the crowds behind us, and his jaw tensed. "You better not be here with a fucking date."

Well, that *was* romantic as far as Dimitri was concerned.

40

DIMITRI

I WASN'T THE kind of man to make grand gestures.

I'd been raised to be tough, uncompromising, immune to any emotion that would make me weak. So it made sense that things like romance, soul mates, and forever weren't anywhere on my radar—until Benoit Olivier waltzed into my life.

Now here I was, having flown thousands of miles across an ocean, standing in some secret location in the hopes that Benoit felt even an inkling of what I did.

What King failed to mention when I'd called to set up this meeting was that I'd be walking into some kind of party. Yes, it was Valentine's Day, but King and his cohorts hadn't really struck me as the types to hold a fancy get-together to celebrate such a romantic day. What with their penchant for espionage and holding arms dealers at gunpoint.

But that was why *I* was here, wasn't it? For romance? I wasn't exactly the poster child for sweeping someone off their feet either, which was why this spectacle had me momentarily faltering.

I'd expected Benoit to be in a meeting room somewhere for this rendezvous, not standing in the middle of a shindig where there were gorgeous men in tuxedos all vying for his attention —and that immediately set me on edge.

I scanned the crowds of people drinking and dancing, looking for him, and when my eyes locked on Benoit standing next to a tall, broad-shouldered man—*wait, is that Shepard Winchester III, son of the former president?*—I tensed.

Blood began to ring in my ears as every possessive instinct began to fire, then I spotted King move up to Benoit and gesture for him to turn around.

That was when it happened, when I saw it. The same emotions that had plagued me for weeks swirled in Benoit's eyes, and my feet began to move of their own accord.

I didn't care whom he was standing next to, whom he had come here with tonight. All I wanted was to be back within touching distance, kissing distance—claiming distance.

Because Benoit Olivier was mine, and no one was going to stand in my way.

I crossed the room, mindful of the crowd parting as I made my approach, just in case someone got stupid and tried to make a move on me.

I didn't think King would be the kind to invite me to an ambush, especially after our business dealings had gone so well, but one could never be too careful.

All the while I kept my eyes trained on the beautiful man watching me. Benoit looked as gorgeous as ever in tailored high-waist black pants, a gold filigree blouse that I would lay bets was silk, and a lightweight cape around his shoulders. He looked almost...regal. His brown hair looked to have copper highlights where it was pushed back from his face, making his cheekbones look impossibly high, and the stubble lining his lips and jaw was just enough to tempt.

I wanted closer to those lips, closer to that man. So I could slide my fingers through his hair and taste him the way I was dying to.

Like a moth to the brightest of flames I moved in, and when I was close enough to breathe in his unique scent, I said, "You better not be here with a fucking date."

Benoit's eyes widened, and I realized that maybe I wasn't cut out for this romance business after all. But then he blinked and that slow, sensual smile of his crossed his lips.

He took a step forward, then looked up at me from under impossibly long lashes.

"And if I am?"

My cock jerked at the silky challenge in his voice, but my heart pounded even harder. He wasn't scared. He wasn't running from my threat. He was indulging me, playing with me, and fuck if I hadn't missed that.

I leaned down until my lips were by his ear and said, "You better send him home or *I* will send him six feet under."

"*Ooh.*" Benoit chuckled and turned his face until our lips were an inch apart. "I do so love a possessive man."

I angled my head, dying to take the kiss I'd so desperately been missing, but I couldn't get past the word he'd uttered—*love*. Even though he was teasing, I had to know...was it possible? Had I come here in vain, or was he feeling the same twisted wrongness I was at being apart?

There was only one way to find out.

"Do you?" I said, losing the battle to keep from touching him. I slipped my fingers under his cape and curved them possessively at his waist. "Do you think you could?"

Those perfect lips parted, and it felt like a hundred breaths passed as I waited for his response, though it probably wasn't more than a few seconds. My chest felt too tight, but I wasn't going to pass out. No matter what his answer was, I could handle it. I hoped.

But then Benoit slid his hands up my chest to curl his fingers around the lapels of my jacket and pulled me in closer. "I think I could," he said, meeting my gaze, the green in his hazel eyes shining fiercely tonight. "I think...I might."

The relief that went through me was so intense that it was a good thing I had a hold on him, or my knees might've given way. That wasn't the image I wanted to portray, especially here in the midst of so many power players.

At the moment, though, I didn't give a fuck about any of them. There was only Benoit and the soft smile on his lips, and...

There might've been one other thing, but I'd surprise him with that later.

"I was hoping you'd say that," I said. "I would've hated to force your hand."

"Hated it?" Benoit arched a brow, and I smirked.

"Maybe I would've enjoyed it."

"Now that sounds more like you." He leaned into my ear, his breath warm on my neck, and added, "Feel free to show later how you would've forced my hands...or any other part of me."

I couldn't help my growl as I grabbed the back of his neck and pulled him against my body. Unable to resist another second of keeping this polite, I took his lips in a crushing kiss that he met with the same intensity. Those soft, pillowy lips I'd dreamed about for weeks—the ones that let fly nothing but smartass, sexy remarks that both infuriated me and drove me crazy—opened without hesitation.

I could faintly hear the sound of voices whispering, but they all faded into the background, until there was nothing but the feel of Benoit in my arms again. His hands slid up my shoulders to wrap around my neck as I slipped my tongue inside his mouth for the taste of him I craved.

The moment I got his text in Germany, I should've been on a plane. Instead I'd spent weeks torturing myself, trying to convince my heart and my brain that I was better off without him, that he was better off without me, that we were too complicated, that there was no possible way we could be together or trust each other, that it would all end badly. Until one night an undeniable truth hit me: I didn't care.

No matter how much it didn't make sense, Benoit was the one I wanted, and being here now, with him wrapped up in my arms, nothing had ever felt so right.

He licked inside my mouth, long, teasing strokes that had me grinning when he pulled back to look up at me.

"Hold on, is that a *smile*?" He gasped, his hand going over his heart. "I didn't even know it was possible."

I tried to force a scowl, but it was impossible to hold for long with the amusement shining in Benoit's eyes.

I leaned in to steal another kiss when I felt at least a hundred pairs of eyes staring at the two of us. I slowly craned my neck to the side, observing the surprised faces of those in the crowd.

"What the fuck are you all looking at?"

Benoit chuckled and cupped my jaw, turning me back to face him. "Now, now, *mon monstre*, no need to scare off the guests."

"They're staring."

"Only because they've never seen such a handsome scowling man before. You should be flattered, considering there's a prince in our midst."

I immediately locked eyes on Prince Theodore Rinaldi, who was casually watching us with a mix of amusement and wariness, a kretek dangling between his fingers.

"A friend of yours?" I asked, turning back to Benoit.

"A brother."

Shit, there was another one, and an influential one at that. No wonder Benoit was so confident. Not only was he a force to be reckoned with, but he had men of high caliber at his back.

I respected that. But even more, it gave me peace of mind over this decision. My job wasn't a safe one, but Benoit was surrounded by family that wouldn't let anything happen to him, and that was only if anyone dared to go through me first.

"Come with me," he whispered, putting his lips to my jaw. "After all, you're here to see me not scowl at them, are you not?"

My eyes came back to his sparkling ones, and I nodded. Damn right I was there for him, and I needed no more invitation than his slipping a hand in mine to follow him wherever he wanted to lead me.

Hell, I was starting to believe I'd follow him to the ends of the earth. That thought had once caused complete and utter panic deep in the pit of my stomach. But as Benoit pushed out of the ballroom and into a smaller, more private room, I closed the door and drew him to a halt.

He stopped and glanced over his shoulder at me, and before I could say a word, he was back in my arms.

We'd tried being apart, knowing this could very well end in tragedy rather than a happy ending, but we were done fighting it now.

I wanted to be in his life. I wanted him to be in mine.

Now the only question that remained was: did he want that too?

"I can't believe you're here," he whispered over the top of my lips, sliding his hands up to touch my face.

I shut my eyes, reveling in his touch. "I wasn't sure you'd want—"

"I do," he cut me off, moving his fingers to trace my scar. "I've never wanted anything more."

I took his hand and pressed a kiss to his palm. "I can't promise it'll be easy. My life is—"

"Yours." Benoit smiled. "I know who you are, Dimitri. I've always known. But I'd rather a life with you than without you. In case you've forgotten, I'm used to a little risk for my rewards."

I pushed off the door and cradled Benoit's face between my hands.

God he was beautiful. I wanted to spend the rest of my life looking at his face. Waking up to it, falling asleep with it on the pillow beside mine. Benoit arguing with me, making love to me, growing old with me...

"Can you do me a favor?" I said, and swept my thumb along his cheek.

"Only if you lock the door." He winked at me, and I grinned.

"Good to know you have some boundaries with your brothers, but it's not that kind of favor." I stepped back and let my eyes wander down his stunning outfit. "Check your pocket for me."

Benoit's brow furrowed. "My pocket?"

He slipped his fingers into the small pocket at the front of his pants and pulled out a small, rectangular piece of paper, and his mouth fell open.

"What— When did— You've been practicing." His grin made me feel like the smartest motherfucker on the planet.

"I have."

"It was when you first walked in, wasn't it?"

"When I was threatening your fake date."

"Fake? You didn't know that."

"Yes I did." I laughed at his incredulous expression. "I just needed to distract you."

"By threatening to kill someone?"

"Seemed the most believable option."

Benoit held up the small piece of paper. "And what, pray tell, is this, *mon monstre?*"

"A new proposal."

He looked at the paper, his eyes narrowing, then back to me. "A proposal?"

"Yes. To replace my original one."

My heart thundered as he fingered the edge of the paper, then he unfolded the note and read over the words I'd written.

Be mine. Now and forever.
And remember, I don't take no for an answer.
~ Your Monstre

Benoit ran his fingers over the paper, once, twice and on the third time looked up, and shining back at me was all of the hope and love I'd been feeling since stepping inside this building tonight.

"I was yours from the moment you—"

"Offered you a million dollars?"

"I was going to say four."

A loud burst of laughter left me before I could help myself, and I reached for his hand and pulled him back in, kissing his lips hard.

"Tell me again," I demanded as Benoit wound his arms around my neck.

"I'm yours. Now and forever."

"Maintenant et pour toujours."

Benoit pulled back. "Been practicing French too?"

"I never go on a mission without doing extensive research."

"And I was your mission?"

"The most important of my life. I love you, Benoit. I didn't think I was capable of feeling that way, but there's nothing I want more than to prove myself wrong. And I will. Every single day."

"That's a pretty strong promise."

"But it's one I'll keep. No matter what continent we happen to find ourselves on."

"Good, because there's no sending me away anymore. I have ways to find you."

"And would you? Come find me?"

"Every day, for the rest of my life. I love you too. And I don't care how scary you and your big bad life are—I want in."

"You think you can handle me?"

"Oh, *mon monstre.*" Benoit began to laugh, that joyous, lyrical sound that told me he was up to no good, then patted my chest. "I've been handling you ever since we met."

"Is that right?"

"Of course. I sent you a text, and look what happened. You showed up to sweep me off my feet. Next plot...rings."

My eyes widened. "I don't know. I spent four million recently on this mouthy dancer, so I'm not sure a diamond ring is—"

Benoit cut me off, pressing his lips hard to mine, and I wrapped him in my arms. The truth was, I'd buy him the world if that was what he wanted, but right now he seemed more than content to be in my arms, right where he belonged.

And that meant my life, for once, was fucking perfect.

THANK YOU

Thank you for reading
IMMORAL (Park Avenue Kings #3)

We hope you had as much fun as we did playing voyeur to
Benoit & Dimitri's dangerous game of cat and mouse. They are
so perfect for each other, and we had such a great time writing
their wild and crazy love story.

Up next, our MERCILESS King.
The only question is...
Who will we find when *his* mask is removed?

MERCILESS
Park Avenue Kings #4

SPECIAL THANKS

We want to give a very special shout out and thanks to some wonderful people who made the writing of Immoral possible.

Hang Le, Arran, Linda at Foreword PR, Gel with Tempting Illustrations, Wander Aguiar and our amazing Brellas in both our Patreon & The Naughty Umbrella on Facebook who helped us out with some much needed translations.
Barbora Skařupová for our Czech, Monika Kaefer-Pravda for our German, Zaza for our French, Vale Giovagnoli for our Italian and last but definitely not least, Elizabeth Agiantritis who helped us with our Greek.

Thank you, to you, our readers. Whether you're in our private reader group, The Naughty Umbrella, on our Instagram or Tiktok, or one of our Patrons, we appreciate each and every one of you so much for picking up our books. It means so much to us that you'd spend your time falling in love with the worlds we have created.

SPECIAL THANKS

We are loving every second of this new world where our kings work behind the scenes to get everything their hearts desire, and we can't wait to bring you each and every one of their stories.

ALSO BY BROOKE BLAINE

South Haven Series

A Little Bit Like Love

A Little Bit Like Desire

The Unforgettable Duet

Forget Me Not

Remember Me When

Hate to Love You Series

Bedhead

L.A. Liaisons Series

Licked

Hooker

P.I.T.A.

Romantic Suspense

Flash Point

PresLocke Series

Co-Authored with *Ella Frank*

Aced

Locked

Wedlocked

Fallen Angel Series

Co-Authored with *Ella Frank*

Halo

Viper

Angel

An Affair In Paris

Lust. Hate. Love

Elite Series

Co-Authored with *Ella Frank*

Danger Zone

Need For Speed

Classified

Dare To Try Series

Co-Authored with *Ella Frank*

Dare You

Dare Me

Truth Or Dare

Malvagio Series

Co-Authored with *Ella Frank*

Forbidden Mafia Prince

Sinful Mafia Prince

Park Avenue Princes

Co-Authored with *Ella Frank*

Infamous Park Avenue Prince

Insatiable Park Avenue Prince

Scandalous Park Avenue Prince

Possessive Park Avenue Prince

Salacious Park Avenue Prince

Notorious Park Avenue Prince

Park Avenue Kings

Co-Authored with *Ella Frank*

SAVAGE

DEVILISH

IMMORAL

MERCILESS

RUTHLESS

UNHOLY

Standalone Novels

Co-Authored with *Ella Frank*

Secrets and Lies

Sex Addict

Shiver

Wrapped Up in You

All I Want for Christmas...Is My Sister's Boyfriend

Jingle Bell Rock

Once Upon a Sexy Scrooge

ALSO BY ELLA FRANK

The Exquisite Series

Exquisite

Entice

Edible

The Temptation Series

Try

Take

Trust

Tease

Tate

True

Confessions Series

Confessions: Robbie

Confessions: Julien

Confessions: Priest

Confessions: The Princess, The Prick & The Priest

Confessions: Henri

Confessions: Bailey

Confessions: Ethan

Confessions: Zayne

Confessions: Chloé

Prime Time Series

Inside Affair

Breaking News

Headlines

Intentions Duet

Bad Intentions

Good Intentions

Chicago Heat Duet

Wicked Heat

Wicked Flame

Sunset Cove Series

Finley

Devil's Kiss

Masters Among Monsters Series

Alasdair

Isadora

Thanos

Standalones

Blind Obsession

Veiled Innocence

PresLocke Series

Co-Authored with Brooke Blaine

Aced

Locked

Wedlocked

Fallen Angel Series

Co-Authored with Brooke Blaine

Halo

Viper

Angel

An Affair In Paris

Lust. Hate. Love

Elite Series

Co-Authored with Brooke Blaine

Danger Zone

Need For Speed

Classified

Dare To Try Series

Co-Authored with Brooke Blaine

Dare You

Dare Me

Truth Or Dare

Malvagio Series

Co-Authored with Brooke Blaine

Forbidden Mafia Prince

Sinful Mafia Prince

Park Avenue Princes

Co-Authored with Brooke Blaine

Infamous Park Avenue Prince

Insatiable Park Avenue Prince

Scandalous Park Avenue Prince

Possessive Park Avenue Prince

Salacious Park Avenue Prince

Notorious Park Avenue Prince

Park Avenue Kings

Co-Authored with Brooke Blaine

SAVAGE

DEVILISH

IMMORAL

MERCILESS

RUTHLESS

UNHOLY

Standalone Novels

Co-Authored with Brooke Blaine

Sex Addict

Shiver

Secrets & Lies

Wrapped Up in You

All I Want for Christmas...Is My Sister's Boyfriend

Jingle Bell Rock

Once Upon A Sexy Scrooge

ABOUT BROOKE BLAINE

Brooke Blaine is a USA Today Bestselling Author best known for writing romantic comedy and M/M romance. Her novels lead with humor and heart, but Brooke never shies away from throwing in something extra naughty that will scandalize her conservative Southern family for life (bless their hearts).

She's a choc-o-holic, lives for eighties bands (which means she thinks guyliner is totally underrated), believes it's always wine o'clock, and lives with the coolest cat on the planet—her Ragdoll/Maine Coon mix, Jackson Agador Spartacus.

Brooke's Links
Brooke's Newsletter
Brooke & Ella's Naughty Umbrella
www.BrookeBlaine.com

If you'd like to join Brooke & Ella's Patreon for a look behind the scenes, to read chapters early, to get ARCs first, this is the place right here!

Brella Patreon

ABOUT ELLA FRANK

Ella Frank is the *USA Today* Bestselling Author of the *Temptation series*, including Try, Take, and Trust and is the co-author of the fan-favorite *Fallen Angel series*. Her *Prime Time series* has been praised as "highly entertaining!" and "sexy as hell!"

A life-long fan of the romance genre, Ella is best known for her steamy, heartfelt, M/M romances.

If you'd like to join Ella & Brooke's Patreon for a look behind the scenes, to read chapters early, to get ARCs first, this is the place right here!

Brella Patreon

You can also find them in their Facebook Group

The Naughty Umbrella
(Facebook Group)

And if you would like to talk with other readers who love Ella's character's from her Chicagoverse, you can find them **HERE** at *Ella Frank's Temptation Series Facebook Group.*

Want to stay up to date with all things Ella?

You can sign up here to join her newsletter and get a FREE ebook.

Made in United States
Orlando, FL
22 July 2025

63168702R00184